MW01233837

HOT SHOT

A SOLOMON KING MYSTERY

L. WAYNE DAYE

authorHOUSE®

AuthorHouse™
1663 Liberty Drive
Bloomington, IN 47403
www.authorhouse.com
Phone: 833-262-8899

Published by AuthorHouse 11/27/2020

ISBN: 978-1-6655-0630-4 (sc)
ISBN: 978-1-6655-0629-8 (e)

Library of Congress Control Number: 2020921469

Print information available on the last page.

This book is printed on acid-free paper.

The man crouching in the car up the street from the house glanced at his watch as he recorded the faces of the men and women moving in and out the swinging door. Through the night he could barely make out the faces on the far side of the street. He watched as his hands sweated with excitement, as the addicts mingled --- in and out the house buying and selling heroin.

The three glassine bags of heroin in his hand were sealed with Christmas tape. He took a deep breath and opened the door. The cold December air caused him to turn up the collar of the windbreaker he wore. A car filled with men, all junkies suddenly brushed pass, causing him to lean against the side of his car. He turned and headed for the dimly lit house.

His heart hammered and cold sweat trickled down his neck. He grasped a long, deep breath to calm himself, and then, very carefully and with perfect form, he entered the company of street people. Mostly men and women who lived and died for the next blast.

A master of disguise and dressed as a repairman, his hair streaked with grey and a neatly trimmed beard covered his face. He emerged out shadows as junkies ran back and forth trying to decide where to get the next shot of dope. He motioned for a boned faced man to come to him. Holding his breath as the man approached.

"You looking? I got a new thing I'd like someone to try. What's your shot?" The man asked.

The junkie suspicious looked around and retorted, "It takes two or three bags most of the time to get my sickness off."

The man calmly passed the three bags from his sweaty hands to the thankful junkie.

"Take these and let me know how it is, I'll be here when you get back."

The junkie grabbed the free bags and scurried away. Without another word to anyone the man disappeared back into the shadows.

CHAPTER 1

July 4th --- Night

WHAT LOOKED LIKE A THOUSAND sky rockets clawed their way upward toward the night sky, scrabbling feebly as they started to lose height, then burst into a cluster of multiple colored puffballs, as fireworks were being set off at Wallace Wade Stadium.

Patrolman Mike Jones, twenty-five years old, watched the sky as he turned the corner onto Chapel Hill Road. This was his second month out on the street on his own and he had other things on his mind. He checked the radio connected to the dash of the cruiser, reassured he could call for help if he needed it.

The clatter of a car caught his ear as it pulled beside him at the traffic light. Two young women, maybe in their early twenties, heavily made up, dressed like street walkers, hair extension, cigarettes hanging from their lips, offering a cloud of cheap perfume. They winked and called to him, blowing wet kisses. On their way to some night club and already stoned. Someone was going to be lucky or maybe unlucky tonight, Jones thought. But not me. He was on duty this hot and sweaty night, patrolling the streets until six in the morning. He leaned his head out the cruiser for a breath of fresh air and watched until the two young women turned the corner. The breeze snatched away the last whisper of fumes from their old Buick Cutlass and he was on his own again.

He cut through the narrow dirt street which bought him onto

Green Street, two blocks of small shops and an empty space that was once a seafood restaurant. The street was dark, its single street- light that was shot out long ago.

The hollow echo of his patrol car bounced off the buildings, giving him an uneasy feeling that he was being watched. Once and awhile he would slow down the cruiser to a crawl, but there was no one to be seen. Outside on the street, in front of the shops, piled up on the pavement, were plastic bags of garbage, ready for collection the following morning. Jones eased down the block flashing his spotlight into the shop doorways, looking for whatever was there.

The end shop, long empty and boarded up, was once Johnson's Seafood Box. Marvin Johnson turned a one window sandwich stand into the most popular restaurants on the Westside in a decade. Then came the drugs, crime and stickup man, killing Mr. Johnson for the money in the till.

Tonight, a swaying sign in the gentle wind announced, "This Valuable Property to Let". The sign had been up for over three years. The shop's door was piled high with bags of garbage which had been dragged there from the adjacent shops. Once more he clicked on his spotlight, watching the beam crawl slowly down the street glaring through the doors of the shops. He half-way expected to disturb someone on the prowl --- maybe a creep thief looking to carry away anything that wasn't nailed down.

Jones stiffened. There was someone there. Someone laying behind the bags of garbage; someone keeping very still. He slowed his cruiser and stopped by the curb. He stepped out the cruiser with his flashlight, leaving the cruiser's door open. The inside light glared on the pavement. "All right come on out I can see you". There was no movement. Keeping his hand on his holstered weapon and flashlight to see, he started pulling bags out of the way. Then suddenly he realized the figure was a man ---laying still, dead.

"Durham Police Department." Police Sergeant Bill Seagroves smothered a yawn as he lifted the phone to his ear and muttered into the mouthpiece. He wasn't really concentrating on what the caller was saying. He was still shuffling names. He had been going through the duty rosters, trying to find a possible switch so he could have the week after July fourth off and was livid to see that Captain Jack Fletcher had yet put him down to work that week. Well, damned --- Captain Fletcher had better reconsider. Let some of Fletcher's blue- eyed boys do their share of the holiday time for a change, because the tide was about to turn. Seagroves frowned at the agitated voice. "Take it easy, lady … just tell me what happened…What? Where? How bad is she hurt? His pen scribbled furiously. "Don't worry; I'll get someone over there right away.

He snatched up the internal phone and jabbed the button for Miss Super Cop's office. Detective Sergeant Linda Graves. Let that slick ass broad do some work for a change instead of painting her fingernails. He'd noticed from the roster that she had the two weeks after the fourth off.

"Yes?"

The impatient edge to her voice always irritated him so his tone was terse, "Fifteen thirty- five Moline Avenue… a rape and stabbing sixteen- year old girl."

"On my way she said." "I'll need backup."

"We haven't got any," said Seagroves, happy at last.

CHAPTER 2

JONES WAS SWEATING WITH FEAR. He had to do things by the "book" or they would never let him live it down. It was a man ---- middle age----and the ashen face was Leroy Watson's. He pulled some of the garbage bags away to get a better look. He froze. The man was propped up against the shop door, with a syringe hanging out of the pit of his arm. He touched it and his hand jerked back as if he had received an electric shock. Jones had never seen a dead man before. Part of his training included a visit to the mortuary at Duke Hospital to view a postmortem but looking at bodies in the morgue was not like touching the cold body of the man on the street. In the morgue the pathologist allowed the recruits to observe an autopsy --- and he'd survived without fainting. But now in front of him he had a dead man.

As he backed away, he thought he heard a grunt. Still alive? Was he still alive? He couldn't be —the body felt to cold.

He put on a pair of latex gloves and fumbled at the cord tied around the man's arm. Quickly, he decided to leave things alone. He didn't want to contaminate the crime scene. Then he stared at the man's face. A middle -aged black man, Kango hat, cigarettes in his pocket, black shirt, cord around his left arm right above a syringe. Vomit dribbled from the mouth and nose. Jones dropped to his knees and gingerly touched the flesh again, ice cold and no sign of a pulse. The brown dribble of vomit had a nagging sour smell. He rose to his feet and shone his flashlight around the body. The dead man's head was to one side and his legs reached forward.

He straightened up and pulled his radio from his belt, then took a few deep breaths and called the station. To his surprise he managed to keep his voice steady. He sounded like a seasoned cop who met death on the streets every day. "Jones here, I'm at the 300 block of Green Street. I've found a man in the doorway of what use to be Johnson's Seafood Box and he's dead. Looks like a drug overdose."

"Stay there," ordered Seagroves, "Whatever happens --- stay there!"

Jones moved back to his cruiser and waited. An eerie feeling seemed to hang over the area; the tiniest sounds were magnified. The rustling of the wind of the exposed garbage bags, the creaking of the "FOR SALE" sign over Johnson's Seafood, the thumping of his heart. Then in the far distant, but getting louder, the wailing siren of a patrol car racing across the city to another crime scene. Seagroves wasn't going to send the Murder Team out until he had checked. Not on the word of a rookie.

At the station over on Main Street it was chaos and Sergeant Seagroves was near despair. Everything was going wrong, a murder investigation and no homicide detectives available. Detective Jon Parker who should have been on call and at home had left a contact number which rang and rang but no one answered. Solomon King was on holiday and that chic Linda Graves must have turned her radio off, as he had called her for the last half hour. He was now ringing the division commander's home number but knew he wouldn't get much help there. He could hear Fletcher's ridicule now. "You're telling me that you aren't competent enough to sort this out yourself Sergeant?" The phone was hot against his ear, ringing and ringing. Then he was aware of someone standing at the desk in front of him. An older looking black man, horn rim glasses, thin and crooked over in a Hawaiian shirt was trying to get his attention. "Be with you in a minute sir." Seagroves said.

"I'm tired of waiting, Sergeant, I've got places to go."

Seagroves groaned, another worrisome little bastard. Just what he needed to make his night complete.

His attention was snatched back to the phone. Someone had answered. It wasn't Fletcher, but his half sleep, irritated wife fretfully demanding to know who it was. "Sorry to disturb you at this time of night, Mrs. Fletcher but is the Captain there? No? Do you have a number where I can reach him? Yes, it is urgent? "Of course, it's urgent, you crazy broad, would I be calling if it wasn't. He thought. "Thank you." He scribbled on his pad and hung up the phone.

The man in the Hawaiian shirt was glaring at him. "I'm still waiting Sergeant."

"Please take a seat sir, I'll deal with you as soon as I can." He looked up hopefully as Officer Blake came in from the control room.

"Still no answer from Parker, Sarge!"

"Keeping trying, if the damn pathologist arrives to find there's only a Sergeant in charge, he'll go nuts. Any luck with Miss Super Cop?"

"Not a thing!"

"Trifling broad's useless." Seagroves tore the sheets from his pad.

"Someone else who's useless ---- see if you can get Captain Fletcher on this number."

Blake took the number with a frown. "This is the same damn number I've been trying for Parker, Sarge."

Seagroves looked at the number again, "Blake you're right. Fletcher and Parker are hanging out together. I wonder where?"

"A cheap little whore house" suggested a familiar voice.

"King! Solomon King, big, tall and black, a bear of a man in his wrinkled brown suit and broke down Stetson hat, stood glaring at them.

"Solomon!" cried a thankful Seagroves. "I thought you were on vacation?"

"I am. I just stopped by for my little black phone book. Did you get the post card I sent you?" He stood there with a smile, "All the show girls pawing over me out in Vegas. I couldn't get them off me.

Seagroves grinned. "I stuck it on the notice board down the hall but Fletcher made me take it down — said it was pornographic."

"So, what's going on around here?" He asked

"Green Street, body found in front of what use to be Johnson's Seafood. The rookie Jones called it in; said it looked like another drug overdose. Oh yeah, and rape over on Moline."

Solomon's stomach turned over at the news. "Why would some junkie crawl in front of an abandon shop to shoot dope? Why not one of the shooting galleries or an abandon house? This is the fourth overdose in little over a week." Seagroves said.

"There must be some high-grade heroin around. "Are the stiffs' youngsters who maybe were trying dope for the first time?"

"No, last week the three of them were all thirty-five year- old men or older. All black with tracks up and down their arms. All had criminal records and been arrested for drug possession and sales ---- and were known addicts."

"What did the pathologist's report say?" King asked.

"The word is high grade heroin --- almost eighty percent pure."

Solomon stopped in his tracks. "That's not dope cut for the streets." He said.

"Not a good sign, I'm glad I'm on vacation. I'll just grab my phone book and go." He disappeared down the hall.

Seeing Seagroves with nothing to do the little old man in the Hawaiian shirt sprang to his feet.

"Perhaps you can now spare me some time. I've lost my car---- a dark blue Chevy."

"Do you want to make a stolen car report?" Seagroves asked, sliding the forms toward him---knowing the fastest way to get rid of the old fart was to ask for details.

"Sergeant, I didn't say my car was stolen, I just don't know where I left it. I was at one of the sip houses having a drink and forgot where I parked it. It's on one of the side streets somewhere. I got confused after a couple of drinks --- and I can't find it."

"Someone probably has taken it by now." Said Seagroves breezily.

"I'm sure it hasn't been taken, Sergeant. It's locked and I have the keys."

"And you have completely forgot where you parked it?"

"If I knew, I wouldn't be in here bothering you, would I?"

Seagroves stopped writing and asked, "So what do you want me to do?"

The little man rolled his eyes as if he thought Seagroves was an idiot. "I thought that would be obvious. I need one of your patrolmen to drive me around the side streets of Buchanan, so we can find my car."

"I've got a better idea." Solomon had returned with his phone book --- speaking while biting down on a cigar. "Why don't you get the hell out of here and look for it yourself. We don't run a taxi service round here. We got more important shit to do."

The little man spun around angrily, pointing his finger at King. "I'll have your job," he shouted. "You don't realize who you are talking to. I've got friends in high places all over this town. I want your name."

"Fletcher," said King, Captain Fletcher."

"Okay, said the little man, scribbling the name down on a small scrape of paper "You haven't heard the last of me." He stormed out the station.

You're crazy as hell, Solomon." Seagroves shouted with a laugh.

"He won't take it any further," King said and was hoping he was right. "Anyway, I got rid of your problem. I'm out of here in case he knows somebody that will call Fletcher."

"I don't care if you're on vacation, he'll suspect you," said Seagroves sullenly.

Blake walked through the door from the control room. "Still no answer, Sarge. I got the exchange trace it for us. It's the Governor's Inn out in the Research Triangle, the bar and restaurant's number."

Seagroves eyes narrowed as he rotated the toothpick in his mouth. "What in the hell are they doing out there? Those two bastards are up to no good. I bet you. So, why isn't either of them answering the phone?"

Blake, shrugged. "The operator says there could be something wrong with the phone. Maybe, we can send one of the patrol cars by."

See if you can locate an officer who's out in that area. We need to get Parker in here." "Okay, I'm on it, Sarge." "Make sure he knows it looks like another overdose."

The front door slammed shut. Seagroves ran outside quickly. Just in time to catch Solomon before he drove off. "Hold up Solomon."

"I'm still on vacation until next week," Solomon hollered.

"We've got to have a senior officer over on Green Street. "No fucking way!" Solomon shouted. Come on Solomon; help me out until we can locate Parker --- just for an hour or so." Solomon bit down on his cigar and eye balled Seagroves without a blink. "Okay, okay" he nodded reluctantly, "you owe me."

Blake ran out the door as it was closing. "I finally got hold of officer Graves, Sarge." Solomon looked at Seagroves and throws his hands up, "you found your help." "Not so fast." said Seagroves "Graves is not a senior officer" plus, she's on the call on Moline Avenue."

CHAPTER 3

DETECTIVE LINDA GRAVES HAD SEARCHED for the house for over an hour. She didn't know her way around the back streets of Durham. The city map she used confused her even more. Many of the side streets were faded out on the map and had similar names. After circling the block two or three times she pulled in front of the house only after being flagged by a lady on the porch. "I'm sorry. I had trouble finding this address. How's the girl?" She asked. "The ambulance took her and her mother to Duke Hospital. She's got a couple of stab wounds in her upper arm and on her hands." The lady on the porch glanced back and frowned at the angry voice that came from inside the house. "That's her father. He's ready to kill the man who attacked his daughter. You better find him first. I tried to calm him down, but he won't listen." "I wish I could stay but I got to get out to the hospital and interview the girl ..."Graves rushed onto the street to her cruiser, relieved to get away from the clamor of the angry father.

At the hospital, Linda cut off her radio. She didn't want her interview with an irritable mother and scared girl interrupted by clatter of her radio. She sat down and homed in on the mother and the girl. The woman was plumpish and looked to be in her thirties, tan skin in a blueprint dress. The girl attractive, jet black hair, mulatto and appeared physically mature for sixteen with a tear stained face had cried until her eyes were swollen.

The mother, wild eyed, at first seemed unaware of Detective Graves entrance, then the women looked up inquiringly.

"Detective Linda Graves," announced Linda, holding out her identification. She walked in and stood at the foot of the bed.

"Took your time getting here," said the woman, wiping tears from the girls' eyes while putting the tissue box on the table by the bed. "Then she nodded at Linda. "Are you the mother?" "Yes, I'm --- Ruby Lee Myles." Then she nodded at Linda, "And that's my child, Trudy. Hush now baby the police is here."

"Try and tell me the best you can what happened. Take your time." The sobbing girl spoke, "Well --- I was walking back from the corner store --- and this man started to walk behind me saying stuff." The girl dropped her head and lowered her voice. "He said he wanted to ----you know used the f----word. I tried to ignore him, and then he grabbed my arm and spun me around. He started pulling me with him. I tried to fight ---- then he punched me in the face ---- started stabbing me with something sharp and got behind me and twisted my arm --- forcing me into an empty apartment. The apartments right up the street from the store."

"Have you ever seen the man before that time?" Detective Graves asked. "No, I don't think so —

he looks like one of the men who stands on the corner by the store all the time. He smelled like alcohol and seemed to be half drunk. He threatened to kill me if I screamed or kept trying to fight with him."

"Do you think you could recognize him in a picture or a line up?" Asked Linda. "I think so---I'll try," said the girl. "How long did he keep you in the apartment?" "About two hours—then he told me to leave—he warned me if I told anyone he'd find me again."

Linda snapped her notebook shut. She would have to come back again tomorrow and show the girl so photographs. "Well, thank you very much. I'll come by tomorrow so we can look over some pictures.

Mrs. Myles walked her to the door. "Do you think you can catch him?" She asked.

"We'll get him," Linda said. She wished she shared her spoken optimism. Sometimes these guys are hard to identify. She realized there was no identification or witnesses that she knew of --- she didn't even know the man's age or what he looked like. And in all her experience --- sex crimes were tough to crack, offenders kept painstaking alibis ready at all times. "We'll get him I promise." The door shut behind her, but she could still see the pain on the mother's face as she walked away.

In her car she switched her radio back on and Blake told her about the dead man found over on Green Street in front of Johnson's Seafood Box. She started her cruiser and headed for Green Street.

"She had her damn radio off?" Seagroves asked scornfully. "What does that broad think we give her a radio for … just to keep in her hand?" The phone ranged. "Yes?" he snapped. It was Fletcher and he sounded tipsy. "My wife tells me you've been trying to reach me Sergeant."

Seagroves clapped his hands over the mouthpiece and yelled for Blake to call back the area car. Then told Fletcher about the dead man found on Green Street.

CHAPTER 4

PATROLMAN MIKE JONES STOMPED HIS feet and wiped sweat with a white handkerchief. It was hot. He wished he could get back into the cruiser and ride the streets with a fresh breeze blowing in his face, but he had been ordered to stand around with a clipboard and ask questions of anyone who came by looking. So far he had recorded notes from himself, patrolman Adams who had arrived, a scant conversation with two teenagers boys who had not seen anything, the two crime scene officers Sharpe and Wright in their white overalls, who had screened the area off with yellow tape, and the coroner who was in and out confirming the man was dead from what looked like an overdose.

An old Chevy Impala puffed around the corner and screeched to a halt. Wright nudged Sharpe, pointing at the man climbing slowly out the car, wrinkled brown suit, broken down straw Stetson, scuffed wing tip shoes looking like he hadn't shaved or changed shirts in a week.

Adams, standing by the corpse, saw the man pull up and let out a sigh. Control had told him that Detective Sergeant Linda Graves was on her way over, but instead he had to put up with Solomon King.

King took a quick look around the scene. Everything seems to be in order --- condoned off with yellow tape. The cruiser driven by Patrolman Jones provided the lighting. Everyone seems to be doing what was needed. He smiled to himself thinking, "Sharpe and Wright can handle all the paperwork."

"Officer Jones come over here and tell me what you got." King said, chewing on the knobby cigar in his mouth, "I'd better know what we got, just in case the brass asks."

"Dead man, aged about forty," said Jones, leading him to the body. "Believed to be Leroy Watson according to a pictured I.D. Known heroin addict --- arrest record extensive ---- mostly for petty crimes ---- did state time for a sale and possession of heroin."

The body was being put in a plastic sack. It wouldn't be moved until the pathologist, a rules and policy man who insisted that bodies be left exactly as found, had examined it. King knelt over ----chewing on his cigar as he looked into the man's ashen black face, the dribble of vomit around the mouth and the syringe sticking in the man's arm. He stood up and bit down on the cigar. "This ain't right ---- I been knowing old Leroy for almost twenty- years, he could never afford to buy enough dope to kill himself. This is the fourth overdose in less than ten days. I don't know it don't feel right. He shook his head sadly. His momma lives around the corner, have anybody told her? We've waiting for Fletcher and Parker." A voice said.

Good, rather one of them than me." said King. "It's gonna damn near kill her, she got to be near eighty." He stared closely at the body as his eyes filled with questions. "Where did ole Leroy get that kinda dope from?" Who's selling dope like this on the streets?" What in the hell is going on?" He'd seen the effects of heroin since it first arrived in Durham back in the late sixties ---- five- dollar bags sold out on a hot dog stand down on Pettigrew Street. He seen it destroy and suck the life out of men and women of all ages ---dying slowly in jails and on the street. But, never had he seen a time where Durham had a string of deaths from overdoses. Maybe, one or two here and there but no time had it been a time Durham had four overdoses in a week. He thought for a second and gave up. It wasn't his case, so it wasn't his problem. It was time for him to get home to Princess. His wife had died on him five years earlier; right after both their children had graduate high school--- succumbing to breast cancer. He'd been by himself since then --- just he and Princess, his Persian cat.

"The coroner says for sure it's an overdose," said Officer Jones. "How long have he been out here?" "The coroner wouldn't commit himself to a time. He said the pathologist will pin down the time." "He's a lot of help." King straightened up and glance at his watch. "What's taking Parker so long to get here?" "He and Captain Fletcher are on their way over now, sir." Sharpe said. "They sent word they want to stay on top of the drug overdose cases --- the Committee for the Affairs of Black People are asking questions. The whole thing is turning political." "I'm only standing in until Parker and Fletcher gets here, so just carry on until the brass arrives." He moved to set on the hood of his car while he waited --- chewing on his cigar.

CHAPTER 5

DETECTIVE SERGEANT LINDA GRAVES CAME around the corner like a bat out of hell. She damn near blew past the crime scene, excited about been called to the scene. She hoped to be assigned to the overdose cases that was unofficially being called by the officers on the street and in vice "The Hotshot Murders." She was hyped and thinking it was her chance to make a real name for herself. Without Jon Parker at the scene, she would be the senior officer.

As she swung her cruiser against the curb, she looked over and frowned. The area was already cordoned off, but there, sitting on the hood of his old beat up Chevy Impala, wiping sweat with a dingy white handkerchief, chewing on his cigar was Solomon King. Why was he there? He was supposed to be on vacation. She flung open the door of her car and sprang out. "Hey ---- King!" King biting down on his cigar, looked up briefly, then, ignoring her, turned to Patrolman Jones and continued talking. Linda couldn't believe he was ignoring her so blatantly.

She scurried across the street, over where King rested on the hood of his car. "you been called in on this case? I thought you were on vacation?" I was called over her as the senior officer."

King barely looked her way. "This is your case, sweetheart if you want it. I'm still on vacation." Then he was shouting at Sharpe and Wright who was moving the garbage bags from where the dead man was found. "Leave that shit alone! I want it checked for prints and each piece of trash in each bag examined." He turned to Linda, "I'll be out your way in a little while."

She managed to keep calm, but inside she was mad as hell. Her one big chance and Solomon King had to get in her way. Why couldn't he have stayed on vacation --- for another few days or a year?

King eyeballed her. In her early thirties, black hair, a little plump but in the right places, her hair pulled back, emphasizing her sharp features ---- not bad for a white girl in work clothes.

"Can I take a look at the body, Detective King?" King spread his hands, "Knock yourself out, sweetheart."

Linda grimaced at the "sweetheart" but tried not to show her feelings. As she made her way to the body, an unmarked white van slithered around the corner. The pathologist and his intern had arrived.

"Oh shit!" Whispered King; "It's Count Dracula. You better watch out sweetheart, he's blood- thirsty." You have to deal with him until Parker gets here. Don't be shy." Lighting the knobby cigar in his mouth, walking away toward the roped off area. Linda following right behind him.

Sharpe, the crime scene officer stopped them. "Do you want every garbage bag out here fingerprinted or just the one's around the body?" "No, just the ones around the body ---- and opened them up to see if you can find the glassine bags the drugs came from."

Dr. Thomas Stroud, the Durham County Pathologist moved with deliberate motion ---- wasting no time. He was out of the car and kneeling over the body in a flash. Stroud studied the face and then examined the man's arms closely; his intern watched each move, as she held the flashlight over Stroud's head. The night air on the street was hot and thick, testing each officer's patience.

The syringe hanging from the man's arm held Stroud's attention. He instructed the intern to lower the light as he removed the syringe from the man's arm --- slow and carefully. He nodded, "Another drug overdose. The autopsy will confirm the cause of death and help to identify the drug type and quality."

"What you got Doc?" Stroud frowned. He didn't have to look up — he knew it was Solomon King speaking; the stench of his cigar was his mark. Solomon King always insolent and direct, wearing what seems like one of two suites each day, wrinkled brown or wrinkled gray, hand pressed white shirt with the top button loose, and a stained looking tie hanging around his neck. Stroud wondered why King wouldn't allow himself to keep a fresh shave and haircut ---- at least he'd look professional. Stroud stood up, snapping at King, "I thought Jon Parker was supposed to meet me here?"

We've finally found him and he's on his way." King chewed on his cigar as he stared at the pathologist. "Parker's out on the town somewhere. He pointed at the dead man being stuffed in the body bag. "To much dope, huh?"

"Looks like heroin or cocaine, based on the syringe hanging out his arm," said Stroud. Stroud's words were captured by a scurry of activity behind them. Car tires squealed to a halt, doors slamming and voices buzzing. Lieutenant of Detectives Jon Parker, in a dark blue dress suit, with a pressed and starched white shirt, made his untimely appearance onto the crime scene, bring with him the smell of smoke and whiskey. He nodded arrogantly to King as he handed excuses for Stroud. "Sorry for the delay, I was off duty and at a fund raiser." He glanced down at the body in the bag, shaking his head. "What do we have?"

Stroud took a deep breath. "Looks like you got yourself another overdose. He held up the syringe in the plastic bag. "From all the signs it looks like a repeat of the others we've had in the last ten or so days. The gentleman looks to have overestimated the amount or purity of the drugs he used. All the symptoms of a classic overdose --- the syringe in his arm, the vomit and dribble around the mouth. We will test the residue inside the syringe and do an autopsy." Stroud stepped out the way so Parker could take a look at the body. He unzipped the bag and looked in for a split second. "Okay."

Must been some fundraiser ---- one where money was raised by the bartender from the bastard's who were damn near drunk, thought King.

"Any sign of a weapon being used or a struggle?" asked Parker. "As far as I can tell --- no struggle or weapon was involved. We'll know more after a full examination. I just conducted an eyeball examination out here. Get him to the morgue. Leave him in the sack --- don't touch a thing."

"How long would you say he's being dead?" asked Parker. "It's a hot night, which tends to speed rigor up, I'd say he has been dead somewhere between three or four hours. I can be more exact once I get him to the mortuary."

"Parker looked up toward the sky, closing his eyes for a second, concentrating doing his mental calculations. "Which would put the death somewhere around … eleven o'clock this evening," offered officer Adams.

"Thanks for your calculation officer Adams." Snapped Parker. "You don't think someone dumped him here ---- do you, Mr. Stroud?" "No" said King; chewing on his cigar, as he walked toward his car. "He wasn't dumped here, he sat right here in the doorway, cooked his dope up and pushed it in his arm. The bottle top he used to mix the dope and a book of matches is right here in your face."

Stroud let out a loud sigh. The question had been addressed to him not King. "You need to come over and work for us, Detective King," said Stroud. "We could use another person to clean the place." King chewed on his cigar before he responded, "You don't need to be a rocket scientist or lab rat to know he set here and killed himself. Just look around a little bit."

Reluctantly, Stroud nodded his head saying "Yep!" He probably came here on his own to 'take off."

A sharp streak of lighten raced across the sky as the thunderclap seemed to shake the earth. A high wind blew, the swinging sign over Johnson's Seafood Box saying "For Sale" creaked, as a gust of sand twirled against the plastic garbage bags on the street. King straightened his straw Stetson and looked toward the sky. "I'll leave you fellas to figure this one out; I've got to get home before the rain starts."

"Solomon hold on for a minute." Parker walked behind toward the street, the sweat dripping under his shirt felt like he'd run a mile, "I need you to do me a favor, if you would."

I know he is not asking me to do him a favor, thought King, "A favor?" "What's a favor?"

"Damned Solomon! He paused, "I'm half drunk, and I'm in no shape to take over here."

"To damn bad," thought King. "You knew damn well you were on duty before you started your party. You'll make it through the night --- get you some mouthwash and a pot of coffee, I'm still on vacation and I'm going home."

"Just this one-time Solomon" --- for a few hours. I'll take over first thing in the morning."

Hell no, thought King. He wouldn't fucking bulge if it was me asking him. King stared at Parker, thinking what a piece of shit.

"Look at me Solomon. Half- drunk ---- dressed in my party gear … How can I go speak to ole Mrs. Watson about her boy like this?"

King bit down on his cigar. Parker had just pushed the right button. Stinking of whisky, in a fancy suit, slurring speech, telling you that your son was found dead …. Overdose from heroin. Parker had him. "Okay, okay, get the hell out of here."

Parker patted him on the back. You're a real brother, Solomon. I owe you one. He headed for his car swaying from side to side. Solomon shouted, "don't pat me on my back again ---- and I ain't your damn brother."

King made it to the street as Parker opened the driver's door. There were passengers in the car, a young black attractive woman in a skimpy dress, setting on the passenger's side ---- Captain Fletcher and a young white woman with bright make-up in the back seat. King chewed on his cigar and pulled on his nose. "You guys must have won first place at the fundraiser? Get your lying asses out of here and sober up." He paused and reached as if he suddenly realized something, looking at his watch, "Parker, you got exactly five hours before I'll be leaving for home."

Fletcher kept his face stern, not giving King the pleasure of knowing he was embarrassed. He stared straight ahead as Parker closed the door and drove away. Fletcher nodded as the car pulled away. King thought, what a foursome.

Detective Linda Graves felt disappointed as Parker drove off. His leaving meant she had to work under King, at least for tonight. King return to the secured area as Stroud was about to drive away. Looking at King the pathologist waved his note pad, "I'll deliver my official report as soon as I have it complete."

As the corner drove away, the white undertaker's van pulled up. King walked over and instructed the undertaker and his helper to put on latex gloves before they touched the plastic sack and took note as the body was placed in a black body bag, then carried to the van.

Crime scene officers, Sharpe and Wright rushed over to take pictures, and to eyeball the area where the body had been resting.

King motioned for Detective Graves. "We got our selves more than a few overdoses. Get back to the station and start a file ---including all the stiffs who have died from overdoses in the last ten days. See if you can find a common thread between them; where they hung out --- their hustling partners --- all the street gossip."

"I'll get the list and file together and touch base with vice to see if there is any word on any high grade heroin around," said Linda. "Someone is selling dope on the street that's killing people --- dealers never put dope on the street that pure, at least not intentionally."

"Sound like you know where we need to start," said King. "Talk to vice and draw the list up. Any new dealers or anyone who used with any of the stiffs on the day of the overdose ---- bring them in. Officer Adams you ride with me."

Linda paused, "Wouldn't it make sense if I came with you and Adams search through the incident reports of the other deaths?" She wanted to stay with King while he was leading the investigation. Solomon looked over at Linda, "Adams and I are going to break the news to Leroy's mother --- something Lieutenant Parker should be doing. You are not going to miss out on much." I'll pass, I'll be at headquarters," she told King.

CHAPTER 6

SOLOMON KNEW EXACTLY WHERE Mrs. Watson lived. It was the biggest house on Kirby Street, two story manicured lawn, white trimmed in green. Mrs. Watson had taught school for over thirty years and was loved and respected by all her neighbors. Leroy was her only child from a broken marriage years ago. She'd pampered and spoiled him --- trying to make up for not having a father around. He'd attended five different colleges --- parting and chasing drugs. He finally returned home for good, a full-blown junkie, living off his mother.

As Solomon's Chevy sailed up to the curb and stopped, he checked his watch. It was right at seven-thirty --- a new day had begun. He still had not made it home to Princess. He could see Mrs. Watson in the front yard by her rose brushes.

He walked to the gate, leaning over. "Good morning Mrs. Watson, got some awfully nice roses here." "Thank you, officer King, what brings you by so early in the morning?" What my Leroy done now?"

Mrs. Watson knew in her heart it was bad. She wrenched her hands as she walked toward Solomon.

"May I come inside" asked Solomon, chewing on his knobby cigar. In the house Mrs. Watson invited Solomon to set and he dropped into an armchair setting on the edge. "Okay, officer King what have happened?" Solomon slightly lowered his head, "it's bad news, isn't it?" said Mrs. Watson. "I know the news is bad this time." "I'm sorry Mrs. Watson," he then exhaled. He couldn't stall any longer, "Mrs.

Watson …. He began. The old woman lowered her head looking down at her clenched fist, rocking slowly from side to side. Solomon hesitated. "It's Leroy," She nodded. He held out his hand, "He was found last night. He's gone from what looks like an overdose. I'm sorry."

The old woman let out a cry like a wounded animal. "My baby ---- Oh God, not my child." Solomon reached for her hand …" "I'm sorry I had to be the one to bring you this news." The old woman whimpered, squeezing his hand like a vice. Suddenly she raised her head ---- clearing her throat. "When can I start making the arrangements?" Solomon caught off guard, "the body will be released to you as soon as you can come down and make an official identification. It will take a couple of days for an autopsy …. If you approve, after that the funeral arrangements are up to you."

CHAPTER 7

"KING!!!"

Fletcher screamed like a drill sergeant in boot camp. Before he could answer he had marched to the doorway of Solomon's cramped office.

"Get that broken own heap of yours out of my parking space." I'm calling a tow truck. I rushed down the freeway fighting school buses and trucks to get here and you're in my space again. Why can't you park where you suppose to park? You got your own spot out there. The sign clearly says reserved for Captain Fletcher. We don't get many perks around here and that's one of them. Hell, the secretaries can't spell and the coffee taste like dish water, but we do get our own parking spots. Move your car or I'll get it towed this time around."

Over the years, Solomon had become numb to all the bitching. He declared, "it's just a damn parking space. You act as if I screwed your favorite whore."

Fletcher carried on. Everyone down the hall of offices paid no attention. The cluster of detectives was accustomed to the cat and dog fights and didn't notice unless the shrapnel flew their way.

Fletcher walked down the hall still fussing to himself. "Why didn't you park in Parker's spot?" Because he's black and I'm white? Because you think he'll raise hell and I won't? Do you ever get up in the morning and plan to follow the rules? It's every man for himself as far as you are concerned. Big John's towing? Yeah, "This is Captain Fetcher at the Police Headquarters downtown...."

Solomon eased down the hall and gave Officer Adams who was looking at a stack of incident reports over Detective Linda Graves' shoulder his car keys, "Adams would you do me a service and move my car into another spot before the fucking moron of a captain have a heart attack?" Thank you.

Solomon turned around to find a wretched looking woman standing behind him. She forced a smile, but it was more like a look of stomach pain. She stood looking like a deer staring into headlights.

"You Mr. King? I'm the one who called about my brother's death."

She studied a balled-up handkerchief that she played with between her hands. Her clothes and hair looked tired, she wore no make-up, her kinky hair hadn't been combed. It was a look that Solomon knew --- the tired, haggard face of a long and tough life.

"What's your name little sister?"

"Clara Banks."

Solomon shifted gears. He became as attentive as a priest during confession. Let's go somewhere so you can tell me about your brother. He moved to the woman's side and took hold of her as if to help her across a busy street.

"We'll go into this conference room where it's quiet. Have a seat and I'll get us some coffee from down the hall. I'll be right back." Solomon walked away chewing on his cigar.

The woman seemed to be drawing her words from deep inside her stomach. "I'd planned to come down yesterday but couldn't find the nerve. I don't want to get into any trouble with people. I'm not like my brother was, he wasn't afraid of nothing. I was always the one who stood in the back."

She leaned in close looking around like someone was listening. Lieutenant Parker passed by the door and laughed silently as Solomon looked him off. Parker returned as soon as he was told why the woman was there. "Solomon do you mind if I set while you talk to Ms. Banks; …

Carla do I have the right name." Parker asked. The woman gave a subdued nod. "You can set in but let's not rush things." Solomon said.

Parker sat on the far end of the long oak table for a dispassionate analysis. Solomon took to the woman with the warmth of a doctor using his best bedside manners. She maintained her subdued smile while wrestling with the handkerchief between her hands.

With a shy tone she spoke, "I think my brother died just like the other men I've been reading about.

Solomon remained relaxed. Parker's ears perked up like a bird dog pointing a quail.

Solomon soothed the woman's nerves with his tone and style. "Yes tell me what happened."

The handkerchief was balled tight in her hands and suffered the pain of her anxiety. "Well...." She lowered her gaze respectfully, "he was a student over at NCCU --- uh, dreaming of being some kind of doctor, and he was always smart as a whip --- loved books since he was a baby. Some kinda way he got himself involved with drugs --- the hard stuff. He started to use the stuff, uh, and changing into a different boy. He stayed in school alright but mostly it looked like he messed with drugs. Then he started having more money than I'd ever heard of --- and all kinds of people knocking at the door. I knew then he was selling the stuff. Then one night I heard him talking to someone on the phone telling them he'd try the stuff and let him know how it was when he came to class. He sounded like he was talking to another one of them college men. One hour later, I found him in the bathroom with a needle in his arm --- by the time the ambulance come he was dead. They told me he took too much dope."

"When did your brother die?" Asked Solomon. It's been six months today ---- his name was Ronnie Banks." Said the woman.

Parker sat at the end of the table on the edge of the chair --- looking like a chiseled linebacker, gearing up for Saturday's ball game. He raised his eyebrows at Solomon suspiciously. The message was that he thought the woman had given them a new timeline for the overdoses.

Solomon seemed lost for words, as he lowered his voice searching for a touch of logic. “Ms. Banks, it’s okay. Do you happen to know who called your brother on the night he died?”

The subdued smile didn’t fade, but tears filled her eyes. “Um, no --- he always was getting phone calls from people.” She said. “Do you know any of the people who use to come by to see your brother?” asked Parker. “No, but they was mostly college folk. His friends were all from the college. About the time Ronnie started with the dope and all, I’d hear him talking on the phone to one of his school friends. They talked about making something --- it sounded like a big secret. I could tell it wasn’t about schoolwork. Something was going on over at that school. I didn’t come in before or tell anybody cause, I didn’t want no trouble with them drug people, plus ya’ll wouldn’t have believed me anyway.”

Solomon patted the woman’s hand. “I understand why you believed that. How many years had your brother been in school at NCCU?”

The woman’s face lit up with a fresh breath of relief that someone was listening to her was followed by, “he’d been over there for three years --- he talked of graduating in another year.” A single tear slid down her face, she caught it with the mauled handkerchief. “He was a smart boy, always in his books --- even after he started with the dope.”

She looked out the window into space, as if she was looking into what was supposed to be the future. Her voice went to a whisper. “He died at such a young age. After momma died, he became my child. He was the first one in the family to go to college. Before all the drugs he was such a good boy, full of life, always talking about being some kinda doctor. He loved basketball and writing stories. He was all the family I had. I never had a husband --- she lowered her head as if ashamed but necessary,” … “and never wanted one, all my hopes was in Ronnie. I wanted a better life for him.”

Parker's eyes grew soft. He didn't know whether he believed her, but she'd touched his heart.

Solomon asked kindly, "And why do you think your brother's death is like the other men you've heard about on the news in the last couple of weeks."

The woman's jaw tightened, "The folk at the hospital who done the autopsy told me he'd died from heroin poisoning --- the doctor said the drugs Ronnie used was not like any he'd ever seen before. He asked me where I thought he got that kinda stuff from .... And that's what said in the newspaper about the others."

Solomon said methodically, "so on the night your brother died, did anyone come by to see him --maybe the person who gave him the drugs or the person who was supplying him?"

"No, no one came by. Ronnie came home like always. Ate the dinner I'd made for him and went in his room to do his schoolwork. Then the phone rang."

The woman slumped. Her listlessness grabbed Solomon's heart. "The medical examiner said he died from some nearly pure heroin, said it killed him almost instantly."

Parker asked, "Have you packed up your brother's personal belongings? And, if so, did you find an address book --- phone number or anything like that?' The tears flooded. "No, I haven't found a thing." She looked up, "I don't know much else about what Ronnie was up to but I know something ain't right about the night he died. One day he was with me and the next day he was gone."

"Have any of Ronnie's friends or the people he dealt with came by since his death?" Asked Solomon.

With the frustration of having to cover details, the woman sighed, "Professor Alford from the school, the one who Ronnie said was his advisor. He came by to say he was sorry and spoke highly of Ronnie.

And that boy who he paddled around with, Trevor Hall came by and was at the funeral along with a lot his school friends."

Parker asked pragmatically, "Did Ronnie ever say who he worked for ----? Did you ever see Ronnie and anyone who appeared to be shady together?"

The woman flinched and turned to Parker as if he had just belched crudely. "Ronnie never brought anyone around me but one or two of his school friends." Her eyes lit up. "It was someone other than his school friends that he got his stuff from. The man that called Ronnie sometimes was no schoolboy. I could tell by his voice --- he wasn't a young person." The woman was visibly tired and angry. "Can you find out who gave the drugs to my Ronnie, Mr. King?"

She brushed her hand over her unkept hair and sniffed saying, "Something bad happened. Please prove it."

Minutes later Solomon and Jon walked down dim hallway, dodging hurried secretaries, winos and policemen; some were coming in from the blistering heat, wiping sweat. Solomon had a few people he needed to see, and Parker had to interview a victim who had been robbed.

Jon scuffed, "She's convinced somebody gave her brother a hotshot. If that's true, we got five deaths from heroin working right now. We need to get on top of this thing." Solomon looked over at Jon, chewing on his cigar, "take it easy Jon, we'll get to the bottom of this thing."

Parker grinned, as he thought. The joy of working with King was that he never let the circumstances of the case he was working on get him down.

Solomon walked ahead of Parker, dotting out the door. Detective Linda Graves appeared out of nowhere. "I'll ride with you," she announced. She had slightly full lips for a white girl which Solomon was finding disconcertingly stimulating.

"No" snapped Solomon, "You got the Myles woman and her daughter waiting on you over at the hospital. If you get your ass over there, they might be able to identify the creep who raped the girl from the photos on your desk."

As Solomon stepped out into the street his radio blasted. "Can you get over to the mortuary? The Pathologist wants to see you urgently." It was crime scene Officer Sharpe.

The mortuary was situated on the ground floor of Durham Regional Hospital at the end of a long hallway. Solomon parked alongside a black Mercedes, which gleamed and sneered at King's rusted out Impala. "Looks like a pimp's car" sniffed King. There were other cars, a dark blue Cadillac which King recognized as belonging to Sharpe, the Crime Scene officer, and a white BMW belonging to Stroud the Pathologist.

Most of the autopsy room was in darkness, but strong lights glared down at one of the tables where a gowned Stroud, with a green waterproof apron round his waist called Solomon over. On the other side of the table with notebook in hand, was his intern. Stroud dictated his notes to the intern. Sharpe, also wearing green mortuary overalls, hovered in the background with his camera.

The still corpse of Leroy Watson appeared as a slab of meat lying on a butcher's table.

"I wanted to be the first to tell you," said Stroud. He reached for the toxicology report from the intern. "The heroin our good friend here used was right at eighty percent pure. It had about twenty percent milk sugar in it. Anyone who sells heroin this pure is trying to kill someone. It's more to this than just an overdose."

"Poor bastard!" said Solomon. "I doubt if he ever felt what hit him."

"We haven't seen any heroin like this since the 1970's when it was shipped in bodies of soldiers from Viet Nam," said Sharpe, peering over King's shoulder.

"You're right," said Stroud. "The stuff that killed this guy is high grade stuff. Heroin like this could kill a horse."

Stroud dictated his findings to his intern. "Deceased is a black male, appears to be in his mid to late forties. Death caused by injecting heroin into the right arm, no sign of external injuries." He bent over the face. "Vomit exuding from the mouth and nose." He took samples and passed them to the intern. "Arm shows scare tissue, indicating habitual IV drug use." He moved to one side then to the other.

The intern with latex gloves, eased the plastic sheet down, amidst a sour smell of vomit and body odor. The man's face had a long sad look, baring his teeth. The flash gun clicked, and the film-winding motor whirred as officer Sharpe took pictures.

The Pathologist had finished. He washed his hands at the sink, while his intern was busy organizing her notes. "Brief finding Doc" Solomon asked. He stressed brief. Stroud wiped his hands slowly with a paper towel. "No sign of anything but too much heroin. If killing him was the intention, it worked." "Okay." Solomon nodded; he knew that meant there was someone out there killing junkies.

CHAPTER 8

SOLOMON THOUGHT IT OVER AS he rubbed his cold hands. It was freezing cold in the autopsy room and his arthritic knees were beginning to hurt. Who had old Leroy Watson bought the death bag from? He had to hit the streets and check with some of his contacts---- Quinine Sam and Red Smith to start with --- to see if they'd heard anything about a new dope package on the street. If there was a bag killing people, junkies would be chasing it like a chicken at a June bug. It doesn't make any sense for someone to sell dope that's killing people. Makes no business sense --- why sell dope that's eighty percent pure and lose money, when dope that's fifteen percent would satisfy any junkie in the world.

Sharpe began to bag up the materials removed from the body --- a pack of Newport's, a Bic lighter, an address book and some pocket change. The mortuary attendant came to take the body back to the storage area, but Solomon held up his hand telling Sharpe to take a couple of shots of the face. "I'll have them put in the file we've started back at headquarters. Why would anyone want to go around killing worthless junkies," Solomon asked biting down on his cigar.

Solomon stared at Stroud. Behind him Officer Sharpe, gasped. "You think someone killed Leroy Watson on purpose? Wonder what he'd done to cause someone to kill him?"

"It was quick and fast." Said Stroud, "almost like getting a lethal injection on death row. He was dead before he got all the dope into his arm."

In the car Solomon settled back and lit the cigar --- looking out into the street, starring, motionless. He slowly reached for his radio …. Calling Detective Linda Graves. In three minutes, she shouted, "What is it Solomon?" "I want you to check and see how many deaths we've had from overdoses in the last five years or so. And make a list with names."

In fifteen minutes, Solomon was circling the "open air" drug market on Dowd and Elizabeth Streets. As he approached the block, he could see dealers flagging cars as they drove by. Dealers moved away from the stashes as the old Impala slowed to a crawl. Solomon parked across the street in Ellis D. Jones's Funeral Home parking lot. He slowly climbed out the Impala stopping long enough to light his cigar. "No need to panic boys, I'm not here to haul you in for selling drugs without a pharmacy degree and a license. I need a little help …. One of your competitors is selling some bad stuff --- killing folk. I need to get em' and the shit off the street. If, I don't get whoever it is soon not a one of you is gonna be able to sale a bag on this corner or any other corner in Durham. I'll have blue and white's parked on every corner in the city. It's bad enough to peddle the poison, but purposely putting shit out that's killing junkies is the limit." All the corner hustlers kept silent --- as if they were afraid Solomon would call them by name. "I'm gonna leave but I expect you guys to call me if you know anything about this bad dope. Don't be shy now, most of ya'll have called me before." "We ain't heard nothing bout no dope killing nobody, most of our customers complaining the shit ain't no good," said Tank, slyly. Solomon chewed on his cigar, looking at Tank, "you boys be good and call me. Remember one hand washes the other."

Solomon slowly walked back to the old Impala, like he didn't have a worry in the world. He moved down Dowd Street, turned right and drove south on Alston Avenue to Calvin Street. Every other house on

Calvin Street was a gambling house, liquor house or shooting gallery. Solomon in his Impala wormed his way down the block...men standing in front of houses, wine bottles in brown bags, cigarettes hanging from their lips, offering sly stares, nervous because of living on the wrong side of the law.

Solomon moved down the block from one end to the other, no sign of Quinine Sam or Red Smith. Five minutes later he was knocking on the door, at 1210 Blacknall Street. He leaned over the railing of the porch and looked around the side of the house. There was no answer or sign of anyone. He pushed on the door and it opened. "Sam, Sam!" Anybody in here?" He walked in the house --- checking the bathroom. He could tell someone was close by. Just a washbasin and a shower; a tube of Colgate toothpaste on the window ledge, a book of matches, cup of water and belt ---- all the signs of a junkie's home. Next to the bathroom was a bedroom, not much more than a broom closet, with a single bed and a old beat up chest of drawers.

No one was home. Solomon walked out the door. As he pulled the door close, he turned into Quinine Sam, short, fat, round faced with salt and pepper hair. Speaking with a whining voice, "Damn man what you're doing? Moving in or what?" Smiling graciously, "You welcome anytime Solomon. What can I do you for?" "Looking to talk to you," Solomon said. "I need some advice, and you're the best source I've known for over twenty years." "My pleasure! Just don't forget who your man is when it's my turn" retorted Quinine Sam, still smiling. "We got some of your folks dying from some bad dope. The shit has killed four or five people in the last couple of weeks. Overdose, shits damn near pure. We got to get it off the street." With a voice cracking from the heroin in his body, Quinine Sam offered a sarcastic smile as he spoke. "It ain't from anybody I know--all the dope out here is garbage. I wish I could find some shit that good. I ain't heard nothing like that, man. Whoever got it is keeping it on the down low."

"Keep your ear to the ground on this one; give me a call if you hear anything. I'll make it worth your time." Solomon puffed on his cigar, looking at Quinine Sam up and down. "Hey man, when are you going to leave the shit alone? You've been at it long time. It's time to make some changes. I've made a career off you." "We are what we are. You a policeman and I'm what I am," said Quinine Same.

"Okay, okay it's getting late ---- I'm not here to peach. I'm going in and get some rest," said Solomon. I'm not going to find whoever is selling the bad stuff today.

CHAPTER 9

IT WASN'T UNTIL HE GOT home, and the front door slammed behind him that he suddenly remembered Princess. She had been in a kennel while he was on vacation and he hadn't filled the litter box. The entire house was a livid stench. He had left her in the house while he went down to the station to pick up his address book. Damned! He'd promised her he'd be only a couple of minutes; that was nearly ten hours ago.

She wasn't in the living room. He looked hopefully in the bedroom. She couldn't be found but her smell was everywhere. The bed was unmade and clothes on the chair. He got on his knees, looking for the source of the smell. "Damned, where is the shitty smell coming from?" What a wonderful day this has turned out to be ---- what a homecoming, after spending the night working on a murder case half the night and returning to a shitty smelling house, and nobody to blame but myself. He finally found where Princess had marked her territory, cleaned it up and freshen the house with aerosol. He undressed, letting his clothes fall on the floor by the bed, and then flopped down on the mattress.

The night flew by! It was a quarter past eight the next morning and hot as hell all ready, as he turned the Impala into the parking lot at the back of the station. The lot was usually half-empty at this time of the morning, but for some reason it was damn near jam-packed with cars. The task force, for what was now being called the "Hotshot Murders" was assembling. Every available officer from Vice, the Cat Team and Homicide had been called in to help, including off duty personnel. All very efficiently organized; Solomon was glad it wasn't his case, officially. Organization, task forces and efficiency were not his strong points. He'd rather work by himself or with a partner ---- using the old way of doing things.

As he ambled along, looking for somewhere to park the Impala, he spotted Red Smith crossing the far corner of the parking lot. Parking space was scarce, but he managed to squeeze in beside Captain Fletcher's Black Lincoln, after bumping it a little.

"Hey Red get over here." Red stopped, looked at his watch as if he had a schedule to keep and walked over to Solomon. "Yeah, if it ain't my favorite policeman, what you call me for?" "Been awhile since we talked, what you been up to, Red?" Asked Solomon. "I've been working and staying out the way. I got a job and an old lady. Been off the shit for about a year." "I'm proud of you Red. In any case we got us some killer dope on the street. It has killed about five people and counting in a month. We got to get it off the street, if you happen to hear a rumble from the jungle give me a call" said King. "I doubt that I'll hear anything ---- I'm out the loop but if I do, I'll give you a shout." "Take care of yourself and the lady." Solomon warned.

In the lobby, a beat looking Sergeant Seagroves --- who should have gone off duty at six --- was directing people to the conference room and the coffee pot. "Up the hall and turn left, first door on the right." "What's all the commotion about?" Asked Solomon. "Looks like a party about to start."

Seagroves beckoned Solomon over, his eyes glinting as they always did when he was about to bitch about something. "Parker and Fletcher putting together a Task Force on the overdose cases --- nothing but politics."

CHAPTER 10

PROFESSOR ALFORD SAT IN A chair in the darkened living room of his apartment "safe house". His eyes were closed, his hands neatly folded in his lap. Approaching fifty years old he was still lean and muscular. His facial features spoke to his Indian and African racial heritage; his years had etched fine lines around his eyes and mouth. His short curly hair was cut stylishly, his clothing was quietly expensive. His green cat like eyes was his most distinctive features, which he had to disguise very carefully when he went out on his missions of revenge. He opened his eyes and glazed over the amply proportioned house. The furnishings rich; English, Queen Ann, and early American antiques mixed liberally throughout the house.

He rose and moved slowly around the apartment which was the place he became a man of many faces. It was his safe house where he became a new man, delivering vengeance and death. The safe house was also equipped with special recessed lights that covered the ceiling. Multiple mirrors placed in every direction covered the walls. A large bar stool sat in the center of the bedroom floor. Clothes, men's suites, formal wear, shirts, hats --- utility uniforms, work boots --- urban gear --- women's dresses, wigs, hair pieces, toupees, falls and all types of shoes lined the walls. In the closet were latex caps, acrylic teeth, molds, synthetic materials, putty and other body parts. The long dresser in front of the east wall mirror contained absorbent cotton, acetone, spirit gem, powders, body makeup; large medium and small brushes with bristles of varying lengths; compacts of makeup, molding clay, collodion to create scars, crepe hair to make beards, mustaches, and eyebrows. Derma wax to change the face, cream makeup, gelatin, sponges, tape and a thousand other things available to reshape his appearance, same as the set up in the attic of his home.

Professor Alford had been an avid student of drama years ago while in undergraduate school. Many of the identities he created for himself came from scenes that ran through his head as he planned his next execution.

This was his recluse ---- his dream world where he could decide who deserved to die and what character would deliver the lethal serum.

The professor sat atop the stool, facing the mirrors. He starred into the mirrors. He scrutinized and observed himself --- his mind toying with who the next character would be. He'd create another character, a man or maybe a woman bearing a gift---death to another sick and pathetic junkie. He had told himself that on all the occasions before he issued out each death bag. Seven years running, all ten of the victims deserving to die. Each one had accepted their gift, willingly with a thankful smile.

Over the last seven years he'd exacted revenge and tasted internal satisfaction --- soothing his pain, sense of lost and anger. Ironically, the professor had grown up in a very loving and caring home. Son of a Preacher respected and admired. His parents died when he was in his last year at Columbia, when he was looking forward to graduate school at Georgetown. His sister, young pretty and a teen mother was all that he had of a family after losing his parents. Then came the cancer that ate his sister's life away. By the time he graduated from Georgetown with a doctorate in chemistry --- he was also saddled with the responsibility of raising the child of his sister. Bridgett came to live with him at twelve years old. He placed her in private schools, provided tutors, dance lessons and kept her from the wrong side of the city --- the drudges of life. He watched and planned her life. Then came the time when he could not protect her from the entire world. She had to find her way, dating boys and finally college at UNC. He saw the changes. The attitude, missed classes, the shady girlfriends, a flashy boyfriend and then the two glassine bags of heroin he'd found in her room during the Christmas break. He then discovered the trust fund he'd set up for her had been raided so many times that there was nothing left. He confronted her with what he'd found. They had their first verbal fight; Bridgett stormed out of the house in the middle of the night. In six months, he was at her grave site, she'd died from an overdose.

The tears from his eyes dried but the psychological damage festered and lived inside, eating away at his soul. His inner rage grew exponentially with each day that passed. The life he'd tried to keep Bridgett from had taken her away. The hustling, drug dealing scum of the world, men out to prey on the young and weak.

He couldn't let it pass. No one seems to give a damn. Bridgett was just another dead junkie, as far as the world was concerned. He decided to free the world of its waste … the drug users and dealers. His Bridgett had been stolen from him, stolen from herself. All the long-held hopes, dreams and plans were abruptly torn away, a precious life lost. The right to live, stolen by a man --- men pushing poison to the weak and innocence.

In another year Bridgett's boyfriend had died from an overdose. People kill one another each day, rarely for any good reason. By comparison, when someone's action takes an innocent life, to seek revenge is with excellent purpose. Professor Alford smiled and found peace when he thought of this. Morphine, acetic acid…. and the correct formula had led him to the creation of synthetic heroin. Eric Graham, Bridgett's one- time boyfriend sick from addiction and greedy for money was easy prey. A call an offer of friendship, a proposal to supply him with heroin, encouragement to test the supply, the overdose.

CHAPTER 11

THE PHONE RINGING ON THE desk caught Solomon in a woozy daydream, thinking of when he had lost his wife and all the dynamics her death had put into play.

Looking over the forensics report he could barely keep his focus on what he was reading. Thoughts of his wife's death, his Louise a big woman with a good nature who always had a kind word for everyone. The mastectomy, then the chemotherapy, the weight loss and night cries from pain. There was nothing to compare to the loss of a loved one, he thought. It was awful when someone who had helped form the foundation of your life was taken away. You are left to determine who you are without them, to deal with the pain and try to go on. The sadness of the lost leaving a stinging in the pit of your stomach and surfacing each time their memory occurred.

It had been almost five years ago now. Both of them were forty-five years old, in the prime of their lives. They had vowed to spend a long life together, retiring to sit on the front porch, rocking and watching the cars drive by. They'd raised a close-knit family, belonging to one another; two children, Sarah Anne and Junior both gone out on their own. From tables filled with chicken, pies and ice-tea, to eating on the run at the greasy spoon restaurants over the city.

The phone on his desk rang again, startling away the heartsick memories he'd held on to for fifteen years ---talking, laughing and hugging.

He snatched up the phone, "King." The voice caught him off guard,

"Ned" he asked. He leaned back and threw his feet on top of his paper filled desk. "What in the world prompted you to dial my number?"

"Solomon you got to be the hardest man to catch up with in Durham" said Ned.

"Why you're hunting me? You must need something. I'm not going to give you something that will violate someone's constitutional rights to privacy."

Solomon could hear papers rustling and someone in the background. "The deaths from overdoses, I hear that maybe it's more than just a case of junkies misjudging what they're putting in their veins. Maybe, someone is putting this killer dope on the street on purpose."

Solomon grinned to himself. "Yeah! Now where'd you hear something like that before the last body got cold?" He grinned because he knew Jon Parker had leaked it in an effort to publicize his task force.

"I never reveal a source." Ned insisted, "At least not unless I get something in return. So now today, I hear that a young man, a student down at NCCU died from an overdose six or seven months ago and it looks like he might have used the same type high quality dope --- according to lab reports. Confirm? Deny?"

Solomon frowned. Parker shouldn't have told that part. "Ned you son of a bitch, you're fishing. You print that and you'll screw up our entire investigation. Goddamn you."

Ned was undaunted, "So that's a confirmation. I just have to find out who the young man was."

"I'm off the record, you bastard. It's not a confirmation, not exactly, but it's a possibility that the kid from NCCU might have died from a shot of high- grade heroin like the others. There's no record of the drugs from the toxicologist." He shouted. "And if you print it without knowing it for sure, then you're a lying piece of shit and I'll never talk to you again."

Ned cringed "My God Solomon, don't take it so personal. Where did you get your communication skills, out the sewer? No wonder you got all the women pawing over you."

Solomon growled, "All the sluts chasing me are journalist. Ned tell me off the record, who leaked you that shit about the kid from NCCU?" Some asshole around here who's planning a political career?"

He shouted back. "You know that one hand washes the other, and the system stays afloat by taking care of those who takes care of you."

Solomon shouted, "Bribing one another, uh."

"No freedom of the press."

"Oh, fuck you Ned. You're full of shit as ever. So, how's the wife and kids?" I see where your boy is doing well running with the Durham Striders. I'm sure he got his athleticism from his mom. If he was like his old man, he'd lose every damn race."

"Why don't you come out to the track on Saturday and watch the kids run, it'll give you a change of scenery in your life? It's good for guys like you and I to get out of the old rut once and awhile." Said Ned.

"Oh man", Solomon lamented, I haven't been to a sports event since Junior played football over at Hillside High School damn near ten years ago," said Solomon, "that's tragic. All work and no play, is a dull way to live." "I've never been the outgoing type since Louise ---- well its best if I stay with the grind."

"I hear that good-looking lady cop Linda Graves works in your Division, now," said Ned. Solomon retorted. "Yeah, she's with us body and soul." "What you think of her?" Asked Ned; trying to get Solomon to forget about work for a minute. "If I was a younger man, I'd be all over her." said Solomon, "She ain't bad to look at and kinda smart to boot."

Ned laughed loudly, "Hey, I like to do the wild thing with her. We met on a story I did when I first started with the News and Observer, some story about a string of convenient store robberies. I swear

I couldn't figure why some good-looking chic like Linda would want to be a cop. I bet every guy she arrests want her to put a choke on them."

Solomon studied the blue sky that had opened to the hot sunlight. Not a cloud in sight ---which made the day even hotter, hot enough to fry an egg on the sidewalk.

"You want a beer, Ned? Met me at the Hauf Brau on Broad Street and I'll buy."

His reply was bland. "I can't. I have to go straight to Shepard Junior High School track after work; this is my day to record times for the Striders track practice. I've committed to the kids --- sometimes I think I bit off more than I can swallow."

Ned sounded like a man who was sentence to life in prison. "Yeah, sounds like you're having fun with the kids." Said Solomon. "I'm having fun alright, some days the only thing that drives me to show up is the commitment."

"Print your speculation on the overdose cases, Ned, you son-of-bitch, and I'll call your boss."

"And tell him what?" That you have department leaks and I'm good at catching the drip of information? I'll take the beer another time. Thanks for your time, although you didn't give me anything."

"What is it you want me to say, scum bag?"

"You could have said whether the kid from NCCU died from the same batch of dope. That would have been enough for me to start a story." "I got nothing for you today." Solomon said, "We'll have to talk later."

Solomon's daughter Sarah Anne was malingering in the doorway as he hung up the phone. She looked at him with a wide smile. "I know you're surprise to see me," she chirped. "I've had you on my mind all day and decided to drive up to see you. The traffic between here and Charlotte wasn't bad at all -- it was a nice drive. Looking around, "you know dad, your office looks like .... looks a mess. It looks like you had a party or something."

"I'm sorry honey" he said snidely, "that I didn't have flowers, air fresheners and a nice tidy desk." "I bet the house is a mess." Solomon looked up with raised eyebrows.

She said menacingly, "let's go home, I'm gonna cook you a good meal and clean the house." Sarah Anne was making her biweekly rounds, checking up on her father. She'd started to check on him right after her mother died. She couldn't watch over him each day and he wouldn't allow it ---- a night or two twice a month did the trick.

Solomon went soft, wrapping his arms around Sarah. Sarah cooed, "Daddy, I love you and worry about you living by yourself. I want to pamper you a little. So, come on let's go before your phone rings."

"Okay sweetheart, anything you say." He looked at Sarah Anne thinking how much she was becoming like her mother.

CHAPTER 12

SOLOMON SAW THE NOTE STICKING on his door. He snatched it down, reading it as he reached for the doorknob. “Meet me in my office in ten minutes --- the door is open, Captain Fletcher.” What in the hell do that poor excuse for a Captain want this time, he thought?

Solomon marched down the hall, turned the corner and let himself into Fletcher office. He took a quick look around and shuddered. The room was too neat and clean, it almost hurt to be there. Desktop clear, wall charts meticulously lined up, and the prissy smell of floral furniture polish. An organized, efficient looking room, which matched its occupant, and which made Solomon itch to get back to the dallying untidy fug of his own office.

As he was observing the place, Fletcher in a smoke grey thousand -dollar suit, starched white shirt and matching tie whizzed in.

“How was your vacation, detective?”

“It was good while it lasted --- I sent you guys a post card and a picture with a couple of chics hanging on me. I heard you throw it out. I understand though, you want all the fun and girls for yourself.”

Fletcher, cut his eyes at Solomon without making a comment. He moved to the business at hand.

“I’m going to assign you to the overdose cases officially. I’d like for you to work with the

Task Force. We need to get these cases solved. And please follow the procedures on this one, Solomon.”

"You know I don't like working with Task Forces and the new style bullshit. Just tell all the keystone cops to stay out my way --- they can do their thing and I'll do mind." Solomon barked

"Alright, alright just don't make me look bad on this."

"No problem," Solomon said.

"The briefing for the Task Force is starting in five minutes. I'll report that you have been put on the case as well. By the way, I'm gonna assign you a partner." Solomon looked at fletcher, grunted and filed out the door.

King wandered down the hall to a side room behind the receptionist desk and helped himself to a cup of coffee from a pot someone had prepared. He didn't want to be bothered with the task force and all the starch collar wearing politicians who were involved. He felt if the case was to be solved it would happen on the street not in some weekly meeting. He sipped coffee and chewed on his cigar, thinking of what if anything he had missed. He stole another cup of coffee and headed back to his office.

He was at his desk studying; thinking of what he knew about the overdoses, one thing was that each man who had died had a history of drug use and sales. What else did they have in common? If the overdoses were murders, what else connected them? What made the killer chose them? He chewed on his cigar and pondered.

He snapped back to life when Detective Linda Graves rushed through the door --- looking like a Vegas show girl, tan, shapely and those sexy lips. He wondered what she wanted as he looked at her, casting his eyes up and down, biting down on his knobby cigar.

"Solomon!" He looked straight at her. "I'm your new partner." Hands across her breast, she sneered down on him.

"You're full of shit" he said.

She rolled her eyes and gave him grit. He sneered. "What in the hell is on Fletcher's mind, you and me partners."

"Yes, I'm your partner. At least until we find whoever is passing around the bad dope." "Look, I don't like this no more than you do but it is what it is. So, are we gonna stand around and complain or go about solving this thing?" She asked.

"What about the rape case you're working?" He asked.

"Fletcher instructed me to put it on the side burner, watch over it but concentrate on the drug case with you."

"What did you do to get me?" He asked.

"You must have pissed Fletcher or somebody off. I'm serious, you might not know it but you pissed somebody off. Most people consider working with me a punishment."

She stood there and fluffed her hair as he spoke. His eyes were on her every move. He had only seen her in the station in the last couple of months. The first time he'd been up close was at the crime scene the night Leroy Watson was found. But he'd heard she was a smart heart-throb cop. Looking at her, she looked like some---five feet seven cheerleader, nice legs, tight ass, and swanky clothes, sparking brown eyes and soft brown hair. Each time he looked he prayed he could be young again. Then she spoke ---- and her toughness shone through. He'd heard she was tough and smarter than most of the men, not backing away from anyone. He watched as she flopped in the chair in front of his desk. Long fingernails, perfume in the air, soft pink lipstick, all the stuff that cause men to yield to women.

She snapped, "How long have you been in the police business?" "Damn near as long as you are old, close to twenty years." He answered. She continued, "What made you want to be a policeman?' Solomon look at officer Graves and leaned back in his chair, biting down on his knobby cigar while starring at her. Finally, after a minute or so he spoke. "When, I was a boy around five-years old or so, my granddaddy was shot, killed and left beside the road out in the country in an area where our family lived call Coppler's Corner. Officer Graves put her hands over her mouth saying, "I'm so sorry." Officer Graves was noticeably knocked off her feet by Solomon's disclosure. Solomon continued the word was he was killed by some white men. Granddaddy was a proud strong man, one of only a few black men who didn't work as a sharecropper during those times. He respected other people and expected the same from them. It been said that on several occasions he had minor run-ins with a few of the local white men who either spoke out of terms to him or attempted to treat him as less than a man because he was black. No one was ever arrested, charged or convicted for his murder. It was all swipe under the rug. My granddaddy and the rest of his family was the victims of a justice system with one set of laws for blacks and another for white folk that acted as if grandaddy and other black people had no value. I left and joined the army as soon as graduated high school and buy a bus ticket. I soon realized the rules for whites and blacks in the army and everywhere I went was just like there were in Coppler's Corner, one set for black folk and another set for white folk, so, I decided to become a policemen and jumped at the chance to be a detective to do my part to try and set things straight for people who are robbed, killed and are victims of crimes. My daughter Sarah Ann is trying to do her part as a lawyer in a corrupt system of justice to balance the scales and that's her effort to set things straight. The two systems were in place when granddaddy got killed and ain't much change since then. It runs from the police to the magistrates, to courts to the prisons. Officer Graves was in shock. Solomon assured her saying, "it's the way it is but you and I will get to the bottom of the "Hotshot" murders as he bit down on his cigar.

"Ever had a female partner before?" "Not a damn one that I know of." Linda could only mutter dumbly, "Oh ...." And shrug.

She looked at him, eye to eye. "I'm gonna tell you what's said about you around here .... So, we can get down to business. They say you're a renegade cop ... doing things your way. That you don't follow any of the rules, refuse to take orders from the brass because you don't care about rank, that you're ornery, mean as hell and probably the best detective on the force."

He starred hard at her, chewing on his cigar. She swallowed. He finally spoke. "It's a bunch of bullshit. Don't believe a damn thing anyone said."

She smiled, "yeah, right. For some reason I believe them." He said, "I heard you cursed like a sailor, had a big heart, a bad temper, don't mix work and play and had a black belt in karate."

She looked at Solomon, "I want more. I want to be on the high-profile cases when I get the chance. I don't plan on being a detective with the Durham Police Department for the rest of my life. I'd like to make it up to D.C and work with the big boys, Secret Service or FBI."

Solomon studied her, "Well, you watch what you say and sleep with the right brass."

She gazed at him, not knowing whether his comment was meant as advice or a put down.

She found herself liking this off beat guy, past his unshaven face and tacky clothes. She wondered did he ever change suites or laundry his shirts. He looked old fashioned, rundown and useless. He smelled like a wisp of Old Spice cologne, mixed with the smell of his cigar --- and didn't deny he had no plan of following the recommendations of the Task Force or Fletcher.

Officer Mike Jones tapped on the door. "Solomon waved him in. He nodded his head at Solomon and spoke, "Detective Graves, there was another rape on the West End last night. It was just reported. I was told to inform you. Linda starred at Officer Jones, throwing her hands up, "thank you Jones, thank you."

"Here we go," she said, "I can tell already that I'm gonna be on a merry go round."

"Take it easy, Graves, go see what they got and meet me later. We'll handle it ... we're partners remember."

Linda's face squinted. "I don't know whether I like the sound of that." Solomon barked, "Don't tell me you're fed up with me already."

Okay, okay, I'll be back, let's say in a half hour." She stomped off as Solomon slammed the door behind her.

He rushed to the door and yield, "bring me a coke back when you come." "I don't deliver" she shouted. He watched as she glided down the hall --- with a cat like bounce. She had a long stride and nice legs. "What a partner" he said to himself.

CHAPTER 13

THE NEON SIGN FROM THE convenient store cast a bright light on the street. The light ricocheted off the glass of the dry cleaners next door. Cars moved in and out the parking lot --- a group of men stood on the corner a half block away sipping cheap wine as they passed a joint.

Alan Winstead waited in the dark behind the cleaners. He could hear himself breath --- feel the pulse in his neck move up and down. Taste the remains of the pint of Thunderbird he'd drunk an hour earlier. Feel the swell of his penis --- as he waited for the chosen one to arrive, imaging the odor and vaginal warmth of her resistance.

He'd started to stalk and rape at the age of fifteen. Inflicting on others what had been thrust on him. A boy being raped and sodomized, becoming the love slave of his stepfather at the age of ten. By age fifteen, hurt, ashamed, angry and with his hormones out of control, he sought satisfaction of his own. By eighteen he'd raped more than twenty young girls and women. By twenty he'd been arrested, identified and convicted for raping two Duke co-eds in their West Campus Dormitory. At twenty-one he was serving a forty-year sentence in the North Carolina Department of Corrections on Caldonia Farm a maximum-security prison, where was known as "Big Bitch" the king of the weight pile and the queen of the compound.

After serving twenty years he was back. Obsessed, angry and waiting and watching for his next victim.

Tonight, he'd chosen a twenty something young looking black

woman. He'd watched her for a week. A student, coming home each night by bus. He'd noticed her books, the NCCU logo sweatshirt. She never noticed as he stood close to her while she stopped in the small convenient store on Buchanan Boulevard. The smooth chocolate skin and liquid eyes, breast like apples, slender waist and rounded ass. She lived alone in a small apartment around the corner on Trinity Park. Bathing late at night, eating microwave food, talking on the phone, sleeping in the nude as he spied through the small opening of the blinds.

She would be his third --- offer of love, since he'd spun out of control. Helplessly roaming the streets each night on the hunt.

The last had been the young girl returning home from the store, not chosen; not planned but carried out through an uncontrollable impulse at the sight of her beauty and the right opportunity.

The first was one he'd chosen, didn't really excite him. It was a practice run --- a trial and error experiment. Checking his nerve, timing and deficiencies.

A nurse, he took her in the morning as she dressed for the early shift. On a cold morning, after she had walked out to warm up her car. With a knife he gained control, carried out his plan, leaving her in shambles.

He was hurt and angry. It all started in his small bedroom as a boy. He'd prayed each night for it to end. The pain he'd carried for all the years had driven him mad --- the dreams and night sweats. In prison they gave him pills --- black, red and orange to control his aggression and to make him sleep. He wished he could stop but once out of prison he'd lost control again. Each time he saw that certain one, she became the next obsession ---- the next victim.

The prison psychologist thought he was a freak who hated women. Probably the result of a youthful experience of being under the thumb of a controlling mother who was a tyrant loving him with inappropriate sexual overtones. The shrinks were wrong. No one knew of his stepfather and the rapes. The resulting fear, shame and sense of lost.

Behind bars he raped the weak and consented to the strong --- searching for acceptance and a feeling of care.

Alan loved women and didn't consider himself a homosexual or a freak. He spent his days fantasizing and stalking women in malls, and on the streets. Following women, girls for hours in admiration, lusting, imagining each one being in love with him, feeling himself discharging inside them during transcendent moment

CHAPTER 14

As Solomon walked through the station door, Sergeant Seagroves was picking up the ringing phone. He nodded sympathetically. Seagroves looked at Solomon and put his hand over the receiver. "Its bad news." "You're always the bearer of bad news." Solomon moaned.

"What we got?" "Another rape on the Westside by the Trinity Park section. She is a young woman and a student at NCCU. It happened sometime between two and three this morning. The sorry son-of-a-bitch broke in on her in the middle of the night."

Solomon chewed on his cigar. "The rape cases are still assigned to Graves. I'm sure she'll be thrilled. We need to catch the sick bastard. He's probably some guy standing on the corner with his tongue hanging out, panting." Solomon whispered.

"You'll probably right" said Seagroves. We'll get him --- he'll forget to zip his pants and we'll have him."

Solomon examined the internal mail on his desk --- by force of habit, Linda knocked on the door. "Enter," Solomon shouted.

Linda flopped down in the chair in front of his desk and stared goggle-eyed, looking as though she owned the place.

"I've looked into the attack --- the rape," she waggled her finger, fuming holding up the yellow folder. "The sick son-of-a-bitch, it's got to be the same guy. It happened only three blocks from where the Myles girl was attacked on last week, and get this, on the same night."

"Where did this guy come from? Out of nowhere, we got a serial guy rapist in the same section of town --- week after week. Two weeks in a row. Look, I'm going over to interview the vic --- the young lady."

"Could be the same guy," Solomon agreed.

"Look, go and check it out and met me when you finish. I got a couple of leads I'm gonna chase down on the drug case." "Hey," motioning with his hands, "take it easy, we can only do so much in one day."

Eleven o'clock, Solomon was sitting on the corner of his desk, staring at the colored stick pins in the wall map, marking the different locations where the overdose deaths had occurred. Since he'd started tracking them, one on the Westside, and one in Bragg Town and there were probably others that had gone unnoticed.

He didn't have a clue; every lead had been a zero. Deaths from high quality heroin. Was it murder or just a coincident? There were no apparent connections between Leroy Watson, Ronnie Banks and other overdose deaths as he could see. One was a street junkie and the other a college kid. No lead to follow on either.

The phone rang. He snapped out of the trance. It was Helen Gaddy, the record's clerk. "Detective King, I'm trying to locate Linda Graves," she said. "I have the old records on the overdose cases she asked me to pull." "Thank you! Ms. Gaddy" said Solomon anxiously. "Could you bring them over?" She's out of the office but I'll take them."

CHAPTER 15

TREVOR HALL HELD ONTO THE small bag of groceries as he walked from the bus stop off Fayetteville Street to his apartment on Cecil. Bread, bologna, Miracle Whip and bananas. He was sick. He needed a shot of heroin. It had been almost two days since his last blast. His stomach was churning feeling like his bowels would break any minute and the cold chills had him shaking. Withdrawals his body aching, felt like the flu.! There was a note on the door. **NOTICE: DUKE POWER DISCONNECT OF SERVICE.** He read the content as he passed through the doorway. He'd received a notice each month for the last eight months --- one each month since Ronnie Banks had killed himself shooting dope. Not only did he miss Ronnie's friendship, but he missed the steady supply of heroin Ronnie had provided for the last year. Since Ronnie's death, times had become tough. No connection, no money to afford the lifestyle he'd accustomed himself to and no way to feed his habit.

School had become secondary and difficult. His drug habit had grown and become the center of his life. His days were mostly filled with schemes ---- methods and means of getting a shot of dope. His grades had taken a nose-dive and he didn't much care. The dream he and Ronnie once shard of medical school seemed like an illusion.

After Ronnie's funeral he found his way to the streets of Durham, partnering up with hard core junkies. In malls and grocery stores watching for clerks to turn their heads so he could steal money for his next blast. He had accepted small packages from local dealers, trying anything offered but failing at every attempt. He had traveled home to Rocky Mount on two occasions, once during the summer and once during Christmas thinking he could lay in bed and kick the habit ---- cold turkey. Nothing worked, he was hooked ---- trapped.

In the slices of the moon as Trevor wrestled with his withdrawal pain, he was being watched. Measured, he'd be the next junkie to receive the gift of death --- the hot shot.

Dressed in oversized blue jeans; black silk shirt, a knit cap, his chicks round and puffy and his hazel eyes hidden by brown contact lens, Professor Alford peered through the window. His hair streaked in grey, blending with his neatly trimmed beard.

He had parked his old Honda, the car used for his missions of death in the parking lot of the NCCU Student Union out of sight, then walking one block to Cecil Street. Easily, quietly.

Not being noticed and known by the students he taught. He'd crossed the street and walked to the back of Trevor's apartment and waited. Ten minutes later he exited from the shadows and tapped on the front door. He instinctively looked around, making sure he wasn't being noticed.

Trevor Hall, Ronnie Banks' friend and partner constituted a loose end that must be tied. His drug dealing partnership with Ronnie, spreading poison to the weak and innocent. Destroying the dreams of their victims. He too had to pay for the Professor's grief and loss of Bridgett. Trevor had earned the right to receive the gift --- the Hot Shot.

"Who is it?' Trevor asked through the door.

"Otis, I'm a friend of Ronnie Banks. I'd like to speak with you if I could." Trevor opened the door. He nodded his head. He didn't recognize the man at the door. The professor spoke with a distinct urban tongue. "I'm a friend of Ronnie's. I met him last year. He and

I did some business for awhile. I heard about what happened to him. Hey! Can I come in?" Trevor motioned him in, closing the door behind him. The stranger continued. "Yeah Ronnie took care of business and was a stand-up guy. He told me if I ever came through and wanted to do some business in Durham and couldn't find him that you were cool."

"What kind of business are you talking about?" asked Trevor.

The Professor looked around, slyly before answering. "I supplied him with a little dope now and then. I've been in town a couple days from Jersey, got a little something - - - I'd like to move."

"How did you know where to find me?" Trevor ask,

"I came by one night, riding with Ronnie, he ran in for a minute and I waited in the car. You know --- I didn't want to meet anyone. That's the night he told me that you were his partner and was cool."

That was enough for Trevor. He had brought whatever the stranger was selling.

"So, you got some dope you trying to get off?" Asked Trevor.

"Yeah, answered the Professor. Just a little something. I'll be in town a couple of days. I thought I'd try and turn a few dollars while I'm here. If it works out, I might try to do a little something here for minute. Since Ronnie died, I haven't had a hook up down here. What you think, you think we can see what we can do?"

Trevor was caught. "So, let me check the shit out. If it's any good, we can roll." Trevor said.

"I only have a couple of bags on me. You got somebody to check it for us?" Asked the Professor. He knew what the response would be. He was playing a game. He loved playing mind games. Role playing, assuming different characters, using his wit.

"Shit, I'm your man." Said Trevor. "We don't need to find nobody. I'll let you know what it is."

The Professor reached in his front pocket and pulled out two small glassine bags with Christmas tape. Trevor anxiously reached for the bags - - - after grabbing them, he held them up to the light, thumbing each bag, checking out the weight. A smile broke across his face. He was moved by the possibility of getting rid of his sickness --- and finding a connection. For that moment he thought his luck was about to change.

Trevor headed for the bathroom. In the bathroom he reached in the cabinet over the stained sink for his syringe and bottle top. He anxiously unbuckled the leather belt that held up his grimy jeans, ripping the belt from around his waist --- looping it around his arm. An arm with tracks, scare tissue that appeared as small dark ropes, starting at the pit of his arm running downward. He dumped the heroin into the bottle top, spraying it with twenty centimeters of water from the syringe. Nervously, he pulled two matches from a book of matches with the face of "Joe Camel" on the cover. He scratched them against the grain, fire exploded, releasing the smell of sulfur. Holding the flame under the bottle top, the heroin came to a boil ---forming into a clear liquid. He drew the drug from the bottle top and thumped the syringe with his finger to get rid of the air bubbles. He pulled the belt tightly around his arm and locked it in his mouth between his teeth. His scared veins popped up. He pushed the needle into his arm as the professor watched - - smelling the stench of the clustered bathroom.

The blood sucked into the syringe, mixing with the heroin. Trevor looked down at the syringe as he pushed the death serum into his vein. In two minutes he raised his head looking at the stranger --- mumbling, "Damn, this shit is to --- much, he tried to rise from the stool, reaching for the professor's arm, trying to balance himself. The small-cluttered bathroom had become completely dark . . . he was going out, scratching the walls, trying to stand. He finally fell to the floor, bumping his head on the sink.

The professor checked his pulse --- the heartbeat was faint. He waited, walking through the small apartment, refusing to touch anything. As he walked, he observed books, schoolbooks. On the table was the next assignment for the one o'clock chemistry lab. The lab he taught. He moved to the window and looked out into the night. The street was empty, quiet, not a soul was stirring. Fifteen minutes passed, he checked Trevor' pulse again …there was no heartbeat.

The professor eased out the door into the night, whistling a soft melody.

CHAPTER 16

Solomon rested in the comfort of his home on Snow Hill Road in Northern Durham County. He reclined on the couch in front of the T.V. as he sipped from a glass filled with Vodka and Orange Juice. In the back of his mind he toyed with the case. The sound of keys unlocking the front door startled him. He turned toward the door in time to see Sarah Anne coming through the door, waving and smiling. Caught off guard he screamed, “Girl you better watch yourself, I thought someone was breaking in one me. You look like you just won the lottery. Why you got that chummy look on your face?”

“Two things,” she remarked softly as she sat on the couch beside him. He smelled her perfume and couldn't help but notice her fresh happy spirit. He starred at her longingly.

“First, I'm so blessed to have you as a dad.” She said

“Alright; what you sweeting, me up for girl?” He asked with a smile.

“No dad, I mean it. Second, I need you to do something for me.”

Solomon looked at her with raised eyebrows. “Do something like what?” he asked.

She sighed, “I need you to go out to dinner with Juan, his mother and I.”

He looked up at the ceiling, laughing. “Sweetheart, you know I love you but I ain't bout to go out on no dinner date.”

‘I'm serious, daddy. Juan and I been seeing each other for a while, we're serious about each other and thank it's about time we all get to know each other. We'll drive up from Charlotte --- it'll be fun. It's not like, a date for you and Mrs. Johnson; it will just be kinda of a get to know you, dinner. Mrs. Johnson has agreed and would like to know more about our family."

Sarah Anne sat back, eyeing him waiting for an answer. "What's her name?" "Mrs. Johnson, Ethel. You'll like her. We'll just have a nice dinner and let the conversation flow."

"Sarah Anne, you know I haven't been out to dinner but one or two times since we lost your mother. I've tried to stay away from the things your mom and I use to do --- anything that remind me of the good days. Tell them I'm busy working on a murder case, right now."

"Sorry, they'll know I'm putting them off. It's only for one night for a couple of hours."

She touched him on the arm, "Daddy do this for me." He couldn't bare it any longer. Sarah Anne's humility was killing him.

"Alright, already'"

She hugged and kissed his face. "You see, that's why I'm, so glad you're my Daddy."

"How can I refuse you --- setting there looking like your momma?" He said.

She winced. He intensified, saying, "Then you will help me and the church next Saturday evening when we go down to feed the homeless. Every fourth Saturday we feed the homeless; trying to do some good. It will help you keep your feet on the ground to see the suffering of others.

She gave a long sigh, "You got me, next Saturday."

"So, when is the dinner date?' he asked

"Let's make it the Saturday after next." She said.

"Fine, that will give me enough time to talk myself into being pleasant."

She gasped. He laughed and asked flatly, "What's going on with you and Juan? Why you guys trying to get your parents together?"

"We just think it's time you guys meet."

He looked at her over his glasses and growled. "Okay, I'll meet momma and be nice. He pointed at her "no tricks now."

CHAPTER 17

IT WAS TWO DAYS BEFORE Trevor's body was found. At the Durham Police Headquarters, a complaint clerk listened while Mattie Smith the owner of the four family units where Trevor lived reported seeing him lying on the floor as she looked through the window.

"You say you own the building?"

"Yes ma'am"

"Where are you?"

"Right across the street, it's 608 Cecil Street, Apartment D." As the complaint clerk spoke, she typed the information on a computer, so she could pass it on to the dispatcher when finished.

"Ma'am, I want you to stay where you are." The complaint clerk told the caller, "Someone will be there shortly."

A mile or so away, uniform officer Bernard Bell, in a blue and white cruiser was parked talking to a couple of guys at the Chalk and Rack Pool Hall on the lower end of Fayetteville Street when he received the urgent call. Immediately, he fired his car up, made a U-Turn in the middle of the street, ties screeching, and with his siren and lights flashing, headed for 608 Cecil Street.

In less than five minutes, Officer Bell joined Mrs. Smith outside the apartment building.

"Who is the apartment rented to ma'am?" He asked. "Marvin Hall from Rocky Mount but his son Trevor lives there. He's a student at the college, pointing up the street at NCCU."

Using Mrs. Smith's key, Officer Bell cautiously entered the apartment. Instantly he drew back because of the stench, and then forced himself to take a look at the scene, knowing he would have to give the details later. The apartment was extremely hot … he located the thermostat on the wall by the kitchen. It was set at 90 degrees. He lowered the temperature. Realizing the stench was from the body decaying from the intense heat.

What he saw was the body of a young African American male, lying on the floor by the bathroom door. His shirt unbuttoned to the waist, no shoes, no socks and wearing a pair of blue jeans. The young man's face appeared to be bloated; and a belt was looped around his arm. In the bathroom was a bottle top, a book of matches and a syringe. The T.V. was playing in the living room.

Officer Bell didn't touch a thing in the apartment. He backed out the door, returned to his cruiser, picked up the portable radio and called Dispatch. His unit number appeared on the Dispatcher's screen. His voice was hoarse. "I need a Homicide Unit on the Tac Two ---- Cecil Street, behind NCCU, 608 Cecil Street and call the CAT TEAM, tell them to send someone also."

Detective Jake Morris from the Homicide Unit was on his way to headquarters driving an unmarked car when he checked in with Dispatch. The Dispatcher alerted Morris, who switched to Tac Two, "Fourteen-ten to one-forty-four."

"One body at 608 Cecil Street," Bell responded, "Possible drug overdose." He paused, finding composure. "Contact someone from the Task Force."

Detective Jake Morris put in a call to Solomon King. He'd heard King was assigned to the Task Force. He didn't know much about the others on the Task Force….so King was the first choice. Solomon was seated at his desk trying to finish a cup of coffee he'd pilfered when his phone rang. "King here!" Jake spoke on the other end. "Jake what in hell would cause you to call me be before 9:30 in the morning. You know it takes me till 10:00 o'clock to finish my first cup of coffee. "Morris told him about the body on Cecil Street. Solomon replied "I'm on my way. Secure the scene. Keep everyone out of the place ---including the police."

Solomon shouted down the hall, "Graves get your ass in gear, we're on the move." Detective Linda Graves ran from her office shaking her hands trying to dry the nail polish she had just applied. King looked at Graves, "you got to do the nails after work sweetheart. We got police work to do around here. We got another stiff." Graves rushed toward the door as Solomon moseyed behind her to the dark blue cruiser assigned to Graves ---with Graves at the wheel they spun out the parking lot as she pushed hard on the accelerator. As Graves gunned the cruiser down the Durham Freeway toward Fayetteville Street, Solomon radioed Detective Quentin Goode of the vice squad's CAT TEAM, instructing him to join him at 608 Cecil Street. Turning off his radio Solomon starred at Graves, chewing on his cigar. "Hey, slow down, the man is already dead. Let's not kill ourselves on the way and join him at the morgue. Take your time, we'll make it there in time for the funeral." Detective Graves cut her eyes at Solomon--forcing a smile. She'd never seen a man---a police officer who appeared so unconcerned.

The last month had been nothing but a media blast concerning the overdose cases. Phone calls ---reporters from the Herald Sun, News and Observer, the story being relived over and over on WTVD channel 11 and WRAL channel 5 ... competing for each new detail. Today would be another day where the media hounds would fight over the tidbit of information like hungry dogs over bones.

Solomon and Detective Graves arrived at the apartment within moments of Vice Officer Goode, and together they stood in front of the apartment. Goode, with a full beard, street clothes and dark shades looked like a hustler. A Durhamite by birth, he'd been on the CAT

TEAM's narc squad for a decade and knew almost every dealer who ever sold dope in Durham.

Goode respected and like Solomon, in part because he was never a threat to anyone's dreams and worked cases the old fashion way. He knew Solomon did his job well and had not sought promotions. Solomon made it clear he didn't want to be anyone's boss and had never taken the Lieutenant's exam which would have been a breeze. He knew Solomon was a good man to have working the case, any case.

As they took a minute for informal chatter, a few of the neighbors could be seen standing on their porches and in their yards, whispering, speculating, and trying to see what had happened. Solomon saw a WTVD News van cruising by … apparently, they had heard the news on their police scanner, trying to beat the other hounds to the scene.

Solomon looked at Goode, "Okay, let's see what we got."

As he turned the doorknob and they went inside, Goode wrinkled his nose, "Damn it smells like he's been dead for a week!"

Linda shook her head and let out a ghastly sigh. The odor of death was in the air, a rank smell that permeated the entire place.

Solomon looked at Graves, "you mind taking notes?" She pulled a small spiral ring pad from her jacket pocket. "First record the time we entered the apartment," he said, "We need every action taken until we close this thing. The old memory sometimes goes bad."

Neither of them was moving ---they stood still, surveying the scene from the front door. Black leather couch, coffee table with what looked like schoolbooks and an ash tray on it, a small color T.V. playing in the far corner, stereo system in the other. Solomon moved forward ---he could see the kitchen area with a small table. In the hallway by the bathroom door was the body of a young looking African American man. Stretched out on his side, legs curled in a fetus position, no shoes and socks, shirt opened. He looked past the body into the bathroom --- instantly he saw a bottle top, book of matches and a syringe.

Apart from the body lying on the floor, the place looked like a regular bachelor's apartment.

He turned to Goode and Graves, "Looks like he was getting high. I see the glassine bags, bottle top and the matches on the bathroom counter. Solomon put on a pair of latex gloves, walked over and turned the T.V. off.

Graves scribble notes. Goode made a series of calls on his portable police phone. "608 Cecil Street --- we got a body and what could be another overdose. I'm here with Detective King and Detective Graves." Solomon stood still … looking around puffing on his cigar.

Goode made contact with the Crime Scene ID Team --- a identification unit would come out and photograph the crime scene and all the evidence including minuscule particles that the natural eye might miss. They would search for fingerprints, preserve blood samples, and swipe the place for clues. Until they came and finished their search, the entire place would remain sealed off --- and left just as it was found.

Solomon made a couple of calls of his own: he called Detective Jon Parker of the Task Force, who was already on his way. And then he called Captain Fletcher asking him to keep the media out of it ---if he could.

As the ID Team worked to make a positive identification of the victim--- the medical examiner arrived to inspect the body and appeared to be insulted having to wait until the ID Team completed their work.

Finally, the body was removed to the Morgue where an autopsy would follow, with pathologist Thomas Stroud attending.

No one said a word while Stroud inspected the body. Solomon surveyed the room. He didn't see anything out of place. He prayed the ID Team would find something after sorting through the evidence. He knew in his gut the young man on the floor was another junkie who hadn't just happened to shoot too much dope….and there was a killer loose, using high quality heroin as his weapon.

Goode finally spoke. "I got to get out of here…and get some fresh air, the stench is about to make me recall my breakfast." He headed for the front door.

Solomon walked over to Detective Graves shaking his head and chewing his cigar. "I don't know what the world is coming to. This kid was a student. There's unfinished homework on the coffee table ---I'm sure his momma and daddy sent him here so he could be better off in the world." Graves looks up from her note pad, "he apparently got himself involved in something other than class." Solomon puffed on his cigar. "Yeah! But the world is becoming a pretty rotten place --- I've never seen it so bad. It's time for me to pass the baton and get out of this kind of work. I don't have the stomach for it much more."

Graves contemplated for a second. "The world's always been or should I say people have always been ruthless and savage, the difference is we got more people now, and we hear more about the killings from over the world…thanks to the news hounds. In fact, they're circling outside as I speak."

Solomon shrugged. "Yeah, yeah, it's still sickening."

The ID Team began photographing the corpse, taking three photos of several angles; an overall shot, a close and a midrange shot. After the body shots, the photographer shot over areas of the bathroom, the counter with the syringe, the small hallway leading from the bathroom where the body was found and a shot of the living room and small kitchen. The photos might reveal evidence overlooked at first sight.

Robin Hart of the ID Team was busy searching for latent fingerprints, concentrating on doorknobs, the coffee table, the telephone and exits, anywhere a perpetrator's might have left his mark.

Solomon glanced at his watch. It was 3:15 p.m., he'd been at the crime scene for over six hours. His shift would end in another hour and he needed to get home to feed Princess. He knew she was getting hungry by now. Plus, there was nothing he could do to help at the crime scene. He had to wait and see what the technicians come up with.

He thought about the young kid in the black body bag, wondering if he knew any of the other overdose victims. The kid's name, Trevor Hall sounded familiar. He couldn't place where he'd heard it before. But he knew he'd heard it.

The biggest problem in the case was the same in the others, no one, not one of the neighbors had seen anyone coming or going from the apartment. Somehow, if the kid was murdered the killer had managed to get in and out of the apartment and area without drawing any attention to himself.

He still could not figure the motive for killing junkies. No sign of robbery, none of the victims were known to carry large sums of money. No dope found at the scene --- so the victims didn't appear to be dealers. Why use heroin to kill. He didn't have a clue, motive or a prime suspect.

Shortly after nine o'clock on Thursday, two days after Trevor Hall's death, Detective Linda Graves walked from the ID Unit to Solomon's office.

"Good morning, Solomon," she said smiling.

"What's so damn good about it?" He asked glumly, "It's gonna get better. Do we have any clues from the Hall's crime scene?" She asked. "Not a one" he said.

"I have the list of overdose deaths you asked me to pull and organized a day or so ago. Plus, a second list of the next of kin for everyone on the list. In the last five years there have been eighteen deaths from overdose and five of those in the last month. Solomon listened carefully. She continued, "Interestingly, on the next of kin list we have mostly close family members, mothers, and sisters. Get this, one UNC student Bridgett Kerns, her uncle is the next of kin." Flipping through her notes, "James Alford." Solomon bit down on his cigar. "Let me see that." Graves passed him the folder, looking as if she had just won the lottery.

Graves asked, "Is that not the same name, James Alford, the man who teaches down at NCCU. The guy that Ronnie Banks' sister said was Ronnie's advisor who came by to give his condolence?" Solomon puffed on his cigar as he pointed, "look over in the cabinet and give me the Banks file." Detective Graves rose from her seat with an unsettled look on her face. She pulled on the old grey file draw and found the Banks file Solomon had started. Solomon reached for the file. He chewed on his cigar as he read the contents. Looking up at Graves he spoke. "Trevor Hall was the friend of Ronnie Banks according to Banks' sister. The both of them were students over at NCCU ---studying chemistry.

Detective Graves' brow shot up. "What? So, wait a minute we got the Kerns girl who is Alford's niece --- we got Banks and Hall who were students at NCCU. All of them knew Alford in some way. Is that a coincidence or what?" She asked. "I don't believe in coincidences" Solomon mumbled.

CHAPTER 18

LINDA WOKE UP LAZILY, SHE'D hit the snooze button twice --- she lay quietly, thinking. She thought about the man she had once married and still loved. The children she'd dreamed they'd have together and the disappointment she felt discovering he was living a double life; one as her husband and the other as a down low brother, loving other men. The news of Ricks' double life had broken her heart, causing her to examine herself as if she was the cause.

She had loved him for five years. Never wandered, never thought about it. He was the perfect man for her ----she'd thought. She had delved into the thoughts on many mornings, over and over again of how she'd missed all the signs. Her heart still ached, and her pride still suffered.

When she met Rick, he was too handsome to ignore. Star football player, brown chocolate skin. Their love broke the rule, black man …white woman. Everywhere they went women were taken by his good looks and class. She fell in love overnight, trusted him completely, and lusted for him on sight. Each day their love seemed to grow. He surprised her with flowers and gifts. He massaged her sore muscles, made her laugh, and served her breakfast in bed. In the night he brought her to feverish orgasms.

She finally set up and sighed, rose from her bed and drug herself to the shower. As she showered, she snapped out of her funk and came to life under the spew of warm water.

Dripping wet and nude, she walked over an opened the curtains wide, filling the darkness of her small townhouse with the beaming morning sunlight. Its heat quickly penetrated the windowpanes of the chilled air-conditioned rooms, taking the chill away. For breakfast she craved toast and jelly and a chaser of black coffee --- her morning shot of caffeine and daily pick - me -up.

She had spent the evening at a Durham Bull's baseball game with one of her sorority sisters, who like her was in between men.

Linda admired herself as she nourished her skin with creamy lotion, feeling proud her thighs, abs and breast still had their youthful appearance. Just as it did as a cheerleader while at Mercer College, down in Georgia nearly ten years ago. She turned on the T.V. from mute to sound, catching the local news and weather as she found her robe.

Looking in the mirror --- Linda smiled as she gracefully combed her hair back and twisted her ponytail into a rubber band. Her eyes sauntered the pictures of her family on the walls --- thinking of how they'd raised her the best they knew and believed --- with southern values. Bringing Rick home had driven a wedge between her relationship with them, in spite of all the forgiveness, things hadn't never quite been the same.

People usually grow up to value whatever was handed to them by the adults around them; the good and the bad --- dragging issues and baggage into their adult lives. She wanted to be a cop because her daddy was a sheriff and his daddy before him.

She was attracted to Rick because her family forbidden her to have a black girlfriend in junior high school. She refused to attend church because she wasn't allowed to miss a day as a child. Much of her life had become a routine of habits learned and decided on from the life she lived as a kid.

She ate her toast, jelly and drank her black coffee while the news anchor told of a murder on Dowd Street, a school break-in in Wall town, an earthquake in Pakistan and warned of another hot day.

In another ten minutes she'd finished her toast and was searching for her car keys. By 8:45 she had arrived at headquarters and headed down the hall to Solomon's office.

She let herself in. "What's cooking Solomon? Where do we start—?" Solomon sipped coffee from the same cup, he'd use the day before. "We've been invited or should I say ordered to suffer through the weekly task force meeting. It starts in five minutes --- so roll your pant legs up and take a pill so the smell of the bullshit won't upset your stomach." He looked at his watch --- "shall we my dear?"

The newly formed Task Force gathered around a long red cherry table with Captain Fletcher at one end and Bill Fisk from the Mayor's Office at the other, along with the District Attorney for the City of Durham, Bill Noel and eight others. Twenty years earlier Noel had been one of the best attorneys in the City --- with a full partnership in his father's law firm. He was bitten by the political bug and ran for the top job in the District Attorney's office. Noel felt comfortable with the police and them with him.

Noel asked, "Since we'll be working together, do you mind telling me what you're doing ---

"What's the plan?" His eyes fell on Caption Fletcher. Captain Fletcher replied, "Honestly we don't have a clue of where this heroin is coming from and who is passing it out. We've been mostly responding to the 911 calls and finding bodies. We've got homicide and vice combing through this thing." Looking at Solomon he continued, "We've pulled some of our most experienced and best officers off everything and put them on this case. We're gonna get a break on this thing --- we just have to keep at it."

"Have you been pulling people in?" Noel asked.

Detective Jon Parker setting across from Solomon cut an eye in Solomon's direction. "We don't have enough to go on." Noel scanned the room, taking in all the detectives. "Since we've been keeping up with this thing, it's unbelievable that we've got five bodies that we know of all dead from heroin and no one has any idea, who's selling this shit --- to select people. Captain, I suggest you use surveillance on every known drug dealer and location in the city until we can come up with something."

Sergeant Colon Allen, a salt and pepper haired black man with twenty years on the streets as a patrol officer cautioned, "we've got to be very careful that whoever is spreading this dope around don't get spooked. Remember, how little evidence we have so far. And if whoever is doing this suspects we're looking for him, he might shut down, leaving us high and dry ---then we'll never catch him."

"We have to move but discreetly" said Allen. As the dialogue went back and forth, Solomon chewed on his cigar and kept silent. Detective Linda Graves opened her mouth to speak but Solomon used his foot to kick her on the ankle. She knew the kick meant she needed to keep her mouth closed.

"With good surveillance we might be able to catch him in the act." Noel said. Jon Parker spoke then paused. "We won't do that; we won't catch whoever this is in the act. I know we sure as hell don't want him killing anyone else. But I doubt we will catch him staking out dope houses and corners. First, we have to figure out his motive --- then maybe we will have some idea of who we're hunting."

"Catching him in the act would be a home run for the Prosecutor's Office but I doubt that will happen." Everybody laughed lightly. Noel quieted the group with a smile and wave of the hand. "I suppose surveillance does have its drawbacks. We know this guy is smart, if it's what we think, so let's not try to alert him."

Captain Fletcher spoke up as he looked at Jon Parker and Quinten Goode from the CAT TEAM. "I do want you to move on all the dealers --- let them feel the heat. Maybe someone will give us something --- anything."

It was agreed that they would apply the heat. Fill the streets with more officers, bust drug dealers and work informants. The group left the conference room whispering without any clues and with only a half- cocked plan.

Walking along side Solomon and once out of the earshot of the others, Graves finally spoke. “I hope you know you owe me a pair of panty hose. You put a run in my hose when you kicked me. What in hell was the kicking about anyway?” Solomon continued walking, looking straight ahead, “You were about to open your mouth and tell them we'd found that Professor Alfred knew Banks and Hall --- and the Bridgett Kerns was also Alford's niece. I'm not quite ready to reveal that tad bit of information as of yet. Fletcher and that “cowboy” of a prosecutor would've jumped the gun and mad a mess of it. We got some checking to do first.” Solomon finally turned, looking at Graves as he entered the door of his clustered office. “I want you to track down all the next of kin on your list. We'll talk to each of them and see what we can find out.”

CHAPTER 19

DETECTIVE GRAVES FELT LIKE SHE was in a circle jerk --- trying to keep up with Solomon and the overdose cases and now chasing down some lady who'd call claiming she knew who was attacking women on the West End. 718 Green Street --- was the address the woman had given. The call came in during the midnight shift --- Sergeant Seagroves shoved the pink slip of paper with the name and address at her as soon as she had reported to work. He'd said the caller sounded like an old lady. The lady had said she knew as sure as the world who was attacking the women. He had promised to have someone out to see her first thing the next morning.

"Okay, there it is --- 718," Linda spoke to herself. Bent over the steering wheel, peering out the window --- she brought the dark blue cruiser to a halt. Linda got out the cruiser --- closed the door, casually looked around and walked up the cracked sidewalk beside the chain linked fence leading to the iron gate. She raised the latch and walked up to the small one-story house painted in white with dark green trim. Flowerpots, and hanging planters with greenery lined the front porch. There was an old fashion bench swing on the right side of the porch. The house and surroundings made her think of the houses back in Greenville, South Carolina on Pegram Street where she'd grown up. It gave the notion that some nice church momma lived there.

Linda was carrying her Glock 9mm. She'd unsnapped the holster. Although this wasn't official, she still wasn't willing to take any chances.

There were two young black men, looking to be in their early twenties swaggered down Green Street --- checking out the police cruiser, and then giving her a suspicious stare. She walked up to the screen door, knocked and waited at the door.

In a minute or two a small elderly black woman opened the inside wooden door and stood on the other side of the screen which separated her from Graves. The woman looked and hesitated. She slowly unlatched the screen door, peeping at Graves. "Come on in. Who are you?" She asked. "I'm Detective Linda Graves. How are you ma'am?" Graves flashed her I.D. The old lady pointed toward a twine bottom chair, "Rest your feet child. I'm having my morning coffee. Would you like a cup?" She asked. "I'd better not, I've had two cups already," Linda said. "You're welcome." The old lady retorted. Linda noticed a pile of old newspapers stacked by the rocking chair where the lady sat. In a matter of seconds, the old lady had completely turned her off as she watched the morning news. Linda quickly suspected the old lady was avid about reading newspaper and keeping up with the news. Linda felt blocked out as the old lady watched the news as if she was in a trance. For a few minutes Linda set still looking around at the room filled with old furniture, inhaling the musty smell of stale air and pine oil. Wrinkled faced and with weary eyes --- the old lady wore a flowered dress and long cotton stockings. Her grey hair was pulled into a French Roll on the top of her head. Linda could see signs of her beauty from younger years. Linda finally cleared her throat, "ma'am if you could I'd like to talk with you about a call we received last night from someone who gave us this address." The old lady shifted her eyes from the black and white T.V. toward Linda. "Yes, that would be me. I made the call." She said. "Do you mind if I write down a few notes as I ask you some questions? Linda asked. "Do whatever you need to do honey." The old lady replied. "Okay, ma'am, let's start with your name. Linda held a pen in her hand as she waited for the old lady to speak. "Emma Peterson, that's me." She said. Linda moved with caution. "Now tell me what you know." The old lady shifted her attention from the T.V. "Little Al, I been knowing him since he was a boy. He been back home for about six months. I been watching him through my window here as he walks down the street looking at women. The same as he did before." Linda looked down at her note pad at the name Little Al. Knowing that wasn't much to go on. "Ms. Peterson, can I call you Ms. Peterson? What is Little Al's whole name and where have he been?" She asked. "He's named after his daddy, Alan Winstead. His daddy is dead now. Been dead for about fifteen years, momma dead too. They both died while Little Al was away in prison. He worried them half to death. He was always into one thing or the other since he was little." She had Linda's attention. "What was he in prison for and how long was he gone?" Linda asked. "He always was messing wit every girl round here. He wouldn't leave them alone. Grabbing and feeling on them. He couldn't be round no other child unless he messed wit dem. His momma and daddy tried to protect him the best they could --- always having to apologize for the boy's mess --- until they finally caught up wit him for raping dem girls at Duke. It was more than twenty years ago. He been in prison ever since then until about six months ago." Linda wrote as fast as she could. "So where is Alan living ma'am, do you know?" "He's down in the house on Ivey Circle a block away from here --- the house he grew up in. His folks left it for him. It used to be a nice house. No body stayed in it for about ten years --- then he came home and moved back in. I know he's the one. None of this, attacking women didn't start til he got back round here. You need to get him off the street." "The talk is that he's doing it" the old lady said. "Word has a way of getting around, all around."

Linda looked at her notes and then at the old lady. The old lady seemed so sure of herself.

"Ma'am I trust what you say and will check it out." Linda said. She noticed the old lady was in another trance --- watching the morning segment of the national news. "Well thank you ma'am. I'll let myself out." Linda walked out of the house toward the cruiser, aware that she was being watched by the old lady who stood in the window as she fired up the cruiser and drove away.

CHAPTER 20

THEY WENT IN DETECTIVE GRAVES' car, Solomon sitting next to her and Detective Roger Tilley from the Sex Crime Unit, in the back seat. The drive was like a Sunday afternoon ride through the city with the kids ---- cruising, in no hurry, listening to the radio, Sunny 93.7. Solomon sank down low in his seat, chewing on a knobby cigar as he read over Linda's notes on Alan Winstead. He looked as she guided the cruiser down Chapel Hill Road toward Green Street ---- "Left here," he murmured. "No right," said Tilley from the back seat. Ivey street runs across Chapel Hill Road, I think the 600 block is to the right." She turned right. "There it is, said Tilley --- 920 on the left-hand side.

Linda turned the cruiser into a narrow blacktop drive leading to a crummy one story house with chipped white paint, trimmed in blue, lost in vines, tall grass, weed filled flower beds and untended shrubbery that dipped and scraped the windows of an old 1980 something Plymouth parked just outside the front door. Linda slowed and parked behind it and killed the engine. Solomon and Tilley opened the doors of the cruiser and wobbled out. Tilley placed his hand on the hood of the old Plymouth --- the hood was cold. Then he noticed the car had a flat tire. Inside the car he noticed beer cans, an old box of Kentucky Fried Chicken scrapes and paper all over the floor. He spoke, "this car seems to be broke down, with the flat and all."

Thinking, Linda's mind rolled back to the old lady. Ms. Walston and how sure she had seemed that Alan Winstead was the one attacking women, again. The old lady was right; he had come home six months before the attacks started. With a look of confidence on her face, the old women had warned it wasn't a coincident. She was convinced it was Alan, the same man with the same rage toward women that had terrorized the neighborhood nearly thirty years earlier. Waiting, watching, playing mind games, searching out unsuspecting victims and making late night calls, forcing himself on them.

Linda stiffened. The sun beamed between the shrubbery. Her tan skin glowed against the sun. The shrubbery scraped the side of the cruiser. She ducked her head as she opened the door and felt her running shoes crunch the glass and debris under her feet. She followed as Solomon led the way to the torn screen door of an old house that had fallen from grace. Solomon pulled the shabby screen open so he could knock on the brown wooden door. The three detectives waited. Solomon knocked again. "Mr. Winstead, Durham Police, anybody home?" Tilley looked toward the window --- peeping, trying to see on the inside. Solomon turned the doorknob the door was unlocked. He opened the door, "Anybody home, Durham Police." They went inside to an abyss of stained walls, rancid trash, empty cans, rotten carpet and dusty overturned furniture. A cot with a pillow and blanket set in the corner of the room what was once the family den. Beside the cot was a table with candles and an ash tray.

Solomon called out again, "Hello. Police." His voice echoed through the house. Tilley had left and returned with a flashlight. The three detectives using the flashlight followed one another from room to room, down the hallway, brushing cobwebs from their faces. The weak rotten floor in the back of the house lead to the bathroom where a small candle was burning. The floor felt like it would give away on the next step. Solomon pointed to a bloody handprint on the wall leading down the hall to the bathroom ---Tilley stopped and examined the bloodstain with the light. Linda stayed close behind Solomon like a kid being lead through the house of horror on Halloween.

The place was cold, damp and awful. As they made their way to the candle lit bathroom, roaches and rats scattered out of the way.

Linda whispered, "it don't seem as if anyone lives here. Maybe old Ms. Walston was wrong. Winstead has to be living somewhere else. No one can live in a place like this." Neither Solomon nor Tilley said a word.

Solomon kept his eye on the drops of dried brown blood leading toward the bathroom. In the bathroom the red burning candle had burnt down to the wick --- the flame was weak and wavering, a thin funnel of dark smoke reached for the ceiling. Solomon stopped at the door. His 6'4", 260-pound frame filled the door, shielding Tilley and Linda outside. In the bathtub was the body of a young black woman --- nude, head turned to the side, blood covered her torso, her right breast mangled, throat slit, the carotid artery severed. Solomon spoke in a low subdued tone. "We got a body in here. It's messy. Linda would you mind going to the cruiser and call this in. We need to get the crime lab people out here." Without looking in the bathroom, Linda turned and headed for the cruiser.

Tilley finally looked pass Solomon into the bathroom. He gasped, "damn, that poor woman is cut to pieces. Whoever did this is an animal. He's over the edge."

Tilley aimed the flashlight at the body, and then around the bathroom. On the floor was a bloody towel, an empty half gallon bottle of Richard's Wild Irish Rose Wine, cigarette butts and a bloody steak knife laying in the corner by the sink. Solomon and Tilley backed out the room making sure not to touch anything --- preserving the crime scene.

They headed to the front of the house. The floor creaked with each step. The rustle of the untended shrubbery and vines seeped through the broken windows. Tilley searched the front room with his light. He noticed a medium size brown cardboard box in the corner by the sleeping cot. He walked over to the box and opened it with the end of the flashlight. The box was filled with women's underwear --- bras and panties, old and new in all sizes. A box of collectibles, trophies, Alan Winstead trophies.

Solomon and Tilley paddled through the darkness. They looked but didn't touch anything in any of the old musty rooms, in the closets, or inside obscure cabinets. Tilley flashed his light against the walls, scanned the floors and sent the varmints running.

Some fifteen minutes later Detective Jake Morris for Homicide had arrived along with two other officers Solomon didn't recognize. They cordoned off the entire house with yellow display tape --- POLICE LINE DO NOT CROSS. Morris approached Solomon who was standing between the house and a carouse crowd. "What we got here?" He asked Solomon. "Graves, Tilley and I came out here following up a lead on a possible suspect in the West End rapes. We knocked on the door, no one answered, the door was open, and we went in. We found the body in the bathtub. We haven't touched a thing."

Morris acted fast; reaching for his portable radio secured to his belt and made several calls.

First, he called for ID Team to identify the body, take prints and gather every piece of evidence. He called the Medical Examiner to view the victim and then State Attorney's Office.

Morris turned his attention to the house. He went in with Solomon and viewed the murder victim and the cruel sadistic fashion she was killed. He scribbled notes and made a sketch without disturbing anything --- on how the victim was positioned, the wound on her breast and neck. Meticulously moving through the house behind Solomon inhaling the smoke from Solomon's cigar mixed with the musty smell of the house, he considered what he saw as he viewed each room.

A few minutes later an ID crew of three technicians arrived, right behind them was the Medical Examiner, Susan Caine.

Within the next four hours the evidence and crime scene were processed. Near the end of the shift the remains were identified as Carla Bennett, a twenty- five- year old woman from the West End known as a drug user and street walker. She was placed in a body bag and shipped to the county morgue for an autopsy.

In another two days study and analysis had been completed on much of the evidence collected by the ID crew. There was no doubt Alan Winstead had left his signature. An identification card for Winstead was found in the contents found beside the sleeping cot --- his fingerprints were found on the steak knife --- his DNA was found mixed with the victim's body fluids. Alan Winstead was now a hunted man --- on the run.

CHAPTER 21

IN MOMENTS OF SELF-ANALYSIS, PROFESSOR James Alford had dissected his soul, seeking the source of his madness. He concluded that it had not come all at once, not overnight but had evolved in time. He remembered the remorseful weeks following Bridgett's death, the loneliness the feelings of loss and then the anger. He felt someone should pay for her death. His anger grew inside, he convinced himself she'd been murdered the same as if someone had put a pistol to her head. The heroin was the pistol, the poison sold by drug dealers to the innocent, anyone with the price of the bag. He lived with the torment of his pain day after day for over a year. The anger ate away his soul---his rationale, his logic. Anger that set off a thirst for revenge.

Using heroin as his weapon of choice came while reading a story in the Washington Post. The story told of a string of deaths in D.C. resulting from high quality, killer heroin. The article called it poisonous. The number of addicts dying from the poisonous drug mounted each day for a month. Deaths after deaths were numbered on the 6 o'clock news. Public health and law enforcement officials warned addicts of the poisonous drugs circulating through the city. Because of their unfulfilled hankering addicts ignored the warnings and sought to buy and use the killer heroin in spite of the risk of death ---- searching for the near-death blast. As the Professor read the article his mind began to race --- thinking of how he could use heroin to revenge Bridgett's death. The answer had come to him. His pain and anger had pushed him over the edge. At home he turned his study into a mini lab creating his weapon of revenge. After weeks of measuring and mixing just the right amount of morphine base, and acetic acid, studying the results, he created his own brand of heroin. He transported it to the University Chemistry Lab where he worked for hours testing the drug for purity, by injecting it into the blood stream of mice, in measured amounts calculated by body weight. He watched as the drug caused their heart rate to slow and stop---each mouse struggling, trying to stand and escape death. The Professor would stand and watch as his imagination transformed each mouse to a man --- a drug dealer. Then he would choose a second one and a third and would watch as mouse after mouse struggled and fought trying to fend off death. That's where and when it all started.

The MONEY CHANGER, Durham's hottest night club. Tonight, the Professor set secluded in the night. The dark green Buick rental sedan he'd driven to the club to add to his disguise. He shielded himself in the far corner of the parking lot. He shook his head and looked out into the parking lot as the thoughts of how and why he'd killed over and over played inside his mind. The soft raindrops cooled the night from what had been a blistering summer day. Cars buzzed by, with tires causing a frying sound against the asphalt.

Men and women of the night, the big money players, dressed in dowdy suits. Hustlers camouflaged as honorable citizens in expensive clothing. Worthless men and women, living off crime, drugs and foolishness. The Professor seethed as he watched. He waited for his next victim--- his index finger tapping the steering wheel. A half hour, forty-five minutes. Where was he?

Raymond Kelly hated Durham — at least the circle of people he was tied in with. The hustlers, dealers, boosters, whores and junkies. A group of rabid, diseased humans living in a cesspool; a sore that feed on itself, mindless, self-serving men and women who prayed on the weak, the human vultures. He knew the type well because he was one of the vultures, a heartless, sponging piece of bacteria preying on the weakness of others... always circling like a buzzard over a dead caucus. In high school he was drawn to the streets --- hustlers and fast money. Twenty years later selling and using dope was his life, his occupation and how he lived.

Raymond answered the door, passed the man the bag and collected the money with his abscessed swollen hands. He rapped the twenty-dollar bill around the knot of money from his pocket tied with a thick rubber band. He slammed the door and counted his cash --- picked up the phone and called Annie Mae. Annie Mae Slade was his woman and partner. It was time to make a pick-up. The rule was to never hold more than a couple thousand dollars at the dope spot. In fifteen minutes, Annie Mae pulled up in front of the white shotgun house on Elmo Street. White 500 Mercedes, long hair piece, painted face, manicured nails, wearing a name brand sweat suit. She hit the horn twice and Raymond was out the steel barred door. They smiled at each other through moist drugged eyes as she passed him a McDonald's bag, bacon and egg biscuit and fries ...he looked around and slide her the knot of cash. "Here take this," Said Raymond. "You know where to put it. I'll call you later --- in an hour." Annie Mae shifted the Mercedes into gear and pulled off. Then suddenly, she hit the brakes and backed up, rolling down the window as Raymond turned, "Ba, are we still going to Big Emmett's birthday party at the MONEY CHANGER tonight?" She asked. Raymond's eyes met hers with a smile, "Just like we planned, pick me out something real fly to wear." He said. Annie Mae was delighted, going out meant a chance to flaunt her stuff --- jewelry, expensive gaudy clothes and her plump body. "Okay, ba! Don't forget to come home a little earlier." She said looking toward Raymond as she drove away.

The Professor set parked down the block in an old tan Honda. Taking in every move Raymond and Annie Mae made. He had stalked the couple for over a month, recording their daily routine during surveillance. He knew the time of each shift change at the drug market --- Little Pete and Smitty, the other two workers, the junkies who came by like clockwork each day, the cars each one drove --- their walk --- the clothes they wore. He watched and waited ...looking for the right time to make his move. To serve his justice --- quench his thirst for revenge. Doing his part to clean the world of its trash.

Raymond checked his supply it was getting low. He'd sold over two hundred $25.00 bags of heroin and a hundred $10.00 bags of cocaine since he came over to man the dope spot for the day shift. He had come to the old white house on the end of Elmo Street at 9 a.m., relieving Little Pete who had worked the night shift. At 6 p.m. he'd turned the house over to Smitty for the evening shift. The single-story shotgun house was a twenty-four hour stop and shop dope market. Business was good. He'd been able to put away over $700,000.00 in four months, afford a swank condo, the Mercedes and feed Black Anne enough dope to buy her loyalty as well as feed his own monstrous habit.

He made a mental note to check around for a new connection. The dope he had on hand had fell off. His supplier was stepping on it, more and more but still charging the same price. He couldn't cut and stretch it as far as he'd like to. Plus, each day it took more and more to keep the gorilla on his back quiet and satisfied.

Raymond walked through the house... a small shotgun style place with low ceilings, chipped paint and cracked moldings. He rented the place from one of the local slum lords who lived outside the city in Bahama. Raymond always paid on time and in cash, the landlord never bothered him.

As he moved through the house, he heard another knock on the door, and two men cursing at each other. Hustling partners --- thieves arguing over how the money they'd made had been cut up. Although he disliked his clientele, it stroked his ego each time they came with their money, submissive, begging for shorts.

Raymond was a tall, thin, blue black man who had just turned thirty-eight a month earlier. He sported a clean bald head, full beard and was fond of sweat suits and expensive running shoes. Today he wore an oversized navy-blue valor Nike suit with matching shoes, gold watch on his arm and two thin gold chains draped around his neck.

He was what most people called a successful drug dealer----- coming from a good family. His father ran his own small construction company and his mother worked at the Veteran's Hospital as a nurse. Raymond had two sisters and grew up in the comfort of a blue-collar family. But he was not satisfied with that type of life. He passed up the opportunity for college and his father's invitation to join him in the construction business and opted for the fast lane.

The Professor saw the white Mercedes turning into the parking lot. The windshield wipers on delay, clearing the moist from the windows. His hunch was right---- Raymond Kelly and his street whore of a wife had made it to the party. They drove right pass him. He didn't move an inch. They killed the lights and exited the Mercedes, both dressed in black ---expensive and classy.

The Professor wore an oversized chocolate silk suit, double breasted, a dark brown crepe t-shirt underneath, dark brown Belgian loafers, and the right amount of jewelry. Tonight, he'd pass himself off as a Columbian or maybe he'd appear Spanish or some other mixture with South American blood.

Before leaving his home in Hope Valley, the Professor took his time changing his identity. He gave himself a nose job, changing his round nose to one with a pointed profile. He used putty, applying the substance to his nose, kneading and pressing until he was satisfied with it shape. He took his time working from a dresser covered an array of makeup supplies, with mirrored walls, a myriad of tools with which to apply color base, creams and powders. He blocked out his eyebrows and created new ones with eyebrow plastic, covering them with sealer, dressed the area with cream stick and powdered it. He powdered his face, overlaying it with color foundation, adding rouge to give it a natural appearance. He used shadow and highlights --- making his cheekbones and jaw lines seem prominent. Then he applied rouge over her entire face to lessen the impact of his overall appearance. Finally, he placed a wig of long fine black hair on his head, fitted as tight as a swimmer's cap, and tied it back into a ponytail with a rubber band. He examined himself in the mirrors, front and back --- he smiled at his own artistry.

The Professor checked his inner coat pocket, making sure he had not left the two bags of heroin behind, just in case. He looked at himself one last time in the rearview mirror. Perfect. No one would ever know who he was --- his name tonight would be Jose. If need be. He opened the door of the dark green Buick sedan and stepped out. It was show time.

The Professor catapulted from the dark into the neon light beaming from the MONEY CHANGER. The dark of the night accented his disguise.

He unsuspiciously entered the door, three men and two chics in sequined dresses and six-inch heels flirted with one another as they waited in line. The matron checked the V.I.P. guess list and waved the group in. The woman at the window wore a low-cut red silk dress, partially exposing her breast. Her chocolate skin appeared smooth as velvet. She blinked her Diana Ross eyes and flashed her pearly white teeth as the Professor stepped to the window. Taken by his good looks, she spoke, "Good evening sir. Are you a V.I.P. guest?" The Professor fully emerged into the role of Jose, flashed a slight smile. "No, I'm paying." He passed her a $100.00 bill, twice the cover charge. When she attempted to give him change, he raised his hand signaling her to pocket the balance. She smiled and blinked her eyes. The Professor's eyebrows went up. He was witnessing how opposites attract. The woman liked what she saw. She quickly scratched her phone number on a piece of paper and placed it in his hand. Two hot looking chics wearing tight mini dresses stopped to ask him the time, forgetting about the watches on their arms. He shyly gave the time and eased through the door. The Professor appeared as an international player, wealthy and classy.

He found a place at the end of the bar and ordered 7-up with lemon. Sipping from his glass, he observed the who's who of Durham's big money players. Crooks posing as businessmen, the vultures who feasted off the miseries of addicts turned thieves, prostitutes, burglars and beggars --- trafficking their poison --- demanding each dollar. They were living large, but the record wouldn't show it. He sat alone, silently thinking how the lust for money, robbed men of their morality, and drove them to desperate means. Players selling heroin and crack to other human beings, robbing them of their lives, stealing a child's mother, spreading disease through the community. Men desperate for the glitter of life willing to do anything.

Raymond and Annie Mae were regaling a small crowd with some sort of story in a corner booth as they passed around a $100.00 bill laced with cocaine. Big Emmett, the host and birthday boy was entertaining a large crowd of mostly men dressed in flashy gear in the dining room area --- laughing and slapping hands, trying to get a crap game started in one of the back rooms.

Ray and Annie Mae were still regaling the small crowd that surrounded them. A glamorous woman, with long silky hair, wearing a dress one size to small continued to cut her eyes in the Professor's direction as she feed Annie Mae's ego. "Annie Mae Slade, you got it going on. That dress is banging girl. Look at your hair, I know who gave you that cut --- you been to Priscilla's." She pointed a finger at Annie Mae noting that she knew her fashion secret. Annie Mae turned round and round, patting her hair, blinking her eyes and showing all thirty-two of her teeth --- enjoying being the center of attention.

The Professor didn't like the idea of being at the party. He knew he was taking a risk he'd never taken before. He felt a little out of control, out of his comfort zone. He'd become obsessed with the idea of serving Raymond Kelly his share of justice. As far as he was concerned, he'd already tried and convicted Raymond, and the only thing left was the execution.

He'd surmised through his surveillance that Raymond Kelly was number one or two on the list of drug dealers in Durham, pulling in the bulk of the money and supplying the little fish. Raymond had become top dog because of an apparent good connection which afforded him an unlimited supply. He didn't seem to run out ... day after day he pumped dope out of the shotgun house on Elmo Street and supplied other street corner car chasers. The quality didn't matter; Raymond's approach was to never run out. His 24- hour non-stop drug market and the string of small- time dealers buying table- spoons and ounces had created a monopoly of sort.

The Professor looked and observed, suppressing a hidden contempt as he set in the midst of the kind of people he disdained most. The who's who of drug dealers --- as far as the street was concerned, they were the powerful, prestigious, and those doing well, thanks to the ships and planes that made it through in spite of the so-called war on drugs.

He noticed the woman who'd been eyeing him all evening coming in his direction. She could pass for thirty something, but something told him she was older but moved and looked younger. He couldn't believe it --- as she got closer, he could tell the full head of hair belong to her -- not a glue and paste job. Her eyes were soft but exciting, jumping out at him. She held a flute of champagne in her hand and came straight to where he had nested.

"Hey, I don't believe we've met. I'm Virginia Talafero, the owner, manager, operator and sometimes bartender of this little place. You seem to be a new face and alone. Is your drink okay? Would you like another?"

The Professor knew the show had begun. So, he pushed his admiration for the woman before him aside and ignored her forwardness.

He responded in a low seductive tone, looking into her eyes, allowing little affect as possible. "Thank you, Virginia, I'm just fine." Raising his glass, he said, "the drink I have is enough for now. You have a nice place here." "Thank you, mister……" She said with an inquisitive smile. He took the cue. "Excuse me, I'm Jose", extending her his hand. "Nice to meet you," she said. "Same here," said the Professor. "You're new around here." She said as her eyes measured him from head to toe. "Yes, I've been in your city for about a week --- visiting some relatives, enjoying some down time." Virginia took a second and then turned to the crowd. The Professor took notice of her trim waistline, backside and great legs. She turned back and looked at him before walking away. "I'll check on you a little later. I'm the hostess so, I must make my rounds." She said with an inviting smile and searching eyes. The Professor ignored Virginia's flirtation, knowing he couldn't allow himself to become sidetracked. He continued to set at the end of the bar watching the party unfold. A rock-n-roll band dressed in urban gear with dreadlocks was beginning to cook, cranking out their rendition of hits from Frankly Beverly and Maze, the electric guitar leading the way, and the floor was crowded as people got their groove on. The Professor being unsuspecting as possible saw only Raymond Kelly. Right about then some man who appeared half drunk took a seat at the bar next to the Professor. He peered at the Professor through thick glasses. "Man, this is a nice party. A man can snatch any kinda woman he likes out of here, uh."

"Yeah, it looks that way" said the Professor. Then he signaled the bartender. He nodded at Virginia as she drifted past talking with some polished man, obviously a player trying to disguise himself with expensive conservative clothing and modest jewelry.

The bartender a tall burley man with a barrel chest, shaven head and thick mustache, wore black trousers, a white shirt and a red bow tie made his way over.

"Yes sir, what you're having?" He asked. The Professor motioned for the bartender to lean closer, "for the next hour, all the drinks in the house are on me." He said. The bartender refilled the Professor's drink, returned to the bar and spoke into the sound system's mike, "ladies and gents, for the next hour the drinks are free, compliments from the gentlemen at the end of the bar in the brown suit." The Professor raised a casual hand as the crowd cheered. The Professor knew he was taking a great risk by drawing attention to himself. The show had begun, and he had to draw Raymond's attention…had to create the opportunity he needed to get close. Raymond had been a greater test, not like the others. The others were poor, broke, sick junkies, who were easy prey ---- each one leaping at the opportunity of a free bag of dope no matter who offered it. But Raymond Kelly was different. He had money, drugs and was surrounded by one of his workers or some other hustler the majority of the time. He was the big fish. The Professor had to catch him no matter the risk.

The bar became swamped by the crowd ordering drinks. The gold-digging women were sizing the Professor up and the hustlers were whispering, trying to figure out who the "nigga" was who'd bought the bar. Raymond and Annie Mae had been on the floor hugged up, grinding to the beat of a slow jam when the bartender made the announcement. As they danced, Raymond whispered, "check this out, I seen that cat somewhere before." "Where?" Around here." Asked Annie Mae. "No, in Atlanta, I believe. I think I met him or someone that could be his twin." Raymond and Annie Mae made it back to their corner table and continued to check the Professor out.

Cheryle Mathis had her eye on the Professor as well. Cheryle considered herself a player; a woman who prided herself in catching men who could afford her the luxuries of life for the benefit of her company. Although she's been tossed around from one player to the next, her game was still tight, especially for someone who did not know her track record. She had more miles on her than an old Mercedes Benz, but it didn't show. Raymond and Annie Mae watched as Cheryle made her way over and introduced herself to who she thought was a man name Jose. Annie sucked her teeth, "that bitch never stops --- she's at every nigga she thinks she can get a dollar from." Knowing he'd spent his share of money on Cheryle, Raymond tried to ignore Annie Mae's comment. "That's what the bitch does. That's how she gets paid. People do what they do." He said. Raymond hadn't taken his mind off the Professor for a minute.

"Miami, that's where I know that nigga from, I met him through another nigga. I was trying to buy some weight and Carlos, the nigga I used to score from put me with some of his workers. That's where! It's got to be him."

As the Professor sat at the bar playing word and mind games with Cheryle Mathis, he noticed Raymond wading through the crowd. He kept a dubious eye on Raymond making sure he wasn't leaving for the night. Raymond was moving in his direction, trying to figure out how to approach the man at the end of the bar. The Professor's heart pumped with excitement at the thought of being within striking distance of Raymond. Raymond stopped one bar stool from where the Professor sat talking to Cheryle. Raymond ordered a seltzer and vodka. The Professor knew it was all a ploy. Raymond accepted his drink, turned his back against the bar and pretended to look into the crowd. He stirred his drink with his finger. Finally, he turned, looked at Cheryle and spoke. "Wassup Cheryle? Enjoying yourself?" He smiled as he spoke. Cheryle returned a mild greeting attempting to set herself apart from Raymond as much as possible. The Professor knew this was his time. He looked past Cheryle into Raymond's face, 'evening my man. Nice party. You guys in Durham know how to throw a party." As he looked at Cheryle he said, "got a few classy ladies too."

That was Ray's cue, he moved in, "check this out, I noticed you from across the room, I think I ran into you some years back down in

Miami, I believe through Carlos. You got to be the same guy I don't forget a face." The Professor felt his heart pound as he turned and looked; he knew Raymond Kelly had taken the bait. "Oh! Carlos, I do know a Carlos. About 38-40 years old by now, Spanish, tall, slim and love bikes." Raymond added. "Yeah! That sounds like the same Carlos," said the Professor as he nodded his head. He felt a little off. He thought maybe the chic Cheryle had thrown the dynamics off. Down below, he sensed that he was being examined and measured he was feeling things his predator's sense of danger was at work as Raymond spoke. "I don't want to keep you from the lady, but I'd like to speak with you before you split." Said Raymond. "Sure, I'll be here for a while longer come back in ten or fifteen minutes so we can talk."

The Professor turned back to Cheryle and noticed she was finishing her drink. He ordered her another --- giving no attention and comment to Ray Kelly's intrusion as he watched him return to his table where Annie Mae was anxiously waiting. Before he could be seated Annie Mae was in his ear. "You know that guy? Who is he?" Ray was feeling proud of himself --- machismo. He felt knowing the guy at the bar was a sign of how well he was known in the world of hustlers, he looked at Annie Mae as he opened the hundred-dollar bill and feed her more cocaine. "It's who I thought it was --- a nigga I met down in Miami a couple of years back. He's a dealer, heavy weight. Columbian or some shit. I can't figure what the hell he's doing in Durham. He knows this Spanish cat I know name Carlos. I'm going back over and talk some business with him --- if that bitch Cheryle ever give him any air." "Well, I hope you don't think she is gonna give him a break --- especially if she thinks he's got money. Ba, you know how that bitch is, umh." Said Annie Mae.

After twenty minutes more of Cheryle Mathis' attempt to get her claws into the Professor, Ray Kelly was making his way across the floor toward the bar. The Professor had kept a watchful eye on Ray since he'd returned to the table where Annie Mae waited. As Ray made his way over the Professor's pulse quickened just a little. He knew he had to be convincing, making sure Ray brought into the game. He closed his eyes for a split second immersing himself, through every pore of his being, transforming completely in spirit and heart into Jose ---his make-believe character for tonight.

Cheryle dismissed herself as Ray made his way to the bar, realizing that Ray and Jose were making a move.

At first Ray did all the talking, taking the lead ---spilling his guts, telling of his illegal drug operation. Talking money and turn over.

"What I'm looking for is a new connection. The stuff I'm getting is steady falling off. When I first cut into this thing it would take an eight and now it will barely stand up under a three. I'm losing money. I need a better package. I'm looking to buy weight on a regular."

The Professor measured Raymond as he spoke, holding a hard gaze. There was no evasion, no furtiveness' of the eyes, none of the things you saw when you had a snitch or a cross artist before you. Ray didn't breathe hard and swallow his eyes, the Professor stood there watching him poker faced and sincere. His only thought was exacting his justice on the parasite of a man that stood before him bragging about selling poison. Finally, he had to speak, "I don't usually cut into my business associates in this fashion. It usually takes place through an acquaintance or some creditable reference." The Professor hesitated, cutting his eyes at Ray. He continued, "how quick do you want to move and how much money we talking?" "I can move in a day or two — I'll spend a hundred grand, if it can stand to be stepped on at least eight times." Said Ray. The Professor paused, "it might be possible to connect you with something like that." Ray stayed cool but was smiling on the inside. "Then it's on! Said Ray. The Professor still did not confirm the deal, instead he studied Ray before speaking, "I don't know. I have my allies, connections and situations. I'd be breaking my own rules if I make a move like this." He studied for a second longer. "Look, since you know Carlos---I'll see what I can do. I'll call Carlos and get back with you. Give me a number. I'll call you when I'm ready to move. First, I'll give you a little something to check out, to make sure you like it. If you like it, we can do business. If it works without any problems the first time---then we're on."

The Professor knew who the tester would be. He only needed to be patient and decided how and when he'd deliver the lethal dose of heroin, serving Raymond Kelly his overdue share of justice.

It was the most fabulous party thrown at the MONEY CHANGER in years. The crowd was festive and filled with deep seething merriment. It was a party in a climactic fog, men in sleek clothing, and chocolate women with silken brown breast "peaking" out of tight low-cut dresses, the tinkle of the glass and ice, the rhythm from the soulful band.

The Professor finally left alone at the bar, decided to ease out into the night as the first wave of men left with the first wave of women --- before the gamblers had won or lost, coming out to celebrate, drinking whisky and blowing cocaine --- sending themselves into oblivion.

CHAPTER 22

THE PROFESSOR DROVE FROM HIS safe house apartment off Red Oak Avenue to mete Ray Kelly, but not directly. Sometimes he drove directly to the agreed upon location and other times if streets were busy, he crosscut and switched back, making sure he wasn't followed. By 9:30 he was parked two blocks from Café Galante facing Chapel Hill Boulevard. He checked the street signs. Parking was okay, lots of cars on the same side street. A light rain had started to fall on the city shortly after 8 o'clock. The man in the car, wearing the black running suit and black ball cap seemed not to be noticed. The Professor's appearance had changed drastically since his last encounter with Ray Kelly. He had aged at least twenty- five years. Heavy pouches hung under his eyes and a shock of grey hair protruded from beneath the ball cap. The nose was round and saggy, the chin and neck equally so. His movement slow and measured, matching his feebleness of character. He'd aged himself as he sat before the mirrors, preparing to make his call on Ray Kelly, he felt compelled to recoil, to draw into the old man, to assume the character. He looked up and across from where he was parked, a young couple in a white Corvette was smoking pot, they gave a symbolic wave as they exited their car. He ran a handkerchief over his damp forehead as he waited.

At 10:45 the green sedan rental eased down the rain-soaked street. The Professor, the old man for the night flashed his headlights. Noticing the flashing lights, Ray had to park three parking spaces away. He didn't want to allow Ray to exit his vehicle. He needed to make the delivery as fast as possible. When Ray looked up the old man was at his window. Ray hit the down button and the window came down. "Jose sent you a little something." He said as he handed Ray the two glassine bags. Ray couldn't get a word out. The Professor had taken control. "He'll call you first thing tomorrow." With that said, the old man raised his hand signaling good-bye and walked away.

It was right at 9:00 o'clock when Ray and Annie Mae finally woke up. The onset of the morning sickness was their alarm clock. Ray had saved the testers for his morning shot. Waking up, he felt anxious. In the back of his mind was the excitement of shooting a new bag of dope and the expectation of having found a new connection. Any business had to wait --- first he had to take care of his sickness. At heart he was junkie first, business came second, and in that order. As was the routine --- Annie Mae, blemished skin, her bottom teeth, a partial plate and out. Sometimes back someone had cut her back to the dark hollow of her immense butt not that her butt was beautiful --- not like the nice round tight butts on the long legged, bikini clad chics in the nuddy books, pulled herself out of bed to get the tools, a cooker, two syringes, a cup of water and a belt. Meanwhile, Ray without a word began to bust open the small glassine bags of heroin until he'd emptied five bags into the mustard top. He sprayed 60ccs of water into the top with the dope, struck the lighter, burning the top. Annie Mae's stomach turned over at the smell of the dope cooking and thought of the blast. She dared not to say a word or ask a question --- she accepted the larger portion and was glad to have it, the same as any junkie would have been. Ten minutes after the blast, Ray waited for Annie Mae to get dressed and make her morning run- driving her cousin's Hazel Ruth over to Durham Technical College. Hazel Ruth a reformed street walker and single mom, was chasing a nursing degree.

Before Annie Mae could drive out the parking lot Ray was at the kitchen table with a cup of water, zippo lighter, mustard jar top and a belt around his arm. He felt like he was about to shit on himself as he rushed to open the first tester bag. He examined the bag, thumping it, it looked to be a street quarter. His greed took over, and he opened the second tester and dumped it into the cooker also. Nervously, he drew 60ccs of water into the syringe, and wiped his face with his hand. He sprayed the water on the dope, turning it into a brownish mud like mixture. He allowed the flames from the lighter to burn the bottom of the top until the heroin dissolved into a liquid. He reached in his trouser pocket for what was left of the cocaine he'd spread around at the party the night before. He poured an equal amount into the heroin. Spicing up the shot, creating his own private party. He sucked the mixture up through the piece of soiled cotton in the bottom of the top with the syringe. Biting down on the belt in his mouth he tightened it around his arm. His scared veins popped up. It measured 75ccs --- he mumbled, "here we go," as he pushed the needle into his arm, not knowing that the inside of his kitchen would be the last thing he'd see in the world.

By 10:30 --- an hour and a half later, Annie Mae after dropping Hazel Ruth at Durham Tech was walking the aisle at the Food Lion on Hillsborough Road, shopping and grumbling to herself about the prices --- thinking of how once in her life she would shoplift all the shit she needed. But she had reformed herself from boosting and the grind of street hustling since hooking up with Ray. Today was the day she'd promised to prepare Ray a home cooked meal. She didn't really like the idea of cooking but felt that feeding him a home cooked meal now and then and fucking him when he liked was the least, she could do. It was easier and the benefits were greater than her days as a street hustler, the time before Ray chose her for his woman.

In another hour Annie Mae was back home and surprised to see Ray's SUV still parked in the same spot. She felt it strange, knowing he should be at the dope house on Elmo Street by now. Her mind raced as she struggled up the steps to the front door of the condo with three plastic bags of groceries, holding the keys in her hand. She cursed like a sailor as she put the bags down to open the door, "damned look like Ray could at least open the fucking door." She said as she was finally able to push the door open. Stepping into the foyer, she screamed "Ray didn't you hear me at the door?" There was no answer. She headed for the den area, "Ray what are you still doing here. You know Little Pete's probably waiting on you over on Elmo."

She walked in the kitchen and dropped the bags of groceries on the floor as she noticed Ray slumped over at the table with the needle in his arm and the belt on the floor by his foot, slouched to one side, looking like the weight of a feather would tip him over.

"Ray, Ray," she screamed as she rushed over shaking him. He tumbled out the chair onto the floor. His eyes shut, droll streaming from his mouth. Annie Mae noticed he'd pissed in his pants. She saw the two empty glassine bags on the table. In her heart she knew he was dead. Justice had been served.

CHAPTER 23

SOLOMON AMBLED AROUND THE CRIME scene after Ray Kelly's death. As he entered the condo, one of the uniform officers spoke as he passed through the door, "Morning King. Look like another dose." He said.

Solomon had steeled himself as he stepped inside the condo at the crime scene. Over the years he'd learned there's a necessary detachment at any crime scene, it's like putting on a second skin. But he also knew the necessary balance --- never letting himself forget that the victims were human beings and not just remains, not just a corpse. He'd promised himself long ago if he ever became immune to that, it was time to move on.

At the crime scene he'd stayed out the way of the technicians in their white sterile suits as they went over Kelly's SUV and condo with handheld USB microscope and evidence vacuums. A few others snapped Polaroid's as well as regular photographs. Another whole squad fanned out, taking exemplars from inside the condo. He respected their work and gave them the space they needed. He knew the less people contaminated and disturbed the crime scene, the more information that could be extracted.

The Hot Shot Deaths, as they were called, had become a high-profile case and everyone wanted a piece of Solomon's, especially the media. He knew he couldn't control the coverage—the only thing he could possibly help control was whatever crime scene information was released. As he pondered the case, he knew it was time to call Captain

Fletcher and suggest a gag order on everyone connected to the case. No interviews without specific permission from the Department.

Later, in his office, he thought of the Kelly crime scene as he shifted through the file, looking at the list of next of kin in each death. There was one connection that jumped out --- which negated the idea of the deaths being random. He noticed in the Banks, Graham and Brigette Kerns deaths, that Banks and Hall were friends, both students at NCCU, both majoring in biology, and taking classes under Professor Alford. Graham was once the boyfriend of Bridget Kerns who was the niece of the Professor. That was too much of a coincident for him. His theory had always been "how plus why equals who." If he wanted to find out who the killer was, and he'd had long been convinced the overdoses were not accidents or coincidences, he had to consider the similarities and differences, and the combinations of the cases. That meant having a chat with the Professor.

The public was outraged. Local politicians demanded answers. The Committee for the Affairs of Black People accused the Department of treating the cases lightly because all the victims were mostly black men of low social status. Screaming institutional racism in policing, the police being accused of not giving a damn, just another black man dead. Captain Fletcher was taking the heat --- reluctantly he'd called a press conference.

The T.V. trucks were double parked outside City Hall when Solomon arrived at Department Headquarters. He parked in the lot off Duke Street and went in the side door and down the hall to his office. When Headquarters moved from downtown to the Chapel Hill Street location, Captain Fletcher had put him down the hall from him --- within reach.

After making a couple of phones calls, he'd planned to get within ear shot of the press conference. He wanted to see Fletcher as he squirmed and bullshitted the crowd concerning his knowledge and involvement in the case.

The briefing room was over-run with equipment, cables, profane language, bored cops and anxious citizens. Cameramen jockeyed for lighting arrangement, print reporters set on the edge of folding chairs scribbling in their notebooks, and television reporters circled the crowd searching for rumors that would give them the edge over their competitors. The podium in the front of the room was surrounded by a half dozen microphones, while mounted video cameras were stationed in each corner. Captain Fletcher stood up front near the right side of the podium scanning his notes.

The bright lights flashed on, Fletcher cleared his throat as he stepped to the podium.

“Good morning ladies, gentlemen, press and citizens. This press conference was called this morning to briefly discuss a rash of deaths we've had in our community over the summer. I know all of you are aware of the recent deaths due to drug overdoses and that many of you are concerned about those deaths --- and would like more information as well as know more of what the Durham Police Department is doing to find the source of the poisonous drugs so we can get it off the streets. Again, the cause of all these deaths we are discussing this morning have been attributed to an overdose of heroin. The Durham Police Department have been keeping quiet concerning these deaths in hope that the less publicity concerning the deaths would further our effort in locating the source of the batch of heroin and those responsible for spreading it around. Since we have been tracking these cases and we have found a couple of patterns. One, all the victims have been black men with histories of drug use and drug sales or have spent time in prison for drug sales. Two, the deaths have all occurred in Southeast Durham and all have occurred on a weekday. Some of you here this morning may feel the Police Department hasn't shown enough vigor in solving this case. I'm here this morning to inform you that we are doing all that's in our power and that we are using all our available resources to track down the source of the heroin so we can get it off the street--- and I'd say we are making progress. We ask that you exercise a little patience with us and support us as best you can. This case is very difficult for a variety of reasons and we're moving on it as best we can." With that said, Fletcher glanced around looking at the audience of people. Okay, I'll take one or two questions," he said, pointing a finger at Meg McDowell of T.V 11 News.

"Captain, have you determined if one person is responsible for spreading the poisonous heroin around?" she asked. Fletcher was pretty evasive, "We are not sure but that could be possible." Right then another hand flew up.

"If It's one person spreading the drug around, do you think he is picking his victims? Do you think he knows them?" Fletcher felt the heat. "We are not sure and don't want to speculate." He said. "What we do know is that the first victim since we've been tracking this thing died about eight weeks ago, then another and another each week since then. I'm asking the public if you have any information that you think might help us find the source of the heroin, please give us a call." With that Fletcher raised his hand and turned away from the podium.

Solomon stood in the back of the room during the entire time the media roasted Captain Fletcher---chewing on his cigar. Detective Linda Graves eased up beside him, "What's going on Solomon?" she whispered, standing close, leaning toward his ear. "Our dear Captain has been dodging bullets for about fifteen minutes, that's all." Solomon said as he glances around. Nobody was paying them any attention. He tapped Detective Graves on the shoulder as they slipped outside.

"I'm glad he didn't suggest that we could have a serial killer running around." Graves said.

CHAPTER 24

It was 7:15 and Solomon had just got out of bed to feed Princess her Friskies. As he bent over to fill Princess' bowl the phone rang. Before he made it to the wall phone in the kitchen it had rang five or six more times.

"Yeah! He growled. He was half asleep, naked and had to piss.

"This is Graves." Said a sultry voice. "Yeah, Linda I know you been wanting me, I've seen the way you look at me but I'm not up to a love confession first thing this morning." He said. "Solomon, you never stop do you?" Graves retorted. "Captain Fletcher has called a meeting for eight o'clock, not eight-fifteen but eight sharp and you have to be there, orders from Headquarters.

"Run that pass me again Graves" Solomon asked. "Eight o'clock in Fletcher's office." She said.

"We just had our weekly meeting two days ago." Solomon shouted.

"Well this is a special meeting." Graves said.

"Shit, we gotta solve this damn case or else Fletcher is gonna run me off." Moaned Solomon.

"You're right, Solomon." Graves added, "I'll see you in a half hour." She was gone.

Solomon looked at the receiver in disbelief, placed it on the hook and headed for the shower. After a ten minute shower he paddled to his bedroom and throw on a white shirt he'd worn on two other days, snatched his trousers from the recliner, pulled a stain felled necktie around his shirt collar and was out the door.

Going off the porch he grabbed the Durham Sun Newspaper. Across the front --- headlines just below the nameplate, it read "DURHAM'S FIRST SERIAL KILLER." Solomon sat inside his car and read the story before heading out. The story was speculative as far as the facts went with no mention of what linked the murders to one killer --- making it a serial case. Solomon finished the story and fired up his old Impala and headed down to Headquarters.

Solomon was five minutes late for the meeting. Fletcher frowned at him when he walked in and motioned at the empty chair beside him. Jake Morris, Chief of Homicide, sat directly opposite of him and Quentin Goode from Vice/Drug Division sat beside Morris. The other chairs around the table were filled by Robbery Investigator Cook, and other Task Force members.

"I'd like to offer a different approach, "Fletcher said. "I think at least one guy ought to know everything that's going on with the cases. Goode and Morris have their Divisions to run, so it's gonna be Solomon." Chewing on his cigar, Solomon paused for a second, cut his eye at fletcher and grunted. Fletcher continued, "Solomon will be working mostly on his own --- independent of the rest of you guys but parallel." Fletcher said. "You don't have a problem working independent of everyone else do you Solomon?" Fletcher asked. With that everyone laughed, knowing that Solomon always did things his way, whether advised to or not. If any of you have a question or some new information run it through Solomon. "I guess most of you saw the morning paper?" Fletcher asked. "You can see they're running with whatever will sale. The media coverage on this thing will probably snowball --- until we find the source of the drugs and arrest the sons-of-bitches who's putting it out there. The Mayor called and I told him we had some leads and that we'll get this shit off the streets soon."

Solomon looked over at Fletcher, "did he buy that, if I was him I wouldn't." "You got to be convincing when speaking to the Mayor," Fletcher retorted.

Fletcher then asked, "Solomon, do you have anything else you'd like to say?" Solomon bit down on his cigar before speaking. "Detective Graves have set up a data base in her office, she has entered everything we know about the deaths into the data base. I'll see that everybody working on the case get a printout every day or so." Solomon said. "We'll go over what we know about the victims. If there's a connection or a pattern, we'll identify it. Everybody must read the printout each time it comes out. If you see something, give me a call. "We'll put it in the data base."

"What do you know so far?" asked Detective Goode. Solomon shook his head, "Not too much. Next of kin, criminal histories of the victims, that kinda shit. There is a loose pattern between three of the victims --- Hall and Banks were both enrolled over at NCCU, taking classes together under Professor Alford and it looks like Eric Graham who died from an overdose a year or so back was the boyfriend of the Professor's niece Bridget Kerns who also died from an overdose some time ago." Detective Morris jumped in, "the Kerns girl was a student over at UNC --- yeah! I remember her." Everybody sat quiet and thought about if for a minute.

"I plan to pay the good Professor a little visit to see if he'd shed any light on a thing or two." Solomon said.

"What's the interval between the deaths?' asked Morris.

"It's running one every ten days or so." Detective Graves said. Yeah! If it's the same person spreading the dope around, he has the tendency of what forensic Psychologist calls a sadistic killer. He's doing it for pleasure. He's not receiving a revelation from God; he's not being commanded by a voice inside his head. He's driven by anger or revenge, but he's not crazy in the sense that he's out of control. He knows what he's doing, and aware of the consequences. He has a plan and he's obviously intelligent."

"If they start to come faster, that means the killer is working off the top of his head, and not with a deliberate plan," said Roger Tilley from the Sex Crime Division.

We don't know if he's picking them out ahead of time or what. That is, if one guy is doing this." Morris said.

"Any other patterns?" fletcher asked. "Just that none of the deaths have occurred on the weekend."

"There are all kinds of variables to look at, but we got to be careful not to get stuck into one way of seeing this thing. The key is communication --- we got to talk to each other. Read the printouts and stay in touch." Solomon said, "And no talking to the press."

"This thing is going to get intense and we are going to feel the pressure. I'll try to keep all the outside and unnecessary shit to a minimum, but if we get one or two more deaths, there'll be all sort of shit flying in the media --- reporters will try to corner anyone they can. If it gets to that point, we will get the City Attorney involved to advise us on what to say and not say. Every word, every interview gets cleared through my office in advance. Does everybody have that?" fletcher asked.

The room of policemen and detectives all bobbed their heads.

"Let's go clean this mess up." Said fletcher.

CHAPTER 25

ANOTHER DAY PASSED --- AND Solomon felt alone with all the meeting, planning and organizing, that a great amount of luck would be needed to catch whoever was spreading the killer dope around. He knew lady luck would have to smile down on them.

He spent the morning on the streets, Dowd, Calvin, Roxboro and Fayetteville moving from corners to barbershops and to a couple of gambling joints. He talked to a dozen of car chasing dope dealers, grabbed a couple of their customers, a few winos and a couple of shopkeepers. Nobody knew a thing or else they weren't saying. He felt he was being spent --- frozen out, someone had to know something.

He ate lunch at the Green Candle off Fayetteville Street in the Phoenix Square mini mall. Boasters, junkies, students, lawyers, judges and regular folk came in and out the door placing orders, talking and minding their own business. No one seemed alarmed or concerned that a killer might be on the loose.

Solomon's thoughts kept coming back to the question of how much intersection was there between the killer's, if in fact there was a killer, his personality --- his persona and who he was. Until he could connect the pieces, it was like chasing two suspects.

By one o'clock he was back at Headquarters, setting in his office, studying the file. "Evenin," Linda jingled. She was golden brown--- a portrait of refinement. Navy blue suit, cream colored blouse, gold locket around her neck. Her deep brown eyes sparkled as she smiled.

She stood in front of Solomon's desk with some type of document rolled up in her hand. "Well, Solomon, what you think of the suit. How you like it, huh? Is it the right color for me? All blue? Does it make me look to ...ominous?"

He bit on his cigar looking out the window. A low cloud floated in the sky as he looked at the manicured lawn outside the five-story complex.

"What's the tidbit of information you have for me?" he asked blandly. She gave a sigh and cut her eyes at him. "I pulled the file on Bridget Kerns. Her mother was Professor Alford's younger sister who died from breast cancer, leaving Bridget to be cared for by the Professor. He was barely out of school at Georgetown at the time. I'm sure taking in a young child, especially a girl, cramped his life. Anyway, more interesting is there's a note here of how the Professor stayed at the Chief's throat for not arresting someone for selling his niece the drugs that killed her. This went on for over a year; day in and day out, phone calls and Alford showing up at the Chief's office unannounced. The Chief at the time was ...Chief Grooms. It got to the point the department had to almost get a restraining order to stop him from showing up raising hell. Then just like it started — he stopped coming around. I checked his background, no arrest, no criminal history, everything all neat and normal. Other than the fact that three of the victims have a loose pattern, tying them to one another and him, there's nothing that jumps out about him. Solomon had set back in his swivel chair, rocking back and forth, chewing on his cigar with his eyes cast on Linda as she spoke.

"Yeah! That's all nice and neat, I don't know but my gut tells me that there's fly in the milk somewhere." He said.

Linda dead serious said, "he was in school earning a doctorate in chemistry at Georgetown almost twenty years ago. Clean cut, highly respected and all. Never been married, no information on anything relating to his social life. He took a job at UNC Asheville. Taught there for eight years and then came to NCCU. The entire time he was mother, father and uncle to his niece, Bridget. Life seem normal until the Kerns girls was found dead from an overdose."

Solomon stopped rocking in his chair and looked Linda right in the eyes. "Some coincidence, huh?" Three or four people dead from an overdose, all in some way tied to Alford.

"The cases were far apart, Solomon. It could all just be coincidental." Linda challenged. He sat up in his chair looking at Linda with a more serious look, "I don't know, maybe there is no real connection and maybe there is. Maybe he's playing judge and jury because of his niece. Before I go asking him too many questions, I'd like to already have some answers."

CHAPTER 26

A week after Annie Mae found Ray Kelly dead from an overdose, Solomon stood in the back of Greater Saint Paul Baptist Church … the only place available as the church continued to be overrun. Many of the people filing into the church were hustlers and street people dressed in fashions suited for a night club. Scattered through the crowd were family, and old school mates who'd turned out in masses to bid farewell to Ray Kelly. He was once a legendary high school athlete grown to be one of Durham's most notorious drug dealers and criminal. The immediate family followed the attendant down the aisle. The choir sang a soft melody and the organist played. Reverend J.C. Davis whispered in the microphone, "The Lord Giveth and The Lord Taketh Away. Raymond Kelly has paid the debt we all must pay." Annie Mae who was seated on the front row with the Kelly family could be heard moaning and sniffing.

Rev. Davis, a huge, dark brown man with a round mid-section wiped his face with a white handkerchief as he approached the podium. He made direct eye contact with members of the congregation as he began to speak.

"Ray Kelly was a very popular man in his days at Hillside High School. He and I attended church together as kids, right here at Greater Saint Paul. Somewhere, somehow for some reason, Ray lost his way. Although, he lost his way he was still a kindhearted man. I'd see him off and on in passing ---although he was living a worldly life, a life that took him down a different path, whenever we came across one another he'd always give me--- a smile and handshake, all of you know the smile I 'm talking about. That big bright smile Ray was known for. He'd shake my hand and we'd talk about the Lord. God works in mysterious ways and in his own time. God saw fit to call Ray on home. Our hearts ache and we are heavy burdened today --- but who are we to question God's calling home one of his children. Don't you weep to long --- Ray's now resting in God's loving arms."

Solomon scanned the congregation while Rev. Davis preached and admonished the flock. He didn't know exactly what he was looking for in the crowd but would know if he saw it. He'd stood in the back of the church as the hustlers and players filed in --- looking and making mental notes.

As Rev. Davis was about to go off on another firry tangent, Solomon was drawn to a disturbance down where the family was seated. Sammy Lee, the brother of Hazel Ruth and Bobbie Jean, who were all first cousins to Annie Mae were at the center of the commotion. Sammy Lee's ex-wife Queenie who was seated on one side of Sammy Lee with his sister Bobbie Jean on the other ---who was high on heroin and accompanied by her boyfriend Willie James, a known gunslinger as well as was his entire family. Shooting and killing was a rite of passage into manhood for the Fosters. The group had arrived and come in the church together. What nobody knew was that Queenie and Bobbie Jean had bad blood between them going back to the time when Queenie and Sammy Lee were married. Through the entire service Queenie and Bobbie Jean had eyed one another --- gritting and giving one another attitude. The commotion occurred when Bobbie Jean reached across Sammy Lee and snatched Queenie's gold necklace from around her neck. Queenie retaliated by reaching across Sammy Lee, slapping Bobbie Jean in the face. Sammy Lee, a nervous and fidgety natured man jumped up to separate the two of them, and in doing so grabbed

Bobbie Jean's arm in an attempt to control her --- allowing Queenie the opportunity to sucker punch Bobbie Jean. Bobbie Jean wailed and shouted, "Willie James, get em off me." Willie James produced a pistol from his waist band ordering, "get off her --- let her go!"

Meanwhile, the people in the congregation began screaming and ducking for cover. Rev. Davis stooped down behind the podium trying to find protection and get out the line of fire. The choir members ran for the side door. Sammy Lee's momma, a slim fair skinned eccentric dressing woman with keen features, was Saintly even when she was tipsy. She was seated up front in a red hat and matching dress saying, "Lord, look at the Devil doing His work."

Buddy McIver, a short thick man in his late sixties and one of Durham's top black lawyers --- and a friend of the Kelly family, who was obviously under the influence, like most other days made his way as quick as he could toward the front door of the church, grumbling and wiping sweat with a white handkerchief.

In a few minutes, things calmed down enough for Reverend Davis to find the courage to raise from behind the podium and finish the service.

Solomon stood in the back --- biting down on his cigar thinking that he'd never seen or heard of people cutting the fool at a funeral like that before ---ever.

Annie Mae had made sure the Kelly and Slade families would be driven to the church and cemetery in style. There were three black limos driven by white men in black tuxedos. After the church service, a procession of BMWs, Benzes, Jags and Cadillac's followed closely in the line behind the limos in route to Beechwood Cemetery for the burial. As they mannered from Saint Paul's Baptist Church through North Durham and down Alston Avenue, people stopped in their tracks, their mouths gapping open at the sight of the procession. At Beechwood Cemetery, the family and friends of the Kelly's made their way to the grave site.

Sammy Lee, Queenie, Bobbie Jean and Willie James finally made it to the grave site by the time the attendants were rolling the coffin down into the grave.

Reverend Davis could be heard loud and clear, praying for receipt of Ray's soul into Abraham's bosom. The men lowered their heads and removed their hats as the crowd assumed reverent posture, tilting their heads toward heaven. Reverend Davis's rich deep voice rolled over the bare earth toward the pine trees that watched over the cemetery.

"And for thee, O Heavenly Father, find a place for this young man in Thy perfect paradise above, take him home to Thee, give him eternal rest—and we pray dear Lord for the parents ---comfort, guide and protect them in their secret way. Spare them the needless suffering and get them ready for the day when they will be reunited with their child, Amen.

Bobbie Jean began to wail and cry. She tugged on Willie James's arm, "Willie James make them roll him back up – I ain't ready for Ray to go in the grave yet --- I want to see them do it from the beginning." Willie James didn't hesitate; he pulled his pistol and barked, "Roll him up." The family and other by-standers were overtaken with disbelief and insult --- but were afraid to say a word.

Solomon watched the crowd through dark sunglasses from under his straw Stetson, as Reverend Davis convinced Willie James to holster his pistol. He chose not to intervene --- he'd save dealing with Willie James for another day.

CHAPTER 27

DETECTIVE GRAVES AND HER FRIENDS Beth and Hope had adopted The Blue Ram Bar and Café out on U.S. 501 between Durham and Chapel Hill as their weekly meeting place and watering hole. The Blue Ram, a regular hang around for UNC students and the younger crowd was a bright hot spot with fifty different brands of beer, hardwood floors, and UNC logons all over the place, serving club sandwiches, burgers, fries, beer and liquor by the drink.

It was the end of September Wednesday night at 9:30; the day had started with an early morning chill but had turned hot and sultry. Walking through the door Linda saw Beth and Hope in their regular booth in the back. Hope was bent over the table, leaning forward like she was sharing some divine revelation, which happened a lot because Hope was the great philosopher, especially after a couple of drinks---philosophizing a habitual carry over from her day job as a school teacher at Riverside High School. Beth on the other hand was more reserved which matched with her profession as an Accountant at Duke Medical Center.

"Girl, you're running behind – we are two or three refills ahead of you," Hope punned.

"I plan to catch up, starting right now." Linda shot back. She took a gulp of chilled tonic. "How's it going?" Asked Hope, "You must have solved the cases that have kept you from meeting us the last two weeks."

"No such luck, nothing's changed – not a clue concerning the drug cases and I believe my number one suspect to the rapes have skipped town. So, I said the hell with it all for tonight and here I am."

"It's a crazy world," Beth said. "I mean the idea of some lunatic running around raping women just because --- and another psychopath running around giving people drugs that kills them. I guess all the nonsense in the world is bigger and more complex than most people understand and care about." Hope said sympathetically.

"It's the damnedest thing I ever heard of," she said. "You wouldn't believe it – in the drug case we don't have a clue of whom or where the dope is coming from. We've talked to every snitch and chased every lead. Nothin!" The only thing that looks a little promising is a hunch that Detective King is following."

"Is King the guy, the black guy you said was kinda off beat and homely?" asked Hope.

"Let me warn you sweetheart, it's only an appearance. He by no means is slow. He doesn't miss a beat. The word is that he has solved more big cases than anyone in the Department. I think he gives that impression on purpose, just to throw people off. He likes doing things his own way at his own pace. The more I'm around him the more I like him."

"Hey! Enough of the work shit, let's enjoy ourselves." She pulled the rubber band from her ponytail, leaned over and shook her thick auburn hair, brushing it back with her hands.

"So, tell me about your new friend." She asked. Beth had recently met a new guy, an intern at Duke Medical Center. Beth's face became flush at the mention of the topic. Linda began probing for details as Bob Marley's voice blasted from the juke box.

The three daiquiris had begun to loosen her up when her T-Mobile rang. It was Roger Tilley from the Sex Crime Unit.

"Grave, this is Tilley from SCU. Meet me on Hillsboro Road. We got a call from a woman on Darden Street off West Buchanan concerning a man outside her neighbor's window. Might be our guy; maybe he's on the move." Tilley said.

"I'm off duty," Linda shouted.

"Yeah! But you're the lead man on the rape investigation ---- everything runs through you. You know how Fetcher is about that kinda shit." Linda let out a loud sigh and cursed. "What's the fucking use." She rummaged through her bag, flung some bills on the table, and through her hands up, "I got to run," and dashed for the door.

She fired up her red Datsun 300 ZX and peeled out the parking lot. By the time she was a quarter mile down U.S. 501, she was up to eighty miles an hour. In her head she knew she shouldn't be driving, especially at such a high rate of speed after four drinks. She passed South Square Mall exit in the midst of the mall traffic like a bat out of hell. Apart from the alcohol, her adrenaline had her pumped. When she hit Hillsboro Road exit, a stretch of fas food restaurants, banks and grocery stores caused her to slow her roll. Roger Tilley waiting in a dark blue Crown Vic blinked his lights. She parked and jumped in the car with Tilley.

I need to ride with you --- I shouldn't be driving."

"Why not --- what's up?" he asked.

"I had a few daiquiris at the Blue Ram; I was working on my fifth when you called."

"Can you handle yourself?"

"Yeah, I'm okay as long as I'm not the driver."

As they turned off Hillsboro Road onto East Main, one block from Buchanan, Tilley radioed for back-up. He gave the location and instructed the back-up units to position themselves a block away from the house at 1505 Darden Street.

As Detective Tilley and Linda approached Darden Street a tractor trailer, apparently lost of misdirected was attempting to make a turn in front of them. A bright red chromed tractor truck with a twin cab, a hulk of a truck with flashing lights and honking back-up alerts, blocked the street.

They waited tense seconds as the truck made the turn, the entire time Linda drummed the dash with her fingers. Detective Tilley radioed the officers who were on stakeout a half blocked away from the house. "King Zebra Two Six Charlie, where's the subject?" Tilley asked. "Subject not visible at present." One of the officers replied. "He probably made us and took off." Said Tilley. "Maintain your position." Detective Tilley was finally able to squeeze past the tractor trailer, they pulled to the curb as they approached 1505 Darden Street – aw, shit!" Tilley said as two shots rang out. Tilley snatched his radio from his side, "King Zebra Two Six Charlie, we hear gunshots. We're approaching the residence."

The blast from the gun sounded like someone had fired a cannon. Detective Tilley ran from the front door and signaled Linda to cover the back.

Inside the house, Alan Winstead laid face down on the floor in a puddle of his own blood. He had miscalculated his move --- thinking the woman of the house, a slim chocolate and attractive thirty something woman was alone. As he slipped through the window into the dark house, Baxter Henry, the man of the house heard the intruder's creeping footsteps. He signaled for his wife and secured her inside the bedroom closet. He knew the intruder had come to harm them. He could smell the scent of the man's body. Baxter felt inside the draw of the bed stand and eased his Waltham 9mm out --- and in a prone position waited for the assailant. Once a United States Marine in Viet Nam with more than ten silent kills, he was now of a killing mind. Not a phony bravado with the capacity to deflate. Rather focused. He knew it would be quick and short, violent and close. Whoever shot first would win. Alan Winstead moved silently, maneuvering from room to room, he cracked the bedroom door searching for his next victim so he could exact his brutal assault --- as he stepped inside the room; Henry fired twice hitting Alan in the chest and neck.

Outside Detective Linda Graves and Tilley slid forward, edging along the wall silently with their pistols drawn on opposite ends of the house. Listening, trying to get in a position of cover. Suddenly, it seemed like every light in the house came on.

The front door of the two-story white house slowly opened. Baxter Henry stood in the doorway wearing a white terry cloth robe. Detective Tilley looked up and saw that Baxter was unarmed. Tilley and Graves both gripped their weapons and approached Baxter. He held both his hands up as he spoke, "I'm not armed; my gun is in the den on the table. The man is in the bedroom on the floor." Linda's heart was booming almost audibly. Both Tilley and Graves holstered their weapons as Baxter Henry lead them inside his home.

CHAPTER 28

AFTER ALMOST TWO MONTHS OF cancellations, my daughter Sarah Anne had me cornered for dinner with Juan and his mother Ethel. Sarah Ann had held up to her part of our agreement by going down to the shelter to help feed the homeless on each consecutive fourth Saturday of the month. In fact, she'd volunteered to help out at the soup kitchen down on 18th Street in Charlotte since then. Feeding the homeless on those Saturdays caused her to see another side of life in America --- the land of plenty. It put her in touch and added faces to the destitute, the poor and forgotten. Men and women living on the street in park cars, under bridges and abandoned houses…most with histories of emotional and mental illness turned out on the streets from mental institutions to fend for themselves.

Sarah Ann had completely taken over. She changed the plans entirely. Instead of dinner at Slugg's Top of the Tower, she arranged dinner to be served in my home ---our home place. Sarah Ann spent the entire week cleaning and redecorating the house. Having her around and noticing how much she had become like her mother caused my heart to ache. I begin to miss Rosa Lee all over again.

Dinner was a family affair, served buffet style, with the Johnsons, Sarah Ann and to my surprise, Junior and a chic, he simply introduced as Sonya. Junior's in the Army and stationed at Fort Bragg right outside Fayetteville, North Carolina wore dress fatigues. He was a sight for sore eyes. I hadn't seen him in over six months and didn't expect him to be there.

At the dinner table, a debate raged about the invasion of Iraq and the government's support of Israel. We were equally divided on whether the invasion was about WMD's or securing the flow of oil or whether it was another example of colonialism lead by the United States and the British.

Sarah Ann prepared all the food black folk loved. The long table in the dining room was overrun with fried chicken, roost beef, cabbage, yams, mac and cheese, potato salad, ice -tea and chocolate cake.

Paying close attention to Sarah Ann and Juan, and by the way they looked at each other it wouldn't be long before my family would expand through marriage. This was what the dinner was about. Softening me up to --- getting me ready for a son-in-law. After dinner we moved to the den and watched a movie: A Time to Kill with Samuel L. Jackson.

I'd had a long day --- and figured I would never make it an hour after dinner. But the spirit and gaiety of the night had given me a surge of energy. Even with a glass of red burgundy I managed to make it through the movie. At night's end the Johnsons were headed back to Charlotte, Junior and Sonya to who knows where and I was left with Sarah Anne.

CHAPTER 29

HE WAS CONCERNED BY THE newspapers.

He knew he shouldn't save them. If someone came around asking questions…but then if a cop saw them inside his home, it would be over anyway. They would know what's what. The articles had been on the second page in the crime section for the third time in a week. The Durham-Herald Sun had Serial Killer Holds City at Bay. He like the word "hold", it reasoned power and control.

The same day the story hit the paper he'd seen it on the 6:00 o'clock news. Meg McDowell, anchorwoman for WTVD, tall good looking in a smart suit, uttered the earsplitting word "murder" into the microphone outside the Durham County Judicial Building. Four hours later, the ten o'clock news replayed a part of the second press conference with Chief Fetcher.

The conference got out of control, real-quick. Chief fletcher had planned to make the conference brief. The first few questions were succinct. Then a member of Durham's Nations of Islam raised his voice, cutting off a question from a reporter, and the whole conference spun out of control. People shouted at one another, photographers stood on chairs snapping pictures, and reporters continued to fire questions at the Chief.

He watched the tape in dismay. He sat still in his recliner with his finger across his lips as to say "hush" thinking of the rouse of his actions.

He got up early the next morning to catch the 6 o'clock news before his morning run. It was nothing but a retake of the news from the night before.

The Professor could barely concentrate at work the next day, he felt on edge. In each of his classes he canceled his lecture and gave a pop quiz. Later he spent time in his office reading journals and correcting the quizzes.

Professor Alford was honored and well respected at the University and it was said he would be chair of the department in a year or two. He was a loner, well-schooled and always smartly dressed, handsome, polite and what his peers didn't know – an ice cool killer in the same package.

At days end the Professor rushed to his Hope Valley North home … 1126 Roxborough Street, for a hot shower, a glass of Remy Martin and dinner before the 6:00 o'clock news. Nothing new was reported, the only thing of interest was WRAL's interview with a member of the Nation of Islam. The tall dark brown man in a tan suit, white shirt and bow tie ranted --- accusing the police department of dropping the ball in the case because all the victims were black men, siting a county with two justice systems, one for whites and one for blacks and browns. He indicated the killings were somehow based on race. In back of the speaker were five or six solemn NOI members. During the segment, the WRAL reporter talked to other people over the city getting their reaction. The people in the community weren't scared and were sure the police would get whoever was poisoning the addicts.

The reporter revealed the special Task Force working on the case assigned the name "Overdose Murders," to the case and the public had picked up on it.

Later in the evening, he spent time cleaning and straightening his meticulous home. He went from room to room rearranging chairs, pictures and dusting furniture. He couldn't sit still for anything. Finally, he went out to do some shopping. He went from store to store, from one side of town to the next. He finally ended up in Wal Marts on Roxboro

Road, cruising the aisles and observing the crowd. He saw women with rowdy children running, crying and pulling things off the shelves. He saw a man and woman, both white and black that appeared under feed and unclean, a team attempting to disguise themselves as regular customers, thieves concealing merchandise in a big shoulder bag. The man dressed in blue jeans held up by a big buckle western style belt with a chain running through the belt loops, dingo boots, a black t-shirt, who habitually brushed his oily hair out his face as they moved down the aisle. His partner looked frail and scared. She had a head of dirty blond hair and dressed in cheap jeans, a t-shirt and running shoes. He looked thinking, two more junkies, and scum."

As he turned the corner, he faced a woman with a familiar face. He was stunned and caught off guard. The woman gave him a sheepish smile and hello. The Professor stopped in his tracks, his eyes locking with the woman's sly fox like eyes. He was so overtaken by the woman's penetrating stare; he had to say something, anything. "Excuse me; it seems as if I've met you before … but I can't place where." He said. The woman was small, plain and looked to be in her thirties. As he observed closer, he found her to be somewhat attractive, a subtle kinda beauty. She wore a modest, navy blue warm-up suit, and her hair was tied back with a white head scarf. The Professor looked at the woman up and down as if he was trying to place who she was. She could feel his piercing stare as she cast her eyes away. Finally, she spoke, "I think you taught my brother over at NCCU." Who's your brother?" the Professor asked. The woman continued to hold her head down, and then she looked him in the eyes, holding it for a split second. "My brother was Ronnie Banks. I'm his sister, Clara. He died almost a year ago. You were at the wake and came by the house after the funeral, if I'm not mistaken." She said. As she spoke and listened, she knew she'd heard the man's voice before. It was the same voice of the man who had called for her brother Ronnie late nights --- continuously, months and months up until he died from the overdose.

The Professor felt uneasy, the way the woman spoke of knowing who he was and connecting him to her brother was a blow to the gut. She seems to know more than she said. He could see it in her eyes. He knew something about him had alarmed her --- woke her up. Maybe she had put the puzzle together. "Ms. Banks its nice seeing you, and again, I'm sorry about your brother. He was a good kid." He said. He watched as Clara Banks moseyed on down the aisle selecting items of food. He caught her as she turned and gave him one more look. In his soul he knew she recognized him and knew the truth--- "maybe it's my voice he though. Maybe her six sense." His predator nature picked up on her fear. He knew she was on to him.

On his way home driving down U.S. 501 between Durham and Chapel Hill, with traffic moving at about fifty-five or so, the Professor was reviewing his "kill list" in his mind. Who would be next before he concluded his mission? Had he gotten enough revenge or was he now hooked on the power to decide on who lives and who dies? His rational mind told him he had to stop or be caught. Stop! Just as suddenly as he had begun. Finished! But Clara Banks' face came into focus. She was a loose end; he had to decide how to handle her.

CHAPTER 30

AFTER FINISHING OFF WHAT WAS left of Sarah Ann's baked chicken dinner from the night before, Solomon switched on the T.V. for the ten o'clock news. Following the news, he dropped off to sleep and was awaken by the doorbell --- he glanced at his watch and saw that it was almost eleven-thirty.

He had no idea who could be at his door at this time of the night. It couldn't be Sarah Anne she had called earlier from her home in Charlotte. Junior was down at Fort Bragg and Solomon didn't have a woman in his life that would be calling at midnight. Taking his time, he moved toward the door with his Smith & Wesson 9mm in hand, with the safety off, just in case.

He stood to the side of the door and flung it open. At the door there stood homicide Detective Jake Morris, he was caught off guard by the way Solomon answered the door. "Hey, it's only me. The bad guys haven't come for you yet." He said. "What the hell are you doing ringing my doorbell this time of the night?" Solomon asked as Jake looked passed him into the front room. So, Solomon invited him in.

They sat on the couch Solomon offered Jake a beer as he ate from a bag of pretzels that had been left on the coffee table earlier. Solomon looked at his watch and asked, "Jake, have you lost your mind, or have nothing else to do?"

Jake let out a long sigh and looked at Solomon. "I just rapped-up another overdose murder." Then he raised his hands saying, "Let me stop, another death that looks like the string of other cases we've had. The body was found in a house over on Red Oak Avenue behind McDougal Terrance. I tried to call you but kept getting you answering service. The tech heads rapped it all up about forty-five minutes ago. Same shit. I just wanted to let you know." He paused. "These deaths are bothering me more and more. I can't figure it. Who the hell is doing this shit and for what reason?"

"You mean to tell me we couldn't have this talk first thing tomorrow morning?" Solomon asked. Jake stared at Solomon without answering. "Look, Jake I've been trying to figure this thing out, also. I got a couple ideas but no proof. So, for now I'll hold my suspicions close to my chest. Jakes eyes went cold and hard.

"I've been talking to as many of the street hustlers and junkies as I can. I went over some stats I had put together on unsolved deaths from drugs, on my free time." Solomon said.

"Statistic like the ones I got coming out of white neighborhood life Hope Valley or Treyburn, people would be hollering and shitting, going nuts. It would all over paper, in the News and Observer every damn day. Every cop in the city would be assigned to the case; money or the budget would be no concern. But, because all the overdoses are in the black part of the city – it's a different story.

"I don't know. It's kinda like a balancing act, especially dealing with family members left behind by the deaths. The time the most information is needed is the time they least want to talk about what has happened. In all my years, I haven't found the best way to interview family members, after a thing like this have happened. Some are angry as hell and others are to hurt to talk."

"I don't know. According to statistics, eighty-one percent of known female serial killers use poison, suffocates or use lethal injections on their victims. Less than ten percent of various types of killers use guns as their weapon of choice and hardly neither group use knives as their weapon of choice. So, there's an outside possibility, whoever is spreading this bad dope around is a woman. But I doubt it."

"Well, I'd like to catch whoever is doing this --- I don't give a damn if it's a man or woman." Morris said. Solomon looked at him and continued, "Let me tell you what I feel about this killer. The first thing I did was to run several theories about our killer through CICAP system, looking for any kind of match to the rash of deaths like we've had in the last couple of months. The only thing that came up was a rash of overdoses in the Washington, DC area sometime back coming from a batch of high-grade heroin on the street. In that case the distributors got busted. It was just another case of a couple of dealers trying to put the best dope on the street and corner the market. No connection to what we got going here."

"Let me tell you what I think. I believe one person is responsible for spreading around the bad dope. I think it's a male. I think he's on some kind of vigilante trip. I don't think he's a regular street person and he's smart as hell. He's organized, patient and careful. He's probably picking his victims ahead of time. He probably has a job and maybe a family – and look like an average citizen."

"He's probably caught up in some type of fantasy or anger trip. Maybe he suffers from a multiple personality disorder and is moving in and out of personalities. I don't know for sure. But what I do know if he stays out there, he's gonna make a mistake----sooner or later."

"I'm guessing that he hates junkies for some twisted reason. Maybe he was robbed by a junkie or had a girlfriend to leave him and take up with a drug user or maybe he wanted to be a policeman and for some reason couldn't. It might be a religious thing driving him or something about law and the government. I don't know for sure, but I got my ideas."

"Damn Solomon, you really have been sinking your teeth into this thing. " "Yeah well, what we've said here tonight is not for the Task Force. It's my own thinking and let's keep it at that."

CHAPTER 31

IT WAS RIGHT AFTER 5:00 p.m. as Solomon drove down Forrest Hill Road amongst overlapping willows and along manicured sidewalks. After traveling ten or so blocks, he made a right turn on Roxborough Street ---two blocks from Professor James Alford's colonial style home. The houses along both sides of the street looked to have been built in the late eighties. They were all huge, spacious and probably costly to heat.

Solomon turned off Roxborough Street into the drive leading up to Professor Alford's place. The drive was paved from the doorstep to the street. It was clean and well cared for. The Professor probably didn't get to many visitors, something about the house said so. From the way things looked, Solomon figure he must spend a great deal of money keeping his yard and surrounding up. On each side of the house were matching flower beds … yellow, red, white flowers mixed softly with green leafy annuals. A profusion of rose brushes formed the background for the beds, and two large magnolias faced each other in front of the house. He had spent a great amount of effort in making the place beautiful. The house and surroundings had a regimented orderliness about it.

Solomon got out of the cruiser and approached the house. The place seemed vacated. There was no answer when Solomon knocked at the front door. He walked around to the back of the house, peering into the windows. It seemed as if he was looking at a magazine. There was a large deck running across the back. He looked on the deck and then through the window at eh back door into the kitchen. The kitchen window was as much a picture book as the other rooms --- neat, clean, well equipped and orderly looking.

Solomon froze in his tracks. Almost in a sneaky fashion, and then an explosive burst something was coming around the corner. He spun to his left and reached for my pistol. In the next instance, he faced a vicious looking German Sheppard. The dog approached wagging his tail. Solomon stood still with relief, feeling like a complete fool. He reached over and patted the dog on the head. Why had he drawn his pistol? Why did he feel afraid? Minutes later, he was still uneasy. His heart was pounding like it would jump out his chest. It was more to it than the dog --- it was the man whose house he was visiting.

Solomon walked back to the front of the house toward his cruiser. As he was about to open the door, someone spoke. "Excuse me sir, can I help you?" it was Professor Alford speaking from the front door. Solomon turned and faced him. "Yes, I'm Detective King from the Durham Police Department. I'd like to speak with you if I could. I rang the doorbell but didn't get an answer." "I was in the shower and didn't hear …I didn't know you were here until I happened to look out the window, sorry bout that." He said. Solomon made a point of not sounding overly pleasant. He wanted to see how the professor would react. By that time, Solomon had walked up to the bottom of the steps, looking the Professor in the face. "I just need a little information --- can I come in so that we can talk? It'll only take a few minutes." Solomon said. Without being uninvited, he walked up to where the Professor stood at the top of the steps. The Professor looked a little uncomfortable as Solomon approached him. In a second or two, he seemed to gather his wits. "Am I interrupting anything? Solomon asked. "No, no please come in." The professor recounted.

The Professor invited Solomon in, offering a chair with an air of great courtesy. They sat in cushioned leather chairs on either side of the den. On the wall over the mantle were pictures by Barnes with eccentric features of African men and women.

"What can I help you with?" asked the professor

'I don't know if you are aware but there has been a string of overdose deaths in the city the last several months. You've probably seen it on the news---it's been all over the news damn near every day."

"Yes, I have seen it on the news," the professor replied.

As the Professor prepared to speak, his eyes stayed focused on Solomon. Solomon narrowed his eyes, up and down, searching for some sign of weakness, measuring the professor. Studying the pleasant, memorable face, clean honest with clear eyes. Solomon trying to keep his pulse calm – with his gut's telling him this guy knows something.

"I decided to come see you once I found that four of the victims knew you or had some connection to you. I pretended like I'm trying to remember their names. Banks and Hall, I believe. I found they attended NCCU and was enrolled in your 2 o'clock chemistry class."

"Yes, Ronnie Banks and Trevor Hall, they were both bright young men. What a tragedy. I would have never thought they were involved with drugs," he said.

"You see or hear anything around the school or from any of the students concerning the Hall or Banks kids?"

"No not a thing." He said.

There was a long pause. Solomon hardly knew what else to ask the Professor, he didn't want to ask him about the death of his niece – and her boyfriend Eric Graham, not just yet. Solomon looked up at the mantle over the fireplace.

"That's quite a collection of Barnes art." Solomon rose to examine it closer.

"Yes, I'm a Barnes enthusiast" The professor announced.

There is silence again. "Well Mr. Alford, I'm just making my rounds…checking with any and everyone who knew any of the victims.

I got two or three more stops to make." Solomon looked at his watch, then at Alford and headed for the door.

"I'm sorry if I troubled you." Solomon said as he walked out of the door.

"No trouble, sorry I couldn't help you more."

Solomon drove away from the house feeling he'd made a fool of himself. He decided to head back to the station. His gut told him the good Professor was hiding something.

There was nothing connecting the Professor to the deaths except that he knew four of the victims, and that could be a coincidence. But Solomon didn't believe in coincidence.

Solomon finished making some notes at the office, trying to put the Professor out of my mind. And went home with intention of getting a good night's sleep.

Princess Solomon's oversized Persian cat rubbed against his leg each time he took a step. He'd been gone all day each day for a week and Princess seemed to have missed him. Solomon somehow loved the attention she gave him each time he'd been away for a while…it was simple unconditional affection on behalf of a feline.

Solomon finally headed to the den with Princess trailing. He was taking the night off from work and the case. He needed some time. Monday night football, the Cowboys and Eagles in front of the big screen with ice cream and cookies was the plan. Life alone wasn't bad on nights like tonight --- no kids running through the house ---" no honey do" list from the wife, just me and Princess. Hell, who was I kidding … no matter what he tried to do or how hard he tried to convince himself, he missed Rosa Lee, her death made life empty and only bearable.

After half of the half gallon of blackberry Ice Cream, a dozen or so chocolate cookies and nodding through the first half of the game ---his phone rang. The sound startled him at first. He looked at his watch … it was 10:15. He had no idea who'd be calling him at that time of the night. He'd talked to Sarah Ann earlier and Junior the day before, so he was sure it wasn't either of them. He didn't have anyone else in his life who'd have a reason to call me after 10:00 o'clock at night and the guys from downtown always paged if they needed him. Oh shit, he thought, I'm not going to answer. I don't feel like being bothered and what good could come from a phone call this late at night.

After three rings he decided to pick up and heard a woman's voice whisper.

"Mr. King? This is Clara Banks. I talked to you back in the summer down at the Police Department about my brother."

"Yes, Miss Banks, I remember you," he said. "What can I do for you?"

"I'm sorry for calling your house and so late. I found your phone number on the card you gave me when we talked about my brother."

"That's okay, Miss Banks," he said, "She sounded like she was scared half to death. Talking to Clara Banks was a constant pull to get her to talk."

"I've been thinking about calling you for a week or so but didn't know whether I should or not. It's about Ronnie's teacher down at NCCU. The one who attended the wake after Ronnie died."

"You're talking about Alford," Solomon said.

"Yes, that's him. Well, the other week I saw him at Wal Marts one night. He didn't recognize me until I spoke t him. Then he said he was sorry about Ronnie again and asked me how I'd being doing. What I wanted to tell you is, I'm pretty sure he's the same man who use to call for Ronnie all the time before he died. I recognized him by his deep voice. He use to call Ronnie and I could tell it wasn't about school work. I always thought whoever that was calling Ronnie was who he was selling drugs for."

"Miss Banks are you certain it's the same voice?" Solomon asked.

"I'm almost sure it is … I'm good with voices since I sang and all. I think he might know I recognized him or something."

"Why you say that Miss Banks?"

"Well, when I finished talking to him in the store, I caught him looking at me in a strange way. It scared me and I've been shaking ever since. Maybe it's nothing but I think he's the same guy."

"I'm glad you called, Miss Banks. If he calls you or come by your house, you give me a call right away. Look you did the right thing every little detail helps."

Okay, Mr. King and thanks for talking with me." After that she was gone.

CHAPTER 32

THEY STOOD SUBMISSIVELY BEFORE JUDGE Frank Williams. He had scheduled to see them at 9 A.M. and wouldn't see them any sooner, so Solomon and Detective Graves waited patiently. By 9 o'clock the hollow wood walled courtroom had been awoken by footsteps of lawyers, defendants, policemen and sight seers. Inside his chambers, Judge Williams a soft-spoken black man approaching his sixties set behind his grand oak desk … covered with a disarray of files and papers. The room had the aroma of pipe tobacco and lemon.

Finally, he spoke in a flinty monotone rhythm using tedious thoughtful manners as he peered over his rimless glasses. His thick southern accent off set his reputation as one of the sharpest legal minds in the State.

He flipped through the pages of the affidavit. "Let me be clear," he drawled. Frowning and with a deep breath, he put his thick reading glasses on. "You two officers, members of Durham's finest are seeking a probable cause search warrant as a part of an ongoing investigation – in the matter of the rash of overdose deaths here in Durham? Alright, then, what have we got?"

Solomon pulled out a cigar the size of salami and leaned back in his chair as he began. "You'll see there that James Alford knew four of the victims, was involved with them in some capacity and may possess evidence connected to the deaths of these individuals who have either died from a self-administered or were killed by someone purposely distributing a poisonous grade of heroin throughout Durham. We contend that in a search of his residence we would fine physical evidence to implicate his knowledge, the source of the drugs or other information concerning at least four of the people who have died as a result of the drugs --- that will further our investigation."

Judge Williams peered over his glasses, looking at them suspiciously. He sank down in his large black chair, "Alright, guys, I advise that we move with caution here. As you may have a reason to suspect this person of being involved or having some knowledge that's connected to the deaths of the individuals listed here, let's not forget that Mr. Alford, if it's the same James Alford, the esteemed Professor down at NCCU, is a highly respected member of the academic community as well as this community at large. He held Solomon and Linda at bay with a long stare for a few second. "I'm sure the Modus Operandi 'of these crimes are distinctive. Let's just suppose for a moment for argument sake, that Alford is somehow involved. That the overdoses are used to disguise homicides that are being committed by Alford or whoever. Detectives I'm not willing to put the Courts' reputation in jeopardy based merely on a gut suspicious. Bring me something I can hang my hat on. Then we can discuss a search warrant. Remember James Alford is a respectable man and have a lot of friends. I advise you to proceed with cautions. If there are no other issues to be discussed, I have an appointment with a couple of attorneys who are in the middle of a murder trial.

"But your Honor!" Solomon shouted, "Let me tell you what we have." "Okay you have five minutes." We believe that Mr. Alford, either has in his possession some related evidence or other materials that will lead to the arrest of whoever is responsible for these deaths."

Solomon in a terse manner said, "One of the victim's sister, Clara Banks came into see me three of four months ago, right after Leroy Watson was found on Green Street ---- back in July. She told me during that briefing that her brother Ronnie Banks had died a couple months earlier from what was supposed to be an overdose. Then she went on to say that she didn't think he'd mistakenly used to much dope. The night of his death, he'd received a telephone call from a man, the same man who had been calling him for months at their home. She says her brother left out to meet whoever had called and shortly thereafter came home and was found in the bathroom dead."

Detective Graves jumped in, "I created a file of overdose deaths going back five years. What we found after talking to the next of kin of the victims was that four out of seven on the list, I'd come up with had some connection to Mr. Alford." Judge Williams raised his eyebrows.

Linda continued, "Bridget Kerns died a little over a five years ago --- you might remember the case, she was a UNC Chapel Hill coed, found dead from an overdose at a friend's apartment --- she was Alford's niece. He'd raised her since his younger sister passed away from what I believe was breast cancer. A year later, Kern's hustler boyfriend who'd turned her out to the streets was the next one to die from an overdose. Back in the summer Ronnie Banks overdosed and then Trevor Hall was found in his apartment on Cecil Street. Both Hall and Banks attended NCCU, majored in chemistry where Alford teaches and was enrolled in Alford's 2 o'clock Tuesday and Thursday classes." Solomon added, "I got a call from Clara Banks two days ago, she said she'd run into Professor Alford a couple of weeks ago in Wal Marts. Something he did scared the hell out of her. She called me at my home a day or two ago telling me about seeing Alford. She says, she's sure he's the man who use to call her brother during the time he was dealing drugs and the same man he'd talked with and met the night he'd died. She recognized Alford in the store as the man who called her home because of his unique baritone voice. Also, I paid Alford a little visit at him home a week or so ago and I'm not satisfied with what I got. I've been tracking down murderers and scum for a long time and something is not right with this guy."

The Judge grimaced. "We are walking on thin ice here. Everything you've told me is circumstantial at best. He sighed at Linda's balked expression. "Yeah! Well, where else can we start? Whoever is poisoning addicts with high grade heroin is responsible for their deaths. I'm sure it's the same for the ones since we've been tracking this thing and I think it's one person doing it. Whoever it is, is clever enough not to get caught yet. He's organized, patient and careful." Solomon said.

"There is an absence of hard evidence and no forensic or scientific evidence that points to Alford, Am I right?"

Linda said "The consistency comes in with the death of the four who had some ties to Alford, the method is the same in all the deaths and the opportunity ---- well we're not sure of that right now."

Judge Williams raised his chin and looked out at Solomon and Graves, "You two have the Department's backing on this, I'm sure."

"Yes, I talked it over with Captain Fletcher on yesterday." Solomon answered.

"We have no hard evidence or testimony from any witness, but Alford keep appearing somewhere in all the deaths." Graves said.

"I'm not sure that validate a motive for homicide." Said the Judge.

The Judge lit his pipe and studied the affidavit, page by page, scrutinizing them. Detective Graves couldn't take this mixture of smoke and aroma from Solomon's cigar and the Judge's pipe; she waved her hand in front of her nose. "I'm gonna walk outside and get some fresh air" she said.

Judge Williams gave her a brief glance as she walked toward the door, "You know there was a time before the health craze and tobacco law suits that a man could smoke his pipe and not run his company away. Before all the tobacco companies were sued and people realized that the labeled warning that smoking was dangerous to your health was true. Now a man can't smoke in restaurants, on a plane, at work or at home without being on the receiving end of an up-turned nose."

"So, you say Alford knew at least four of the seven people who have so happened to die from overdoses since you been tracking this thing?

"King so you think that Alford is somehow involved. He gazed over the top of his glasses and made imaginary puffs on his pipe.

"Off the record, why do you think a man like Alford would be involved in a mess like this? It, don't seem to fit."

Solomon chewed down on what was left of his cigar. "I haven't figured it that far yet. But you never can be surprised on what drives a man to do what he does. All of us have a face for the public and a face we try to hide."

Judge Williams got up from his desk, put one of his hands in his trouser pocket and walked slowly to the window looking down on Durham's Main Street and across the City. From the window that towered down, the cars, buses, trucks and people appeared as small as dolls as they made their way to different destinations. He spoke solemnly. "The same laws that protect the innocent from a police state where the police violates the rights of its citizens, also protect the accused. Detective King ---- you're looking to fine evidence from Alford's residence that connects these deceased people to him, giving you some type of physical connection to him. If that's all you find, it will be hard to prove he had anything to do with the deaths based solely on the fact that these people were perhaps in his home or the like."

Solomon responded, "What I'm looking for is method, motive, opportunity and an established weapon, the drugs. Also, I want to put a little heat on this guy --- pressure him to get careless."

The Judge countered calmly, "you seem sure he's your man."

"Judge if I was a betting man .... I'd put my money on the fact that he's involved in some way. However, he's involved will help us solve this thing ... I'm thinking."

Solomon bit down on his knobby cigar and stared into the Judge's eyes. The Judge said dryly, "What I need, as you well know and you've made a valiant attempt to give here this morning, is for your investigation to positively foreclose on any other possibilities for these deaths, leaving Alford the sole standing likelihood. I hate to say it but you haven't done that Detective."

He walked back toward his desk. He puffed on his pipe again, "Hear me out King, I think you're on a search and pray mission. It could falter or flourish. It would allow you to prove or disprove that Alford is your man."

He twinkled a kind of dignified mischief at Solomon and concluded, "King, I know you and of your work. I believe there is a good chance you'll on the right track and frankly I've kept up with the murders all summer --- through the media. It's a travesty --- the deaths I mean and all. I'm bound by the law and required more than you have given me. I cannot issue a search warrant at this time. He looked at Solomon long and hard. "Have a good day Detective."

CHAPTER 33

THE PROFESSOR PACED FROM THE den to the kitchen. She recognized me but how? He knew in his gut that Clara Banks knew something---- her eyes gave her away. The eyes— mirrors to the soul. He had trouble focusing.

The real issue he had to remember. She had possibly made the connection with him and her brother. She'd somehow remembered --- something, small and insignificant. Was it something Ronnie had said to her in the months he sold drugs, heroin, supplied from the university chemistry lab.

A supposedly class project and experiment as told to Ronnie after with his brilliance discovered the Professor's notes and supply of synthetic drugs, the threat of exposure and then Ronnie's price for silence. It had all gotten out of hand. Ronnie's experimental use and finally his decision to deal drugs on the street; serving junkies who afforded him more money than he'd ever imagined. There was no other way to stop him --- just like with the others. He'd become another drug dealing parasite, not caring whose life he ruined, no different from the man who turned Brigette out to the streets. Causing her to overload on the junk, justice had to be served.

He chewed on his nails, pacing back and forth. Pain flashed through his ankles. He bent down and massaged it --- turned and wiggled his ankle from side to side. He'd somehow sprained it running through Duke Forest on his early morning run. Cursing, he stumbled to the kitchen, removing an ice pack from the refrigerator. He flopped down on the hassock to apply the ice pack, his hand shaking. After five minutes, his ankle was throbbing; he wrapped it with an ace bandage and went to the television. Weather, sports and local news. He punched the sound and watched only the picture.

His mind turned to the obnoxious detective Solomon King. What did he suspect? Was his visit just routine? The thought of being found out stirred him.

He had to develop a plan. Clara Banks, he needed to do surveillance ---- he had the time. She was the only possible loose end. She wasn't worth his freedom --- his life he'd worked so hard to build. She would be the last one. Debt paid in full. Bridget could rest in peace. He paced more rapidly from room to room, limping, thinking, smiling, and thinking of the end.

His mind moved in and out. Clara Banks. Would killing her be suitable? She moved through his sleep and his rousing fantasy. She drifted in and out of his mind. He had seen her twice, the night before the funeral and in the grocery store. She lived by herself since her brother's death----in a clapboard house on Belvin Avenue in Bragg Town. Five minutes from downtown. Quiet. Easy. Fragile.

The Professor would scout her home. A home once owned by her parents in the middle of one of the oldest black settlements in Durham. Neighbors on both sides; on the right side an old lady, Mrs. Hattie Riley, a widow who'd lived there since Clara was a child with a half dozen calico cats. Bill and Vivian Scott lived on the left side. They had fifteen grandchildren, kids in and out the house all day.

He paced around and around the house for another fifteen minutes and then he grabbed his car keys. A warm and bright morning, he drove over to Belvin Avenue, down the block, down the next, pass Clara' house, the yard neat and clean, rose bushes. He glanced at his watch. Ten o'clock, she had to be at work. A job. What a job." He gripped the steering wheel tight. He didn't have a chose. He continued his drive, down Belvin, then Cooper Street and another and another, the vision of Clara rolling through his mind.

Linda Graves bounced off the steps, up and down. The instructor, taut black man, young sexy in biker shorts shouted, "on four give me a knee up and a tap, knee, tap, knee, tap and on four we're going to backward lounges. Pump your arms, left, right, pump, and pump." Monica her aerobic workout partner bounced beside her, dripping beads of sweat, her Carolina blue shirt and shorts soaking wet.

Linda joked, "Had enough Monica?"

Monica panted as the music blasted, arms pumping, leaping off the steps with cadence, left, right, up, down----pump your arms --- left right." She said between huffs. "We got five more minutes. Last round in a championship fight." The sound of the Spinners blasted, "Burn baby burn, disco inferno"

"Good work, pal. Linda bent over with both hands on her knees. "I can't believe I'm still standing."

"Oh, okay." Monica wiped sweat with a white towel.

"Then I guess they want have to call an ambulance for us." She gave Linda a thumbs up. "Could we start running around the Duke wall --- I think I might live longer." Linda said.

Monica squawked, wobbling to her feet, "some good rough sex would be more aerobic."

Linda laughed. Monica gave her a nudge on the shoulder. They headed for the showers.

They lounged at one of the back tables at Pan Pans, a good soul food restaurant across from Gold's Gym, not facing each other and talking until they had wolfed down most of the baked chicken and apple pie.

Draining all the cola from the ice filled glasses, looking like two gym rats in oversize workout gear. Monica asked, "So how is the investigation going in the drug case." Linda leveled a grimace. "Please, it ain't. I'm not allowed to talk about it. Not a word. We all have been put on notice not to discuss the case until we solve it. It's a media control thing,"

The waitress bought the check, Linda picked it up saying, "Ante up, you. I'm not paying for your lunch today.

Monica plunked down the money, "Yes. If you buy my lunch I might be inclined to tell you that the guy you met from my job likes you and want to ask you out, but his a little intimidated by your badge."

Linda smiled, "Who that guy, Sean? Well for him I'll take my badge off along with the rest of my clothes."

"So, you want me to start a sex scandal? Headlines, the world is desensitized to sexual scandals now days." Linda said.

"Yeah! Right! Only when it's not about a hot police officer." Monica shouted.

Linda looked at her watch. "Damn, I've got to get moving. My sexy partner Solomon King asked me to meet him at the office."

"Please!" Monica smirked. "Solomon might be a lot of things but sexy … I don't think so."

CHAPTER 34

IT WAS EARLY DECEMBER. Six months had passed since Officer Jones had first stumbled upon Leroy Watson's body on Green Street with a syringe hanging out of his arm. The suspicious overdose deaths of five men still had not been solved.

Clara Banks opened the front door while drying her hands on a green apron that was tired around her waist. She was the same as Solomon remembered from the first day he saw her at the police station months ago, shy, withdrawn and with a perpetual smile that seem to hold back some kind of embarrassment.

"Office King." She finished drying her hands hurriedly and shoved them into her jean pockets. "Come in. I've been sorta waiting to hear from you since the last time we talked. The night I told you I'd ran into Professor Alford at the grocery store.

Solomon took off his hat and welcomed the warmth of the snug kitchen with its yellow laced curtains and embroidered place mates. "Would you like some coffee? I was just about to have some right before you knocked."

They sat with two steaming cups of coffee. Solomon laid his cigar on the edge of the saucer. He looked at Clara and spoke — he went straight to the point. He knew no other way. "Ms. Banks, I'm going to be honest with you. Since you called me about seeing James Alford in the grocery store, I've become more convinced than ever that he is somehow involved in this thing. I've been chasing leads like a duck at a June bug. I still don't have anything but circumstantial evidence at best and my gut is telling me that he's in the middle of this mess waist deep. All I got is theory and a lot of speculation. I think I owe it to you to tell you what my instincts are telling me ---even if I'm wrong and can't prove it. I think your brother was somehow given a lethal dose of heroin by whoever is behind this thing just like the others. The quality of the drugs found in your brother and the others are not what people sale on the streets. That causes me to think that someone deliberately served your brother and the others this particular batch of heroin."

Clara Banks' eyes got teary. She shifted in her seat. She took a moment to recover from Solomon's candidness. She perched in her seat, hurting and sedate.

'I want you to understand that I'm not going to give up until I get to the bottom of this thing. There's no statue of limitation for murder. Something can always happen to help break the case wide open and that's what I'm banking on. I'm not here to tell you this is the end but to be honest with you and assure you I'm still on top of this thing. I'm not going to back off and I'm not going away. My suspect knows I'm onto him. He's a little nervous right about now, so I'll just wait ---he'll screw up. Then, I'll be right there when he does, with the handcuffs. Another thing, I want you to call me if Alford contact you in anyway or if you happen to run into him again. I don't know --- but I don't trust him. Just call me if you see him again."

Solomon finished off his cup of coffee and picked up his cigar, lit it and stuck it in the corner of his mouth. He looked at Clara for a long second before he spoke. "Captain Fletcher and the Brass think I'm pissing in the wind with this case. I really don't give a damn what they think — never have. And the Task Force, I don't know what to say about that group of white shirts. I'm keeping most of my work on this thing away from them. But I have to agree that I don't have any science to support my speculation right now, but don't worry about that ---- that's my worry,

Clara Banks nodded obediently. She frowned and shifted in her seat. She said, "So, you think whoever Ronnie met that night gave him the drugs that killed him?"

"Yeah, that's what I'm thinking. According to the autopsy report the drugs he used were the same high quality as the drugs that killed the other men over the summer. So, it means whoever he met gave him the lethal drugs that night and it makes me think the same person gave drugs to the others." Solomon said.

Clara asked. "You think the Professor might have given Ronnie the drugs, don't you? Solomon stared at her without answering as he bit down on his cigar but didn't offer an answer.

"O My Lord!" Clara said as she wiped a tear from under her eye. "But why would he have done that?"

"I haven't put all the pieces together yet?" Solomon said while waving a dismissive hand. Ms. Banks I can't really call the names of who I think gave your bother the drugs that night --- I could get my ass sued. But I think we're barking up the right tree or close by it."

"But how are you going to prove all of this?"

"I'm going to wait, watch and try to get inside Alford's house and see what I can find. I'll keep looking at a few other suspects and leads. One way or the other it will all break."

Clara's face became constrained as her eyes watered. "This is all so crazy. Why would --- would anyone do such a thing?" "Ronnie admired all his teachers --- he never hurt anyone. My Lord, Mr. King."

Solomon felt a little choked up. "I can't say much more, except I'll do my best to get to the bottom of this whole mess."

Since Ronnie's death, Clara Banks had been angry and smothered in grief, the kind that made her wonder why other young men could live if her Ronnie had to die.

After Solomon left, Clara wailed in new pain. Her eyes were filled with tears that ran down and spilled on her face. She wiped her nose with tissue and cried some more.

CHAPTER 35

THERE WAS COMPETE SILENCE EXCEPT for the rustling mass of trees standing in the backyard of James Alford's home. Winter had arrived and brought with it, cold nights in the low thirties and frosty mornings.

He sat in front of the fireplace amid the oak, pine and hickory mixed aroma in pajamas, slippers and a maroon smoking jacket. His curly close- cropped hair was mussed over his head. His reading glasses hung over the bridge of his nose as he read the Raleigh News and Observer. The T.V. played softly as the anchor woman on CNN ran through the news of the day. He pulled on a cigarillo, sipped scotch from a goblet and squinted his eyes in the curls of smoke and dim light from the shaded lamp. Through the window he could hear the faint howl of the wind — signaling the upcoming storm promised by the WTVD meteorologist.

He read the newspaper front and back looking for anything related to the overdose deaths. It had been almost a month since the newspaper carried anything related to the cases.

The only thing he knew was that Detective King was still snooping around. Invariably he's spotted him on campus, setting in his old Impala chewing on his cigar and on a few days, he'd happen to notice him riding down Cornwallis Road as he exited Duke Forest while on his daily run. His common sense told him none of this was just a coincidence. Detective King had his eye on him. He couldn't figure out what had given him away --- what had drawn the Detective's attention to him. Detective King and Clara Banks both caused him to feel uneasy and threatened.

Alford finally folded the paper and put it away. He placed his chin between his hands, looking like the statue of the thinker. He thought and analyzed. No one had ever seen him or been close to him or seen him with either man --- except at the MONEY CHANGER, with Ray Kelly. But he'd hide himself well that night behind a disguise. Ronnie Banks, Trevor Hall could only be tied to him through the University and being enrolled in his third year Chemistry class and lab. No problem when it came to Leroy Watson. He gritted his teeth as he thought, and nothing to give me away when it comes to that no-good use to be boyfriend of Brigette --- Eric Graham.

But he knew there was something he'd missed. Detective King knew something. He could tell from the way he acted the day he'd come by on what he termed a routine call. Something was up. Then he thought of Clara Banks. The way she appeared and looked at him in the grocery store that night. Her eyes told the story. She had recognized him something had given him away and he knew it. He finally decided that Detective King was playing a hunch, but the Banks woman knew something more.

For three weeks no one had said a word about the cases and King had not been back. But he knew he was being tracked. He knew King was laying, and waiting, out of sight. He could feel it, Solomon's smell, his cigar, his breath blowing down his neck, hot ---quiet and patient.

King knew that all the men had died from the same batch of heroin. The old drudge had somehow figured it out. He couldn't swoop down, not yet. He'd lie still, sniff the air. Stare. The mark of a hunter. Alford knew that was King's way.

He jumped up suddenly from the chair and walked to the kitchen, his mind racing. He cleaned the countertop. Hand washed the dishes in the sink. Flipped off the lights and returned to the den to his chair.

One the northern side of town, in the suburb of Durham on Roxboro Road, in solitude, Solomon smelled the stench of sweat and muscle rub of the gym rats at Wayne's Hall of Fitness. Detective Graves through her off handed quibbling had somehow convinced him to get a gym membership and hire a trainer. As he changed from his street get-up into sweats and gym shoes, he thought of his many years of chasing crooks. One thing all crooks had in common was --- none ever thought they'd get caught. But most did.

He stretched from side to side, tried to touch his toes, jumped up and down in place for a few seconds and headed to the tread mill. On the tread mill he looked out and saw the chiseled body builders in tank tops with muscles that had been honed down to look like rocks. Triceps that looked like hunks of marble. Men and women who appeared to be made of iron.

Across the floor Solomon could see Dobbie, his trainer with the personality of a pit bull checking his watch. He looked toward Solomon giving him thumbs up ---signaling Solomon to step up the pace and meet him at the free weight area in thirty minutes.

In what seemed like no time at all, Solomon was on the flat bench pushing the barbell--- with Dobbie's calm voice saying, "Good push, give me two more. You're on target Mr. King. You're moving right along. Take your time between sets --- you want to give yourself one minute between each set. Don't worry about the weight; let's concentrate on form and intensity.

"I feel better than I did two weeks ago." Solomon said. The first week I thought I'd die. I couldn't scratch my head, tie my shoes or hardly get out of bed." Solomon said with a proud smile.

"Yeah! That's how it is for anyone who haven't used their muscles in a while. The key is working through the soreness. Once you do that, then it becomes easier and you won't dread the workout." Dobbie smiled at Solomon as he spoke.

"Let's go to the fly machine. We got three sets of ten to do, three sets of inclines, three sets of declines, some abs and we'll be finished for tonight. Let's go, don't let the iron get cold."

Dobbie was growling. Damn what everybody says, you're never too old to be in good condition, Solomon. The ones that say that are just lazy and looking for an excuse. You might, can't move as quick, jump as high or be quite as strong, but you can get in great shape if you put in the work. Nice and slow, flex at the top."

In the bottom of his safe house apartment, James Alford worked surrounded by walls of mirrors. He'd used pads building himself a great girth, he sported a waxed mustache, a salt and pepper toupee that covered his head of black curly hair --- contrasting with his olive brown skin. He had protruding teeth --- the final piece would be heavy, black eyeglasses with extremely thick lenses.

Solomon huffed and strained through the last set of decline benches. Dobbie watched so he wouldn't quit on the last rep as he recorded the number of sets and reps.

In the ceiling mirrors Professor Alford could see himself and could barely recognize the man in the mirror. The thick coke bottom lens in his glasses caused his eyes to look huge and mystical. His padded girth, waxed mustache, mixed gray hair all created at stranger --- he began to transition into the man he would be for one night. He completed his disguise with a wobbling restrained gait --- he was now a fat old man struggling to move and not the fine-tuned taut athletic specimen he was less than two hours earlier.

He uttered to himself as the howling wind whistled outside his window, "it's time to pay Clara Banks a call."

Solomon looked at the clock on the far wall of the gym --- it read 8:35. He lumbered on toward the showers. Drained, wondering whether it was all worth it. He hadn't worked that hard since his days as a boy on his daddy's tobacco farm out in Rougemont. At the moment, he wasn't sure he wanted to get fit ---- lose his gut or up his chances for a healthier life. Slouching around on the couch smoking cigars and not worrying about calories felt better. In thirty- minutes Solomon had showered. He couldn't believe it, but somehow the hot shower had bought a burst of resilient energy.

The fall night was cool and still; not a ripple of air swept over the parking lot. Solomon's buzzing pager greeted him as he stepped into the night. The office, he thought, another crime in the Bull City.

CHAPTER 36

THE JUKEBOX SQUALLED. ERIKA BADU, as only she could, crooned "Tyrone." Solomon walked into the tavern on Ninth Street amongst the younger crowd like he hung out there each night. Detective Graves set up straight, looking up from her can of beer.

He said off the top, "Do you ever go home after work?" She exhaled heavily. "Can a fitness guru sit down and have a beer .... or will that break your training?"

He sat down beside her. "I was on my way home to feed my cat. You said you need to see me ---ASAP. So, spit it out before Princess shits on the carpet."

Linda looked like a college chic, long haired and ready to party. The low cut top she wore barely held back her breast, and Solomon thought her eyes gave the message that she was ready for whatever might be suggested. Her long auburn hair was down around her shoulders. He studied her beauty thinking, only if I were twenty years younger.

"Two things," she said, slurring from one too many beers. "First off, old stuff shirt. Captain Fletcher seemed irritate that you missed your second straight Task Force meeting this morning. He's hollering that you're not a team player; like you ever were."

"The hell with Fletcher and that damn Task Force." Solomon grumbled.

On the other side of the city, Professor Alford turned off the ignition of the old rust colored Honda. A car he kept stashed at Burton's Garage, only using it as an extension of his disguise and criminal rendezvous.

From a block away he could see the lights in Clara Banks' home through the drawn curtains. He took a final look at himself in the mirror and eased out of the car.

Detective Graves glanced up at Solomon and continued. Second thing is Clara Banks called the office right after you left asking for you. She seemed afraid to tell me what she wanted. Why is she so damned secretive? What's going on with you two?" Solomon didn't attempt to give an answer. "Anyway!" Linda continued "Finally after some probing, she said that she thinks someone's been spying on her. She has spotted a man following her in a rust colored Honda and her dog barked for an hour a couple of nights ago like he saw something or somebody in the back yard. She seemed scared to death."

Solomon pulled a cigar from his shirt pocket and stuck it in the corner of his mouth. He looked at Detective Graves with a furrow in his forehead. "Did she say how long this has been going on?"

"No, she didn't. She said the man have followed her for the last two days as she drove from work."

"I don't know --- there maybe something to it. I'll check it out. It might have something to do with the brother's death."

"Hey, do they have a waitress in this joint or what?"

"No, you get what you want from the bar yourself."

"So, where's the damn bartender?" Solomon said looking around.

"Oh, he's around somewhere." Linda remarked.

Solomon raised from the table and headed for the bar. In a few minutes he returned with an incredible hulk. A mixture of Hypnotic, Hennessey and fruit juice, poured into a beer mug. Linda was impressed by Solomon but not surprised.

"Now back to the case." Solomon said.

He sipped from the beer mug as he looked her in the eyes, "As far as the Task Force is concerned, the only thing they have done is take up my time each week — discussing theories, similarities and coincidences of drug related deaths in other cities. Believe me, if we're gonna catch who's doing this --- it's gonna happen on the streets, not in some meeting. The method of the deaths we've had let me know that we're looking at one man being responsible for what we got going in Durham --- I don't know what's happening in the rest of the country." "We just have to stay on top of things and stay with it. Believe me when I tell you, every criminal leaves something of himself at the scene of the crime --- something, no matter how minute—and always take something from the crime scene with him. Souvenirs hidden some place, that he keeps as a trophy from each killing. Every good detective knows this. We just have to find that thread of evidence and connect it to our guy."

"We got a file downtown, File 1006, a file on drug overdoses going back damn near ten years. Recently we got reports coming into the Task Force --- reports from people who say they've seen a man hanging around trying to sell drugs in their neighborhoods. Different descriptions from different callers. One or two callers said they think its cult killings. There widespread publicity, kooks advancing theories all over town about this thing. "Linda said with a slur.

"All the victims as we know had one common denominator, heroin use; something that made them easy prey for our killer. He's a stalker, predatory, clever animal that cut the weakest from the pack, killing at his leisure." Solomon said as he gulped his drink down.

Solomon had circumstantial evidence, block upon block piled up, there was no doubt in his mind that James Alford was the man he sought for the six drug deaths --- all murders. But didn't have as much as a single hair, a button, a fingerprint, nothing that locked Alford tightly to any of the victims. He knew no prosecutor in his right mind would even take a look. He had to wait Alford out ---keep him under the scope. A man like Alford, if he was the guy, was likely to be in sort of a mind-prison he himself could not escape. Out of control from the exciting challenge of the kill game and chess match with the police.

Linda smacked the table. "Come back Solomon, your mind's wondering." She drained her bottle of beer and poked her finger into his chest. "By the way when are you going to talk to Judge Williams about the search warrant again? Seems like its nut cutting time for you guys. You two have been dancing enough."

Linda rose from the table, brushing her hair back with both hands, looked at her watch and swished toward the door.

Somebody in the joint loved Erika Badu, "Bag Lady" blasted from the jukebox.

Solomon headed for the men's room as Linda passed through the front door. He relieved himself and while he washed his hands decided that a cruise by Clara Banks' house was in order.

Professor Alford shivered as he hid behind the brush by Clara Banks' bedroom window. It had turned chilly. He wished he'd worn more clothes. When he left home, the temperature was in the low sixties. It must have fallen fifteen degrees since dark.

He'd planned to wait until Clara's neighbors on both sides of her retire for the night. The Professor checked his equipment: the gauze he would use as a gag was stuffed in his front pocket and the masking tape that he would use to bind the gag in the other pocket. He had the last of the lethal batch of heroin and hypodermic needle; just enough to send Clara Banks to meet her Maker in his coat pocket. He also had a .38 revolver tucked in his belt. A weapon he didn't intend to use — but necessary to take control of the situation when she answered the door.

Finally, both the neighbors' lights were out. He peered through the window again. He could see Clara Banks setting in her den, dressed in a white bath robe setting in a cushioned chair in front of the T.V. Everything looked perfect. He took the gun out and held it by his side and thought of the order; knock on the door, grab her, put the gun in her face, force to floor, kneel down, pull head back, stuff gauze in mouth, tape mouth, arms and legs. Then relax and administer the shot of heroin. Wait until there's no pulse. Leave.

The Professor vaulted from the hiding place. His stomach turned and tightened. His heart pounded as he headed for the door. He held the gun with a tight grip beside his legs.

Out of nowhere a car appeared. It slowed as he crept close to Clara Banks' house. Solomon King was making his rounds. The Professor in his weighted disguise dashed behind the tall hedges just in time not to be seen. He recognized the old Chevy Impala as it slowly passed the drive. At the end of the street, Solomon slowed to turn around. He knew he had to make his move before Solomon came back. He took on last look and ran.

Running, bending low watching the old Impala trying to make it to the side of the house by the tall hedges. Finally, he was out of sight. The old Impala moved slowly by the house — he could see Detective King leaning, looking toward the front of the house. In a couple of minutes, the old Impala's tail ights were out of sight. King had moved on.

Amble, he thought, walk don't run.

Although the night was airish --- beads of sweat dripped from his forehead. The Professor hunched his shoulders and moved with the gait of the old man he was disguised to be. He moved down the street to his old rust colored Honda, slipped inside and drove away.

CHAPTER 37

SOLOMON KNEW IT WAS BAD news when he looked up and saw Ned Herndon standing in front of the treadmill. He signaled trouble anyway you cut it. He mumbled through breathless strides as he looked down at the timer. He'd been running for twenty minutes with ten more to go.

"Well, Ned, your presence here means, I won't need to purge the food I ate after all. What do you want?"

Ned moved beside the treadmill with a jocund look, groomed in rimless glasses, leather slippers and dark blue gabardine slacks and a tan blazer. "Solomon when did you start hanging out at the gym? It took me two weeks to find your afterhours hangout."

"I needed to change my pace of life --- find something to help me relax, an outlet."

Ned moved in and looked at the timer and then at Solomon. "You have been going for damn near thirty minutes. You're serious about this treadmill running, huh? Did you thank about chess or relaxation therapy?"

Solomon finally begins to slow to a walk. "If you gonna worry me, it's gonna be through the shower door --- I'm on my way to the water. Watch out for the trainers. They'll have you signed up with less than ten words."

Ned stepped around a chic sporting a Toni Braxton hairdo, a pair of black skintight biker shorts and a body that caught the eye of every man and woman in the gym. "Damn, I see why you hang out in here." Ned whispered as he trailed Solomon to the locker room.

The shower steamed the stall. Solomon called out. "I'm not here to look at chics in biker shorts. No that's not why I hang out here. I figured it was time for me to work on getting some of the extra weight off. So, tell me what the hell you're fishing for this evening."

Ned pulled out a small size green note pad from the inside of his jacket pocket.

"You're on the record, my man. I hear you got a suspect in the drug cases --- and that you're closing in on him."

Solomon ripped the shower door open and glared furiously at Ned, with soap all over his face. He spoke, "Ned you son-of-a-bitch. I don't know where you get your information, but you can't print any shit like that. Tell me who told you that Bullshit."

He turned and slammed the shower door close. "I'm off the record right now! Ned you low life, I'm telling you if you print that, I won't ever talk to your ass again and someday I'll screw you for it. Don't mess with my investigation."

Ned cleared his throat. "That I will take as an admission." Solomon stepped out the shower buck naked, cursing. The moment was so fervent neither on seem to care that he was completely peeled. Ned asked, "So how come if you've got a suspect the Task Force doesn't know anything about him? At least I hear they don't. Knowing you, if this person is a suspect you got the goods on him --- or have something that ties him into the crime." "So, tell me the truth?"

The locker door banged. Solomon slipped his right leg inside his blue jeans. He frowned with anger. "I'm gonna find out who you been talking with, and I'm gonna stump a mud hole in their ass before I get a warrant for obstructing my investigation." He slipped into a burgundy and gray NCCU sweatshirt and turned to Ned brushing his hair with a wooden handle brush. "I don't have anything that needs to be talked about. I have a couple of leads that might pan out if people like you would stay the hell out of the way. If you guys could be patient, maybe this thing could get solved."

Ned took off his glasses and wiped the lens with a paper towel. The room was steamy. "Why is it that you suppress the evidence of your suspect from the Task Force --- off the record?"

Solomon was madly slapping musk oil onto his sweatshirt in front of the mirror. "Think about it for a minute. If I release all my information to the Task Force and people like you --- the entire city will know who I'm looking at including the perp. Like you don't know he'd probably leave town immediately.

Ned nodded his head at Solomon's logic. "So, tell me about your suspect, and let's make a deal to hold it. I won't breathe or print a word of it until you give me the okay."

Solomon stared Ned in the eye with a seriousness that said, "I'll kill you if you betray my trust." "I have a suspect that's connected to at least five of the victims on the list of people who died from drug overdoses. Of that list four died over the summer from the same batch of shit. I've talked to the suspect and visited his home. His explanation of knowing or how he's connected to three or four of the victims don't jive. Plus, my gut tells me he's more involved than he's willing to admit. Plus, there' more."

"So, who's the suspect Solomon?"

"I'm not telling! You got to wait until I say the word and I'll give you a statewide exclusive, blow by blow of how I tracked down the bastard."

Ned throws up both his hands. "I'll take the exclusive." Ned put his pen and pad into his jacket pocket. He was at least four inches shorter than Solomon with a collegiate Joe college look. His mellow voice resonated. "Solomon you're the best, they say. I respect you and I promise I won't do anything to impede your work."

Solomon's mind felt at ease. It sounded as if Ned would keep his mouth closed and pen on hold.

"Solomon, one more thing, does anyone else know about your suspect?"

Solomon grabbed his gym bag. "No; only Detective Graves."

"She isn't my leak." Ned replied. I figured you were on to something on my own." Ned looked at his watch and he moved for the door. "You take care, Solomon, and by the way thanks for everything."

CHAPTER 38

Detective Linda Graves was setting across the desk, scowling as she suffered indigestion from the lunch she had at Mable's Dinner, a West End greasy spoon take-out. She moaned openly, "Solomon, I think I need to go home. We're not going to solve any major crimes today --- I'm feeling terrible. Plus, it's only an hour before quitting time."

Solomon looked at Linda with raised eyebrows, "Go on home. And what did you have for lunch? You came back from lunch looking like someone feed you something laced with quinine?"

Linda said gruffly, "It's the damn pork barbecue I had. Something was wrong with it." She tossed a wad of papers on the desk. "There's nothing shaking round here that can't wait til tomorrow. I'm out of here."

Solomon rocked dangerously back in his chair like Ray Charles does when playing the piano, chewing down on his cigar. "You had a bad lunch date, uh? The food was bad, and the date was bad. And we can't catch the killer Professor. But you did bust a credit card and identify thief threesome yesterday. You're still in the ball game."

"Don't try to make me feel good, Solomon. No matter what you say, things are slow when it counts." She said.

He took a breath. "All we have to do is stay with this thing --- forget about what people are saying about not being able to get to the bottom of this thing. The perp can't undo what have already happened. The trail he left behind is what it is. We just need to work the little evidence we have and listen to our gut on this thing."

Linda deadpanned, "What you get when you talked to Trevor Hall's parents?" She looked at her watch. "And don't take all day. I spent the better part of the day getting to the bottom of how the infant child over on Hardee Street fell off the bed and died --- the mother's boyfriend finally admitted he beat the child to death. Tomorrow I get to go review the pictures and read the autopsy report. So, if there's anything new, spit it out."

Solomon grinds on his stubby cigar, hesitating before he spoke. "The Hall's has to be two of the nicest people in the world. They're just two sweet, unassuming and honest people it seems like. All they could tell me is that their son was a good boy --- who left their home in Rocky Mount, came to Durham to attend NCCU. After his first year they noticed a drop in his grades and then a change in his character. Finally, he told them about the drug use — mind you only after his mother found a hypodermic syringe in his blue jean pocket while washing some of his clothes. They tried to get him to get help but of course he argued that he didn't have a problem. Bottom line is they don't know who or where he was getting his drugs. They only knew he was close friends with Ronnie Banks. Banks had come home with him a couple of times. The Halls said Banks seemed like a very decent kid as well." Solomon took his cigar from his mouth and laid it in the ashtray on his clustered desk. "The Hall's ready didn't give me anything new. If anything, talking to them was kinda depressing--- they're still hurting awfully bad."

Detective Graves took a note pad from her shoulder bag and looked through it with a sigh. "What about the Grahams? Have you talked to them about their son, Eric? What do the Grahams think about the good Professor and his niece, Brigette?"

Solomon stood up and walked over to the window with his back to Detective Graves, for a couple of seconds. He turned back facing Graves. "Okay, Uh, the Grahams. When I spoke with them — they didn't have anything good to say concerning the Professor or the niece as far as that's concern. It seems like there were issues between the Grahams and Professor Alford. Seems like Alford indicated that the Graham's son was not the guy he wanted for Brigette. It appears the Professor may have thought Eric Graham was not somehow good enough for Brigette. Although Eric was in college, he was a street wise kid. Not the preppy or yuppie type. Then when Brigette got started on the hard stuff, the Professor blamed Eric. He even advised the Graham's to keep Eric away from Brigette According to the Graham's as it usually happens, the Professor's open disapproval of Eric drove Brigette to him the more. The Grahams didn't say --- but they seemed to have some doubts on how their son actually died."

Solomon made it back to his chair and flopped down. He stretched his arms over his shoulder and moved his neck from side to side. "Aging is hell. Being a gym rat comes with a cost. I got aches in places I didn't know existed. But it's a different kinda ache — I think I'm hooked on the fitness thing."

Detective Graves applauded. "Good, go for it."

"Yeah, just don't fall in love with me when I become a hunk."

"Now, Solomon" she squinted and said somberly, "we'll just have to wait and see the hunk."

Solomon's phone rang. He yanked it up. "King! Who? She has what? Well, yeah, let her come on back here." He looked up at Graves. "Clara Banks. She has a phone bill for us."

Linda mumbled, "Who? She has what?" And then she smiled and said, "Just when I was about to make my move on you."

A woman appeared in front of the door, a subtle pretty, shy, well cared for, stand offish woman. With a Smooth dark complexion, kind eyes and slim taut looking body. Her hair was neatly pulled back in a French roll, her clothes loose fitting and traditional. She appeared to be somewhere around forty.

"Detective King," she said, and Linda saw a glow in her eyes as she looked at Solomon, "when you talked to me the last time here at your office, you asked me to contact you if I thought of anything or found anything that might could shed some more light on Ronnie's death."

She completely ignored Detective Graves as she spoke. Linda was thinking, "This chic gotta thing for Solomon, I can't believe it. She comes by in person to see him — after hours, she could have called. Well! Well!"

Clara Banks opened her leather shoulder bag, fished around and thrust a stack of phone bills at him. Solomon took the stack of bills, mumbled, and peeped up at Linda. As he said, "thank you."

She preened. "I was looking through these bills and I found that Ronnie had been calling Professor Alford quite a bit. The bills go back six months before Ronnie" then she hesitated "died. They're dated. The last call was the night Ronnie died."

Detective Graves, who had gone a little pale around the gills, reached for the stack of phone bills from Solomon. "Did you know Ronnie made calls to Alford before you looked at these bills?"

Sternly, and with unmasked irritation, "No. I never knew who Ronnie talked to on the phone. It wasn't a concern. Why would it be? He was just like any other young person --- as far as I was concerned. Dating, talking on the phone to girls, his friends and all. Yesterday I found the bills in a box of things while cleaning and packing away some things from Ronnie's room." Clara said.

"Thank you, Ms. Banks." Solomon said crisply, "We'll look into it."

Clara Banks stood for a moment, uneasy and blushing. It had been years since she actually had found herself interested in a man, much less an older man. She didn't know exactly what drew her to Solomon. She cleared her throat, said goodbye and left.

Detective Graves said, handing over the stack of bills, "Looks like there are calls from the Banks kid to Alford."

She went over to the window and looked down on the street. She could see Clara Banks as she scurried across the street. Solomon rocked back in his chair and rubbed his cigar out in the ashtray. Detective Graves mused. "So, this is his pattern. Alford kills addicts acting as a self-assigned prosecutor, jury, judge and executioner. He's driven by the grief turned anger — insanity and hate for addicts because his niece got hooked on the stuff and overdosed, or did he kill her also? Was it his niece's death that started him down this road or the fact that heroin ruined her life before she killed herself? So, he has set out to rid the world of drug dealers." She turned and looked at Solomon. "It's all making more sense to me now. As timed passed he got crazier and bolder — stalking and killing dealers at random. He's out of control and will kill again if he's not stopped."

She dumped herself in the armchair in front of Solomon's desk. At a gut level she, like Solomon knew Alford was the one passing around the deadly heroin and was the killer. "Sherlock, we can't prove any of it. And he's out there, maybe stalking his next victim. Getting more rabid, getting away with it. Where the hell do you think he's getting heroin with such a high quality?" She asked. "I haven't figured that part out yet." Solomon recanted. "No telling who he knows."

Linda's stomach turned over. A subtle sense of rage went through her. "We can't even put him at any of the crime scenes. We can't do anything but wait and hope he'll screw up. Meanwhile, Captain Fletcher and the Task Force has got their feet up our ass —hollering for us to solve this thing, hoping their political asses will be spared."

"You sound like we've lost this thing --- peck up. We'll nail his ass sooner or later. My gut tells me his a little nervous concerning a couple of things." Solomon said with a raised eyebrow.

"Nervous about what kinda things?" Asked Linda

"Well Ms. Banks says she ran into him a couple of weeks ago in Wal Mart. After she saw him, she called me saying they'd had a strange conversation concerning her brother. She said she'd recognized him by his deep baritone voice and right away knew he was the man who had been calling Ronnie for months. She said the good Professor seem to pick up on the fact that she somehow recognized him --- and knew he and Ronnie were connected in some kinda way. She said he gave her a scary cold stare and she felt afraid of him. He didn't threaten her or anything, but I don't know … maybe she's a lose end. It might be smart for us to keep an eye on him and see if he trys to make a move on Clara Banks. I think he's running a little scared."

Linda muffled "If we just could put him with one of the stiffs. We don't have anything to connect him to any of the deaths. Not a one. If he is our guy, he's smart."

Solomon lit his cigar again and leaned back in his chair, gnawing on the stud in his mouth. "We could always do like the police in the O.J. Simpson case --- try and plant some evidence. You ever thought about that?"

Linda sprung from the chair like a jack-in-the-box and grabbed her briefcase, answering, "You damn skippy, I think about it a lot, and somehow come to my senses. I know if I do that, I'm no better than the creeps I'm chasing." She looked Solomon straight in the eye.

"I'm glad to hear you say that. If you hadn't said you had thought about it, I would have questioned your determination to catch the bad guys. But the fact you wouldn't say a lot. Look all we got to do is fight clean and keep the gloves on. We'll get our man."

CHAPTER 39

IT WAS DECEMBER. DAY ONE. The drab sky settled beneath its own gravity. According to the WTVD weather report, rain would bleed from the sky by night fall, a sure sign of a 5 o'clock traffic jam. A clapping bolt of lighten which was uncommon in December, flashed wickedly across the sky--- cracking across the blue yonder, dragging with it an outburst of thunder.

At home, the Professor looked in the refrigerator, grabbed a pack of deli turkey, sliced cheese, mayo and reached for the wheat bread on the countertop as he headed for the dining table. His face reflected in the kitchen window from the light over the sink. His mind was obsessively occupied by Solomon King. King had become a thorn in his side --- showing up unexpected, parked in the lot in front of the Physics' Building on the University campus --- and cruising by the jogging trail once or twice each week as he ran the obstacle courses in Duke Forest. He could still feel the fear that gripped him when King showed up at Clara Banks' house on the night, he'd planned to silence her.

He felt King's squeeze. The constant pressure---and was haunted by his uncanny stare. King had become the enemy. He had to be neutralized. No longer could he be underestimated. At his deepest cognitive level, he knew King had unraveled the mystery of the heroin deaths …and if wasn't stopped, he'd make a case against him.

The Professor's mind shifted into the legal mode. He sat at the dining room table and thought. What did King actually have? King knew of his connection to four of the victims. So, what! Hundreds of other people knew the victims. I'm a white collar and a respected member of the academic community. But on the other side, if King is bold enough to arrest me --- the story would grow like wildfire, incorporating every scandal, pick up every piece of dirt around, damaging my image and given respect.

Would I seek a jury trial? A conviction would be hard to get. Not a chance. Or very little of a chance. No jury would ever convict me on a fumbling detective's theories alone. The Professor weighed the odds.

The telephone buzzed. Sarah Ann answered.

"Mr. King, please."

A man was on the other end. "He's not available. May I ask whose calling?",

"I'm Mr. Martin from Crabtree Plumbing. Mr. King called in today, said he had a busted water line."

Sarah Ann walked over to the kitchen window and peeped outside and closed the blinds. "Mr. King is not here he hasn't come in from work yet. You'll have to call him later, maybe the first thing tomorrow morning."

"Thank you, madam, I'll try him tomorrow." His tone was mild and direct.

Sarah Ann thought, "Crap, we don't have a plumbing problem." She knew her dad would have told her if a plumber was supposed to come by. She knew him like a book. He hadn't said a word last night --- and didn't say a thing about a plumber or a plumbing problem before leaving for work.

The phone clicked in her ear. The man had hung up. She walked into the den and looked out the window. Rain beat against the window as gusty winds caused the trees in the yard to tremble.

In their suburban neighborhood people felt safe and protected. The streets were quiet. People jogged casually morning and late evenings. In the summer they pushed their babies in strollers after the sun went down. Most of the families were middle class — working to pay the bank.

She could always drive from Charlotte to her dad's place and find peace and stillness. The house was cozy and filled with memories of her mother. The backyard was lined with beautiful green and purple shrubs, and rose bushes outlining a manicured yard with a high cedar fence that closed off the world. She looked at the clock in the kitchen. For some reason she felt on edge. It would be at least an hour until her father came home. She paged him and waited calmly in the faint lit den in front of the big screen with the phone in her lap.

The Professor dressed in a navy-blue work uniform, clad in a pair of soiled work boots, sported a waxed mustache, a short like grayish afro wig and harnessed his face in heavy, black eyeglasses with thick lenses.

He put the pay phone in the hook and eased out the booth. So, who's the lady answering King's phone? He thought. He's not the lonely old fart he appears to be. In reality, he has a life. A career cop ---respected detective and got himself a lady. He's used to prank calls he'll think nothing of it. He headed toward his old rust colored Honda.

He drove. The rainy night made him uneasy. Block after block, on both sides of Roxboro Road, with sporadic exception, it was dark and unrelenting. It seemed he was crossing into the great beyond. The small sprinkle of cold raindrops painted a dissimulation of patterns on the windows. He could hear the frying splash of the tires churning against the rain-soaked pavement.

He was a man of the city, his soul in tune with the urban bustle. Wide avenues, the concrete jungle surrounded by tall buildings, amongst all kinds of mortals where he could blend — not be known or remembered. He had fallen in love with the city while a student at Georgetown University years ago. Becoming comfortable in the forest of high rises, where sidewalks merged with the souls of the inhabitants and where streets were jammed with buses and cars.

Her T-Mobile cell rang. She popped it open, answered. "Daddy, you got my page?"

"Yeah! About ten minutes ago. What's going on?"

"Did you call a plumber?" She heard the tone of her father's voice change.

"A plumber --- no?"

"Some man name Martin said you called them earlier about a busted water line."

"Listen carefully, I want you to lock all the doors --- don't answer the door for anyone. I'm sending one of the deputy sheriffs by ---."

She wasn't accustomed to her father's professional tone of voice. Never been involved with his work. She felt a nervous fear. She commanded, "Dad what's going on? Please! I'm okay. It was just some man ---he probably made a mistake. What's the big deal?"

"Listen, it might be nothing or it could be connected to a case I'm working. So, do as I say. I'll be home shortly. In the meantime, I'm sending a deputy to cruise by just in case."

Solomon didn't know what was going on or who had called his home. But he knew he hadn't called a plumber. His gut told him it might be somehow connected to the overdose cases. Maybe, the Professor was panicking. He didn't think the Professor was the commando type. The type to scale a fence --- and snipe from a tree or at least he hadn't shown that side of himself.

Sarah Ann could hear the noise from the station house as her father gave orders to someone. He finally spoke back to her, telling her to stay on the line. Then he put her on hold. She wanted him to come home.

Solomon said firmly to Officer Joe Blake as he came out of the control room. "Send two blue and whites out to Professor Alford's house in Hope Valley North ---- here's the address. Tell them to check on whether his home or not. Then you come with me. He might be trying to take a hit on me --- to get me off his back. I don't really have anything on him. But I've been riding and watching him so he might be running scared. It would be all we need if he made a move on me. Maybe he's been watching me --- the same as I've been watching him

He got back on the line with Sarah Ann. She wanted to know what was happening. She hated the drama. He said "sweetie, everything's alright, relax, I'll be home within the hour. When I get there, I'll fill you in. If you see a cruiser out front --- it's my guy. Did you fix something to eat? I'm as hungry as a bear. If not, I'll order a pizza when I get there. See you in a little bit."

She didn't argue or ask any more questions. But she knew something was going on out of the ordinary. She trusted her dad. Period. She turned back to her chair in front of the T.V. and waited.

CHAPTER 40

OFFICER JOE BLAKE HAD NEVER actually worked the streets. He had worked the control room from the first day he'd taken the job with the Durham Police Department. He was thrown off when Solomon yanked his chair, throw him a set of keys and ordered, "Called Detective Graves, tell her to meet me at my place ASAP and then you follow me."

Solomon eased his old Impala out the Police Department parking lot. Officer Blake was behind him in a plain dark blue Crown Vic. His pulse raced as he gnawed on the cigar in the corner of his mouth, his hands gripped on the steering wheel as he pushed his way through downtown. Finally, they charged down Roxboro Road --- by the time they reached Infinity Road they were up to almost eighty miles an hour. The slush of the wet pavement was like driving through a levee of surging high areas.

In his car behind him, Officer Blake watched as Solomon's Impala swished like a fish, he cursed and stayed on his tail.

I've got to get there --- move, move, move." Solomon talked to the other drivers who were navigating through the rain-soaked streets as if they could hear him. "I got to get to the house, he's coming. I feel it in my gut. I got to get to Sarah Ann."

Ponderous pellets of rain hit the windshield like sprays of gravel. He didn't bow; he put his feet to the metal once they turned on Snow Hill Road. The wipers danced across the window back and fourth barely clearing his view. He turned and glided into the driveway of his home and was out of his car before the engine shut off. Officer Blake bounced out his cruiser and ran to catch up.

The blue light in the grill of Blake's cruiser flashed on and off. Solomon ran to the ornate iron barred door and hastily inserted his key. Lights shown from the front porch and inside. The surroundings appeared calm and settle, his key let them in. Sarah Ann sprung from her seat as her father walked in. Rain poured as a loud thunderclap was followed by a strike of angry lightening.

He called, "Sarah Ann! Sweetie, are you okay? Have anyone come to the door, since we talked?"

"No daddy --- no one have come by." Flinching her shoulders, as she looked at him. I haven't seen anyone, what in the world is going on?"

The Professor had parked three blocks from Solomon's house, facing Roxboro Road. He'd checked and made sure he wasn't parked illegally. There were two other cars parked down the street. He left the car door unlocked. Not risking a waste of time in case he had to make a quick getaway.

The weather had turned worst, rain felled for a while in the early afternoon, died away, started again --- and now cold rain poured in the night as he spied on King's house. He turned the collar of his black raincoat up and dug his hands deep into the pockets --- in the right pocket he felt the cold medal of the Smith & Wesson 9mm. The latex gloves under his driving gloves kept his hands warm. A scarf partially covered his face, giving him more protection from the weather and a better disguise. This was new and against the grain, he hadn't planned to resort to using a gun, ever. But King had forced his hand.

The arrival of the deputy cruiser and then later King and his posse ruined the night. He had to abort his plan. He'd knew taking care of King would have to happen on another day --- not tonight.

Solomon signaled for Officer Blake to conduct a walk around the outside of the house. In the meantime, Solomon went through the shuttered doors that led to the kitchen. Blake headed for the back door to the deck and down the stone steps, lit by two bright lamps, passed the flower beds toward the back fence. After a cautious trek around the house, he returned inside feeling things were secure.

Detective Linda Graves had arrived and was hyped ---- ready for action. She faced off with Solomon, "Do you really think he's crazy enough to come after you?"

"I don't know, but in this business, we can't afford to gamble with a guy like Alford." He said.

"We can rap this up for tonight." Then he looked at her. "You need to be on your toes, no telling what this guy might try --- if he's running scared. I'm going to call it a night. We'll pick up from here first thing in the morning."

"Okay, if you sure everything is safe around here. "I'll mosey on home and see you in the A.M."

The Professor headed out to Roxboro Road. He felt a tremendous pounding inside his head. His blood was pumping. He was excited at the kill game. It had now become like a game of Dungeons and Dragons. He was going to do it, two more, King and Clara Banks. He looked for a telephone booth. He saw a phone on the wall, outside a Seven Eleven. A teenager was inside with a cigarette and beer in his hand. He needed the phone. The teenager dashed away as if he could feel danger. The Professor pulled by the phone, dialed King's house. He got the answering machine. "Leave a message." King's voice said tersely, without identifying himself. There was a beep. The Professor was disappointed. He wanted to hear King's tone. The fear.

CHAPTER 41

OFFICER MARK HARRIS SET IN his cruiser and steadily wiped off the windows so he could see. He was parked down the street from the Professor's house. After an hour and seven minutes, he saw a car pull into the driveway. It was James Alford, the Professor. No doubt about it, athletic, fit and ducking under his umbrella. Wearing what looked like a UNC sweat suit. He reached for his key, looked around and opened the front door. In a minute or two the lights in a corner downstairs came on.

Officer Harris got on the radio. "Bravo one to King nine - eleven."

Solomon came back at him, "I'm rolling. Go ahead."

Solomon knew Officer Harris was in his car. "Okay sir, your subject has just been eyeballed returning home, about five minutes ago driving a late model white Mercedes. He's alone, dressed in what looks like some type sweat suit." Just for good measures, he scratched down the tag number of the Mercedes.

Solomon said dryly, "Okay Harris you're clear."

Solomon looked at Sarah Ann and his watch almost at the same time. Deciding to run out for a six pack of beer before he sat down to the steak, potato and garden salad Sarah Ann had prepared for him. "Sweetie, I'm gonna run up to the corner Seven Eleven and grab a six pack of beer. I'll be back in five minutes." He said. His used and abused Chevy Impala lurched into the street as he pulled out of the driveway. He laid his Smith & Wesson 9mm on the seat beside him. Somebody had caused chaos and he was sure it had been Alford. If it was Alford, he was getting bold — or out of control. He knew it was time to make his case against Alford or leave it be. He knew playing hide and seek with a psychopath was a dangerous game.

After he left the Seven Eleven, impulsively he headed for Dearborn Drive in route to Clara Banks house. His gut told him he needed to cruise by ---- just to see what things looked like.

Once in front of Clara's house, he pressed the brakes, slowed the Impala to a crawl and rolled down the window, canvassing the house and yard with a keen eye. With the window down, the night air and his damp clothes brought an instant chill. His clothes were still soggy from the gully washing rain, and he didn't care.

The Professor couldn't figure out why King didn't know he came for him. Somewhere in the back of his head, he couldn't believe it, he thought Detective King would have known.

He sidled through the front door out of the rain, took a step into the den, realized he was tracking water onto the polished hardwood floor, and stopped. He stood for a couple of seconds, breathing, looking around, and then slowly stepped back into the foyer by the front door and slipped out of his wet running shoes. He carried the bag filled with wet clothes .... A utility uniform and a pair of muddy boots to a utility sink in the garage and washed the mud off and put them into the washer.

In his mind it was all a moment from a fable, straight out of a novel or screenplay, and the Professor saw it as such. Having made his way to Detective King's front door, that close to him ---unscathed. When the time was right, he would return, confident of his safety, ability to disguise and knowing somehow the psychopath he'd be for that night would appear.

In his other mind he knew real life was neither as cavalier and colorful as a Hollywood film or whimsical novels nor half as drab as the life of the average academic --- and less predictable as either. His lack of fear in returning to Detective King's home or lying in wait for Clara Banks was irrational, the product of a too-fertile imagination and a part of his aberrations, perversions and hunger for drama, excitement and tragedy at every turn of his affairs --- and as entrenched in his mind as any killer ever known.

Rain began to thump against the skylight in the den. The thumping sound snapped him out of the trance. Thump, thump, tump ----- incessantly.

He headed for the shower, to wash off the grit --- smiling, transforming back into the distinguished Professor. The switching back and forth from one character to the other now called for incredible effort.

The parameters of his characters were constructed with such care; one misstep he could become confused of who he was for the day and it could all come apart.

The man the world was allowed to see was handsome, his body taut and cultivated, a barrier of strength in character concealing any glimpse of madness on the inside. Brilliant, a respected academic, witty, glib, and persuasive. He loved to run, workout, write music and date. He grew flowers in his backyard and prided himself as a gourmet cook. On the surface James Alford was the epitome of a successful man. Inside he was twisted.

He had traveled through life focusing on himself, with very little empathy, always in control of himself, mute, and blind. He had no conscious. A conscious is what make men human, the factor that separate men from animals. He had lost that trait long ago.

The Professor lavished in the sauna. He finished and dried with a soft towel, and slowly oiled his body. Then he went into the bedroom, dressed in silk pajamas, and walked to the small washroom in the back of the house. All the clothes he'd worn were common and available at any discount store; a dark blue service type uniform, black rain slick purchased from an outdoor store, a pair of work of boots and an unmarked blue ball cap. He carried the arm full of clothes to the laundry room and dumped them in the dryer. He returned to the den, turned the T.V. on and set in his overstuff recliner and waited for the 11 o'clock news.

After the news, he got a small bucket of water and mop, went to the entrance of the house and cleaned the floor. Some of the mud was still on the floor. When he finished he went and checked on the dryer. The cycle was done; he folded the clothes on top of the dryer. Then from the kitchen closet he got a roll of black trash bags, took the mop head off the mop, threw it in the trash bag and returned the handle to the utility room. He then emptied all the trash bags inside the house into the black trash bag and deposited it outside by the curb.

By twelve thirty he had finished with the clothes and cleaning. He went into his study and begin to correct test papers from a test he'd given a class of freshmen chemistry students earlier that day. An hour later he'd finished correcting test papers. By one o'clock, he was all done and in bed, lights out, soft music played from the bedside radio.

Thinking — pondering, he lay awake in the dark and walked back through the night that had just passed; the rain, the dark street, Detective King's house, the woman who answered the phone, the arrival of the deputy and his retreat ---- the getaway.

In the beginning the Professor didn't think about getting caught. But all that had changed. He knew the way things were going he might someday be found out --- and get caught. He had no delusions when it came to that. He supposed that if he were caught, it would be through a lose association of uncontrollable circumstances. Different times of the day and night the faces of all his victims flashed across his mind as if on a screen. Faces with a look of shock and helplessness as the powerful drug stole their lives. He imagined a crowed of policemen; a lynch mob chasing him waving clubs in their hands. In these images, the mob tracked him through every street he'd stalked and laid in wait on his victims.

In more settled moments, he still convinced himself that no one had any idea of his tie to the murders. He reviewed in his mind how he'd disguised himself each time he'd stalked his prey, leaving no evidence. He had done a good job but there was Clara Banks and her suspicious eyes. Was it really possible she knew anything? Did her brother Ronnie tell her something on his death bed? What was, that look in her eyes about?

With the event of the last eight months stirring in his head, he finally dozed off.

CHAPTER 42

The morning duped everyone, without warning the rain ceased. The sky turned Carolina Blue and the sun came out. Sarah Anne was in the kitchen by 7:30 making eggs and bacon. Solomon thought of so many of these types of morning, the prefect kind before he'd lost Louise to breast cancer. On those days she made breakfast, fussed over the children and rushed him out the house so he could get to work on time; kissing him on his way out --- her heart fluttering with love.

Sarah Anne turned to her father. He was watching her. She said, "What?"

"I feel like I'm watching your mother all over again." He said.

"Well, I'm not her --- just a rendition of her. I know you still miss momma." She walked over, placing her hand on his shoulder kissing him on the cheek. "Now just like mom would say, sat down and eat your food. We can't afford to waste all these scramble eggs."

She soothes him. "Dad, you did good by mom and by Junior and me. I'm happy to have you for a father."

Solomon looked at her with kind eyes. "Honey and you are the prefect daughter."

She looked at her watch. "I have to get out of her by 9:30. I need to be in Charlotte by twelve. I'll do some cleaning, wash a few of the clothes and hit Interstate 85."

Solomon waved a big hand at her. "You just need to move on back home, so you can stop running up and down the Interstate." He'd spoke before he'd thought.

Sarah Anne looked up with surprise. "Now where did that come from?"

He pushed his plate away testily and fished for the cigar in his shirt pocket. "I don't know. It kinda slipped out. But it wouldn't be bad to have you around all the time, is all."

But dad I'm trying to make a life for myself in Charlotte." She said.

He stood and folded himself around her. "Never mind what I said. It's just a daddy's love speaking. I better head to the office --- or I'll be late as usual."

Feeling a little guilty, she touched him, a finger in his chest, looking up with puppy dog eyes. "Dad, I'll always be around for you --- always. And never stop loving you."

He was getting teary. He couldn't look at her when he said in a low breath, "Sure, sweetie, I know you will. Never mind the words of an old man --- what I said came from my heart not my brain."

Solomon walked over to the phone and called Detective Graves. In three rings she was on the other end. "Get your ass in gear --- met me at the station in a half-hour. We got work to do." He said. He hugged Sarah Anne and headed for the door.

CHAPTER 43

THE CAPRICE JAMAICAN RESTAURANT, LOCATED in the heart of downtown Durham on Main Street was empty by 6:00 P.M. All the red, black, yellow and green checkered tablecloths and pristine place settings were fashioned for the dinner crowd. But it was empty this early. The matron, a tall, oversize woman, with dreaded hair, wearing colorful African like clothes made her way over to where Clara Banks and her ten- year-old god son Travis were seated. She ordered curry chicken, black beans, rice, yams and ice-tea.

Travis was looking around the restaurant at the ceiling, the tables, examining the place --- fidgeting while talking idly about one thing to the next. "My favorite basketball player is Iverson-----.

"Yeah, he can shoot, and nobody can stop him. Man, he's bad, I saw him last night. He scored 42 points. He kept making all kinds of shoots." "Some guys say. Clara interrupted, "stop jumping around. Do you have to use the bathroom?"

"Some guys say he shoots too much. They call him a hotdog. Say he's not a team player."

"Keep your foot still, that's my leg you're kicking." She said

"I wish I could see him play in person. I'm gonna be like him when I get older. My daddy is getting me a new basketball for Christmas. He told me so. I wanna play rec ball next year, Mom says, if I do good in school." "My friend who lives next door plays rec ball already. He has a uniform and all. Its dark blue trimmed in white. I got to get bigger --- then, I can play and get a uniform like Gerrod. That's only four more months."

"It's more than four months, Travis. Next school year is almost nine more months. You'll have to wait until spring and summer passes. Then it will be time for school again." Clara said.

He was putting sugar into his tea slopping it around with a spoon. "So, will that be a long time Aunt Clara?"

Clara grinned. "no, it will be here before you know it. Just make sure you continue to do good in school, so you'll be able to play when the time comes."

"I can hardly wait. No, don't put that napkin under my chin! I hate it, mom does that! I'm big enough to eat without spilling food on my clothes. Travis said without prompting as he chewed. "Mom says she want me to be smart in school like uncle, Ronnie was. She says he was always smart in school, even in elementary. I'm gonna go to college like Uncle Ronnie."

Travis's face was full of enthusiasm. His chin and cheeks were speckled with yellow curry sauce. Clara didn't know what to say --- Ronnie's name hadn't been mentioned in months by family and friends. "Yes, Ronnie was smart, and you are as well." Clara finally said.

More silence. Clara watched Travis as he drank his ice- tea and soaked the front of his shirt. "Be careful before you drown yourself. Slow down, the food is not going anywhere."

Travis said in his way, the ten-year old way, so blunt with words. "Why did Uncle Ronnie have to die?"

Clara's throat cramped. "Travis" She frowned profusely, as she eyeballed him; he wiggled and blinked his eyes. "Do your momma and daddy talk about Uncle Ronnie a lot?"

"I don't know, not all the time."

"Do they say bad things about Uncle Ronnie?" Clara's eyes became intense, "Well, do they?"

"Well no. They just say they miss him and all. Can I have some apple pie? Mommy says I can have desert if I clean my plate. See, I ate all my food."

"Sure, you can have apple pie. Why don't we have some ice cream along with it?"

Clara contained her voice but her hands trembled. The thought of Ronnie caused her heart to ache. She signaled the matron for the ice cream and apple pie.

"After I eat ice cream and apple pie, I'll have to run in place for thirty minutes when I get home." She said.

"Can we go to one of those gyms like my daddy go to? They have a big playroom with Nintendo. We can't tell mom because she says I'm too young to go to the gym --- she's afraid the heavy weights will fall on me."

Clara sighed heartily. "No, Travis not tonight, we'll go back to my house and I'll put in one of my aerobics videos."

I miss having someone in my life. Clara admitted in her simmering thoughts. I'm alone, Ronnie is gone, mom and dad gone, no child of my own --- no man in my life. I need someone she muttered as Travis finished off his glass of ice-tea. I need to move pass what happen to Ronnie, she considered as she drove home through heavy traffic and brisk night air. Travis jabbered more, but Clara was ensuring her own privately dashing thoughts.

I've been lonely for years. I never had anybody in my life for me; to take care of me. Mom got sick and I took care of her. Dad got sick and I took care of him. The streets robbed me of Ronnie. No one ever thought of my feelings or was ever committed to me. I've lived to serve and please everyone around me --- I haven't been allowed the happiness I want.

Travis stopped fidgeting as they pulled in the driveway. He was still wide awake and hyper. "Can I do the aerobic video with you? You said I could."

She walked in the house with Travis, feigning chit chat as they went inside the house and slammed the door.

CHAPTER 44

It was right at 1:00 p.m. on Wednesday. Clara Banks had taken a vacation day off from her job at Duke Hospital. She was dressed in a beige full-length cashmere coat with scarf and gloves to match as she sat on the back steps of North Carolina Central University's Alfonso Elder Student Union, facing the staff parking lot on George Street. She'd been there for almost an hour when the white Mercedes pulled in the parking lot. Her sparkling hawk like eyes concealed by dark sunglasses followed Professor Alford's every move. Her eyes were keen and focused, like a narrow tunnel from the time he exited his white Mercedes.

She had to get one more good look ---a undisturbed survey at the man her heart said was responsible for Ronnie's death. Somehow, she had to make sure to settle her own mind.

Her instincts called his name. Sometimes in her dreams, visions of the Professor and Ronnie setting in some meeting place with plush leather chairs, dim lights and half nude women dancing as they exchange words---conducting business. Business between a schoolboy drug dealer and his supplier. The apparition would shift from scene to scene like a motion picture. The final scene was always of the Professor passing Ronnie the poisonous drug. The dream enhanced features of the Professor's face transformed from calm to sadistic in the last scene. Each time Clara suddenly awoke from the nightmarish dream at the juncture----setting straight up in her bed, drenched in sweat.

Solomon got to the restaurant and thought immediately of the

Cripps and Bloods. There were red tablecloths on wooden tables, and a towering kid behind the bar. Mr. T with dreadlocks, a red bandanna tied around his head and a black tee shirt with the sleeves rolled up. He buffed the white marble counter. Quinton Goode from the CAT TEAM Drug Division was wrapped in a bulky leather coat and scarf even though the place was well-heated and the doors closed out the December chill. His full beard covered his lower face, causing him to look like a shit kicker. Detective Linda Graves sat on the opposite side. He poured red wine into her glass from a big gourd on the table and lit a Newport.

He said to the young dreaded, Mr. T, "Hey, young brother we ready. Our other party just arrived. You can bring the chow now." To Solomon he said, "We're having baby back ribs." "You look great Solomon. What you dropped twenty pounds?"

"Did you invite me to lunch for me to give you a workout plan?" Solomon asked.

"No, I called you here because the waiters are all gang bangers, and I need someone to stand watch while Linda and I eat." He grinned, his beard hiding his facial lines only allowing his white teeth to smile through. "I heard about the scare at you house last night. Do you think it had anything to do with the drug investigation, or just some prank or wrong number?"

Solomon put his cigar in the ashtray and sipped the wine. The wine was good and cold, Chianti. He was surprised Office Goode knew of Chianti, he looked to be a Richards Wild Irish Rose man --- at least judging from his undercover and street get up. "I'm sure it wasn't just a prank. I don't have any proof but …."

Goode pulled at the hair of his thick beard. "Yeah; that's why I asked you guys to meet me for lunch. "I'm trying to see if there's enough evidence for a drug investigation --- or anything the CAT TEAM can do with this thing."

Mr. T set down three glasses of ice-tea, stood back with his arms folded like a warrior until Linda tasted and then nodded at him. "On the one." She said.

"Whoever called was trying to either put some fear in me --- or was checking to see who was at my place before coming to take a look around. Why and for what, I don't know."

Mr. T played some soft Ragga from behind the bar. He didn't know if they were into Ragga and probably didn't care.

"Officer Harris staked out Alford's house right after I got the call ... said Alford came home wearing a UNC sweat suit and carrying a bag around 10:30. Makes me more suspicious of what was in the bag ---- maybe a plumber's uniform. Goode asked, "How do you know it was Alford who called your house. He came home driving a white late model Mercedes --- the car he drives daily. The Deputy cruising your neighborhood didn't remember seeing such a car, .did he?"

"Maybe he has another car he drives and changes up before coming home. Hell, I don't know ---it don't match." Goode said.

"I'm almost positive it was him." Bob Marley crooned "Who Shot the Sheriff?" Mr. T balanced the tray of ribs on his shoulder like a pro. Linda looked at Goode and added, "We know it was Alford ---you know how you just know something."

In a split second, Goode's face went from jovial to serious, throw his head back with his wine glass and poured more. He ate like he was in a prison chow hall, scooping food, wolfing it down and riding on his elbow. He said, "Check this out, this brings us to the shit." His big brown eyes danced at Solomon. "I'm gonna give it to you straight, bottom line. Solomon, it looks like you're obsessed with this guy Alford. Like you're fixated on him or some shit. Everything that comes up, you think it's him. Some of the other guys are saying it must be personal or some shit. Like you're at him for some reason. So, I've bottom lined it. You might think about backing off a little. Not that, I'm your boss but because people are talking, like maybe you're trying to put those OD's on him. Hell, all the people that died were junkies --- maybe they just got hold of some bad shit. Maybe it's all a coincidence."

Solomon picked up his cigar and shoved it into his mouth. The idea of other officers thinking he was driven by some personal reason made him a little irate. "Personal! That's absurd. That sounds like some of Captain Fletcher's theoretical bullshit."

With barbecue sauce in his beard, Goode said seriously, "What do you really have besides a theory of your own concerning this guy Alford and the overdoses? Reckon a serial killer would turn to prank calls or scheming on how he could break into your house?"

"He was doing his surveillance. Jesus Christ, Quinton, he's smart, he's after me."

Goode gloated, "Why Solomon?"

Solomon gazed at Goode as he rolled the stubby cigar around in his mouth. "Because the psycho knows I've figured him out. Because his scared I'm gonna bust him for what he's done." He didn't batt an eye. "You don't believe me?"

Alford moved the large box. He was doing a spring cleaning of the Chemistry Lab in December. He had to make sure there was not one particle of the synthetic heroin in the Lab. Nobody would be able to tell that some of the drugs were manufactured in the university lab. Nobody would ever believe such a thing. He washed and sanitized the glass tubes, bottles, vats and countertops. Later he would request the floors be stripped and waxed. There, he looked around with satisfaction.

Solomon drove, slowly going nowhere, through North Durham's Dowd Street, Canal Street and through Few Gardens Housing Projects. Then he circled McDougal Terrace and then down Fayetteville Street by North Carolina Central University. He final turned into the only place he could possibly find some reasoning ---Crystal Barbershop. He'd talk to his old friend LeRoy.

CHAPTER 45

On the street you could hear the yelling from inside the gym, the Professor thought to himself. The women are still playing. He'd decided to get out for the evening. What could be a better way to relax and put some variety in life than a basketball game between North Carolina Central and A&T State University? The fanfare, the cheerleaders dancing, jumping trying to out-do one another. More good-looking women in one building than he'd be able to find anywhere in the universe.

He knew the scene. Students dressed in leather and fur. Gucci, Phat Farm, FUBU, Tommy, Sean John.

He sat in the second row, mid court. Relaxed, enjoying the sight of the women playing at a slowed paced. It was good to be out for a change. Out of his home —what seemed like a self-imposed prison at times. Boredom had set in. His passion to rid the world of parasitic men who lived off the miseries of others hadn't been fed and burned inside. Detective King was in the way, but, only for a while.

Convinced his motives were altruistic --- working in the interest of society he was anxious to resume the kill game. He was addicted to the power his crimes gave him. Causing the police to debate his wisdom, talk about him and his life.

After the men's game, NCCU winning 78-75, he impulsively drove by Clara Banks' house. He couldn't put her out of his mind. The pressure was building. His need to silence her grew. Then he would continue. If he had the nerve, he could pull it off. He imagined being free to roam at his will. The police would never know. Each day his mind shifted from thinking he'd be caught and arrested to how he'd never be found out.

Alford drove down Dearborn Drive slowly by Clara Banks' house, found a place to park a couple blocks away, got out, and walked along the dim street of modest houses. He passed three teenage boys setting in a Carolina Blue Chevelle smoking pot ---peering through the window as he passed.

He walked another block without a disguise --- it was unplanned, impulsive. He paused at Clara's drive, debating whether he should ring the doorbell or not. He backed away cautioning himself not to overplay it, he thought; someone could be watching ---- sense something. He turned and left.

He rethought his plan during the night and decided to let it go. By six a.m. he ran the Duke obstacle course. The run carrying him into a zone, he changed his mind again, and decided to go ahead to rid the world of Clara Banks, the sooner the better.

CHAPTER 46

SOLOMON SAT ALONE --- SURROUNDED by a mix of hand clapping Sunday morning Saints. In the middle of the dramatic and showy service his mind raced backward to a time when he attended Greater Saint James each Sunday with Louise and the kids. A time when the word of God was delivered through old fashion preaching --- and not the new style ministry through music and dance. Sunday morning when Reverend Pettway spoke to the souls and conscious of his flock. After the musical display ended, and while men and women congregated in the lobby eyeing one another spreading Saintly gossip --- slyly accepting pay-off for ball tickets and repaying local loan sharks --- he stayed and prayed a personal prayer.

The young Associate Pastor, Barry Hinton strolled down the aisle toward him, showing pearly white teeth and a gracious smile wearing an ebony robe and black suede Steeple Gate slippers beneath.

He reached to shake Solomon's hand as he sat down beside him. "Morning Mr. King, how are things? Beautiful day and great service, wouldn't you say?" He gleamed with confidence.

Solomon looked down. "I haven't quite got use to this new style of worship. It seems almost like a backstreet night club. The music and show is a little over the top as far as I'm concerned. I think it might be running the older folk away from the church. But otherwise all's good."

How are Sarah and Junior?" Barry asked.

"Sarah Anne drove up from Charlotte on Wednesday ---- stayed overnight, she's fine. Junior is still at Fort Bragg, living his own life. We talk every week or so. He's fine --- if he wasn't, I'd know. My phone would be ringing.

"I haven't given up on Sarah, yet/" Barry forced himself to say. "I'm sorry about our breakup. It was all my fault. I was l a little too pushy. I pray God will bless me with another swing at her." He grimaced. "I'm really pissed at myself" —. Then he glanced at Solomon.

"Remember what coach Hayes always told you football players. The madder you get, the worse you play." Solomon said.

Barry signed, lowering his head. "I don't know what I can do. I'm flipping out about it. Standing around doing nothing, waiting on the Lord to move ain't getting it."

Heartsick, he stared at the floor momentarily --- making Solomon recall him as a boy, playing with Junior in the backyard. "Yeah, I thought you and Sarah Anne would have given me grandchildren by now. If I had my way, it would have never changed." He patted Harry on the shoulder. "Just be patient --- the fat lady hasn't sung yet."

Barry waved his hand. "Enough of that, whatever will be will be. If it's meant to be it will happen. I've done all I can do to correct the situation. I'll have to trust in the Lord. It's one of many tests I'll face in this life."

"Thanks for your patience this morning," the flight attendant announced. "As soon as we've reached cruising altitude, we will begin our beverage service…."

The plane had been delayed for an hour at Miami's Apo-Locka International Airport. Linda Graves had whisked to the airport at 9:30 A.M. only to wait for an hour to get aboard. She sat back enjoying the in-flight movie, Sword Fish with Hallie Barry and John Trevolta. Half of the other passengers flying miles above a slumbering country watched the movie in a trance and the others quietly read magazines and newspapers.

For two days she'd forgot she was a cop. She had been up most of the time partying with her sister Chelsie and her friends—since arriving in Miami on Friday. They crisscrossed the wooded forest of Georgia and South Carolina. Beneath she could see rivers snaking below, feeding small cites with water. She landed in Raleigh-Durham International at 11:14 waited for thirty minutes and was picked up by her girlfriend Hope.

After being in Miami for two days, the December chill in Durham rose up and seemed to freeze her to the bone. Two days of Miami's constant heat and then swinging back to the North Carolina chill of December seemed to shock her body.

By 1:30 she was on the phone with Solomon. "There must be something." She said thoughtfully. "Bring him in again for questioning. Maybe he'll trip up. If anyone can shake him loose --- it's you."

She felt a surge of frustration. "How'd you know I plan to talk to him in a day or two? I'll bring him in --- sorta informally. I gotta be careful how I handle this guy --- legally. Just me and him for a talk. Keep your fingers crossed --- maybe he'll get sick of me and screw up."

She chuckled, "Yeah! I'll keep my fingers crossed and stick pins in the little voodoo doll on my desk." "Solomon you can't let this guy get under your skin. Like you always say, you think better if your head isn't clouded by your feelings. This thing ain't personal. We both know that. Right?"

"Yeah, I'm okay on the personal side. I'm just waiting for him to do something that will break this thing open. My gut don't fool me too often." He said.

CHAPTER 47

PROFESSOR ALFORD CALLED IN SICK from the Charlotte Marriot. He'd impulsively driven to Charlotte to watch the Hornets play the Lakers. He laid in bed flipping the T.V. from channel to channel. He finally dressed and checked out of the Hotel right before noon. He got back to Durham in the early afternoon, cleaned up, ran Duke Forest, stopped by his office at the University and said he was feeling better. He tried to work but couldn't.

The misstep at Detective King's house was constantly on his mind. He knew when the Deputy's cruiser showed up King was on to him. The Professor took no delight in being beat at his game and felt no superiority seeping from it. He had barely gotten away.

"Where is he?" Solomon spoke into the headset as he pulled to the curb a block away from the Professor's house.

"Just parked in the staff parking lot at the University; looks like he's on his way to the Chemistry Building. We are setting on the corner across the street next to the Fire Station off Fayetteville Street."

There was a four-unit net around the Professor, nine cops. They'd followed him from his home to Duke Forest and from there to the University. They watched him when he started his run and when he finished. They watched him stop by 7-Eleven on Chapel Hill Road and buy distilled water. They watched him as he drove from the 7-Eleven to the University, walk through the parking lot to his office on the first floor of the Chemistry Building.

While he fumbled around in his office, a technician fastened a small radio transmitter under the bumper of his Mercedes. When he left the University later in the evening, the look-outs followed him back to his car. He returned home, stayed in for an hour, and then left out again. Heading North on U.S. 501.

"He's on Dearborn Drive ---he's slowing down at the Banks house." The officer said.

Solomon parked outside the Professor's house --- and looked at his watch. The night was chilled, so he buttoned his coat. It took twenty-five minutes. "Keep your distance." He said through the headset. The Professor passed Clara Banks' house and turned around at the end of the street, it would take him the same amount of time to drive back home if he decided to do so.

"I'm out of the car, going inside." The radio squawked. The look-out team was to make sure Solomon had enough time.

Solomon turned the radio's volume down as low as it would go and stuck it in his coat pocket. He didn't want it shrieking. He pulled a power lock pick and a small flashlight from the pocket of his ruffled London Fog. He pressed the doorbell twice and listened to the phone ring. No one answered. The house was empty. He took out the lock pick and pushed it into the lock. The pick made a rattling noise. The door popped open.

Solomon walked directly inside the Professor's house, slowly moving through the den, living room, kitchen and a small office all neat and clean. He removed a small camera from his inner coat pocket and began snapping pictures, books, paper, bills and magazines and a small IBM Computer. He turned and hurried up the steps, snapping pictures as he moved. He didn't know what he was looking for but if he saw it, he would know. The master bedroom looked like it had been cutout of a book. The furniture alone appeared to cost more than Solomon made in five years. Walk-in-closet, click, click. There had to be at least thirty expensive suits, blazers, shirts, ties, shoes and accessories. All lined up neatly. He pushed the closed door shut, flip on the hall light. He took out he headset, turned it on, and called his look-outs. "How we looking?"

"Everything's fine. My man stopped off at Golden Corral to get a bite to eat---it looks like. We're in the parking lot. I got him in my sight. You're in good shape."

Solomon turned down the volume of the headset back down and started to check for anything specific---an obvious indication that the Professor was in fact involved with the overdose deaths.

Down the hall from the master bedroom were three smaller bedrooms. He checked all three. Nicely furnished, matching drapes and comforters. In the last one was an Olympic weight bench, at least four hundred pounds of iron, a treadmill and assortment of dumbbells. At the end of the hall was a solid oak door leading to an upper loft. Solomon used his small flashlight to find the light switch. The place looked like a makeup room at MGM. Special lights, mirrors placed on the wall in every direction, a large bar stood sat in the center of the room before make-up mirrors. Hats, shirts, dresses, uniforms, urban gear, work boots, wigs, hair pieces all hung against the wall. Powders, body make-up, molding clay, beards, wax and sponges, you name it --- it was there. In the back of the closet was a stack of newspapers tied in a neat bundle. On the front page of the outer paper he could see the headlines "NCCU Student Found Dead." He snapped pictures from every angle. Why the make-up and costumes? He asked himself.

He shut the closet door, walked back down the steps, passing the other bedrooms, went back to the bottom floor checking each bathroom as he went.

He took out the headset. "Where is he?"

He's moving."

"I'm finished over here." Solomon said.

He put the radio back in his pocket and flashed more pictures. He went in the kitchen look in the cabinets and under the sink. Solomon searched for anything to tie the Professor in with the crimes. Trying to build a case with circumstantial evidence was aggravating. The house was clean — to clean. He must have another place. He thought.

"He cleans up behind himself. He's organized, and careful." Solomon said to himself aloud.

"he spoke into the headset. "I'm out."

CHAPTER 48

CAPTAIN JACK FLETCHER WALKED IN without knocking. Solomon lifted himself up from the chair and bit down on his cigar. He calmly walked over to the window. “I have to be in the interrogation room in five minutes, what’s shaking?” He asked.

Fletcher hesitated, “Solomon I’m against you bringing Alford in like this --- but I trust you. Be careful not to cross the line with this guy. We can’t afford a lawsuit.”

Solomon headed to the interrogation room. Ten-year old grey winter suit, white shirt, he’d attempted to press before work, burgundy tie and brown wing tip shoes. He wanted to show a sign of authority. He pinned his department name tag on the pocket of his jacket in view and unbuttoned his jacket so his Smith & Wesson .38 revolver would be in sight. This was his “if you make one mistake, I got ya look.”

Detective Graves met Solomon going out the door as she came in. She offered a wide smile. “it’s D-Day, uh?” Solomon looked at her without a word --- heading straight for the interrogation room. Graves clipped down the hall behind him. “Can I set in with you?”

“I’m gonna dance this dance by myself. You can watch through the two-way.” He said. “Maybe you can see something that might get by me.”

“Let’s roll. This might take all day. Nobody in or out, unless I give the sign.” Her eyes sparkled with excitement. “I’d like to look him in the eye.” She said.

The radiance in the green pastel interrogation room was sharper and harsher than it looked from the two-way mirror. Officer Blake brought him in. Solomon came in and dropped down in a chair on the other side of the table. Alford was still standing. He looked up twice as he poured them coffee. "Hi, have a seat. Cream or sugar? I appreciate you coming in this morning. There are a few things I need you to help me with." The interrogation room clearly took Alford out of the comfort zone of the classroom. The intense lighting in the small room caused his face to shine.

"No, nothing for me, I'd like to know why you requested to see me in the middle of my morning schedule. Am I arrested or something?"

"In the middle of the morning ---- Solomon glanced at his watch. Well, sir in police work we usually don't consider schedules. We kinda move as time and cases call for us to. Oh, by the way, that's a two-way mirror, but nobody's spying on us."

"Detective King, do I need an attorney?" Alford asked.

"I don't know, maybe so. But not right now." Solomon countered.

Alford smiled sly and kinda boyish. "I guess I've watched Law and Order one to many times. So, why am I here?"

Detective Graves paid close attention. Solomon played the clumsy detective routine to make himself appear slow. He pulled his chair around to Alford's side of the table and propped his elbows on the table as if he was lost for answers. Graves smiled thinking to herself, "eliminating barriers." The Professor set with his arms folded and legs crossed --- closed himself off from Solomon.

"I'm looking into the deaths of four or five people who've died from heroin overdoses. We talked about this awhile back." Alford relaxed just a bit. He nodded his head as Solomon spoke. "This thing got me stumped. The Banks kid, the Hall kid, Leroy Watson over on the West End." He smiled, "Ray Kelly and your niece Brigette and her boyfriend Eric. That's a bunch of people dying from dope around you."

Solomon saw Alford relax. "That thing has been eating away at me. Just the coincidence of you knowing all them people, like that and all."

"You don't think they'll coincidences?"

Detective Graves smiled to herself as she viewed the sparring match through the interrogation window. He's trying to find out what Solomon is thinking. Good shot to the body Solomon.

"In my life I've learned not to believe in too many coincidences. I mean, how in the world could a group of loosely connected people all have some type of a relationship with you and the same group all die from shooting to much heroin? I mean that's about the strangest thing around."

Hands locked and legs crossed. Solomon was getting to close for comfort. He looked away from Solomon's stare. He moved in his chair. "You getting warm, Solomon." Graves said.

Solomon looked straight into Alford's eyes. He smiled on the inside. "I know these people were murdered." Solomon didn't blink an eye. "I'm certain about that. I know someone been spreading around some high-quality heroin to each of these people." He glared at Alford.

Graves threw her fist in the air, bingo! He's looking at his watch and picking lint off his shirt sleeves. He's about to tell a lie. Solomon was good, very patient, and as crafty as Columbo. But, so was James Alford. He was well spoken; cool as a fan under fire; even a little conceited.

"I know you read the papers and is aware of the string of recent deaths in the city --- starting what we though was six months ago but it looks like it might to back further."

Alford smirked, at least from Detective Grave's position from behind the observation mirror ---. His faced was filled with insult and his hazel eyes stayed glued on Solomon. His black curly hair was cropped close with not a hair out of place. His wore rimmed glasses, starched white shirt and a three-hundred dollar tie made him look high-handed.

"That son-of-a-bitch is going down!" Detective Graves thought to herself. But she knew they didn't have anything solid on the Professor.

After nearly an hour of sparring back and forth, Solomon had established little more than that Alford knew four of the people who'd died. And that he knew of Alford's costume studio inside his house. Graves noticed the fact of Solomon knowing of the costume studio caused Alford to appear nervous. But Alford didn't inquire of how Solomon knew of the studio.

Alford was dry mouth and hungry. "It's getting late detective, so what do you want from me?" He didn't appear intimidated.

Solomon bit down on his cigar and gazed at Alford. Then he said, "A number of people you know ended up dead."

Alford shifted in his chair. Solomon saw fear instead of arrogance. Then Alford caught himself and became composed. "Detective, I come in contact with a great number of people, young and old. Unfortunately, many of them are gifted but have many emotional problems that include drug use."

Solomon stayed calm, "okay, let me tell you. I got a lot of people who are helping me unravel this thing. DNA experts, fingerprint people, forensics scientist, you know about that don't you? Criminalists, you name it." He jumped up from his chair and looked down on Alford. Crime scene experts and I got a woman who knows you had some contact with her brother the night he died in her bathroom."

Alford jumped up from his chair. Irate. "Detective that's it. I'm not going to sat here and be accused and insulted by you any further." His mind was racing. He had to settle himself. This nigga is making up shit, lying. I left no clues --- no one could have recognized me. I made no mistakes. He has nothing or he'd arrest me. He thought.

"You either arrest me now or I'm leaving. Don't bother me again unless you plan to arrest me." Solomon and Alford sized each other up. Toe to toe.

"We ain't through with each other." Solomon said.

"Good-bye Detective King." Solomon sat back in his chair and lit the cigar.

Detective Graves saw it all. Alford almost lost it. Officer Blake came to the window beside Graves drinking a Coke.

"Solomon rung his neck. He knows he hasn't gotten away. The pressure is on. He's being exposed. All we got to do is wait and see if he panics." She said.

CHAPTER 49

Essie Bagley had been a maid at North Carolina Central University for eighteen years and hated it. Scrubbing out toilets and dust mopping floors at the crack of dawn behind a dormitory full of ungrateful students was not how she'd planned to spend her life. But two more years of this crap, and she could retire with full salary. She was thinking about retirement as she wedged opened the east wing second floor bathroom door at Childley Hall.

At the moment, there were two other people on the second-floor balcony, both of them men from campus facilities. Pushing her cart through the doorway, Essie realized she had her work cut out for her. The rank odor of the place slapped her in the face. Someone had left a faucet on clogged paper towels; water was running onto the floor. The overhead light above the sink was flicking on and off.

Essie reached down and picked up a trash can lying on its side. Waste was strewn across the floor. She looked over toward the sinks. Checked the towel dispensers and walked to her cart for refills.

She tip-toed across the floor dodging puddles of water. By the toilet, something on the floor caught her eye; a belt lying on the floor. She pushed open the stall floor, picking up the fancy reptile skin belt. Beside it was a hypodermic syringe.

In the next stall, Essie glanced down at what looked like two or three small glassine bags and a bottle top. She moved on the next stall, expecting it to be empty. Her howl could be heard over the entire floor.

A young man sat on the commode, his head hanging down, almost touching his lap, and legs spread apart. His blue jeans' top button was open; the sleeve of his blue Oxford shirt was rolled up; spattered with brownish throw-up.

At first Essie though the young man had passed out, but then, after forcing herself to look --- she could see the ashen color of his face; with his tongue drooping out his lips, and the distant look in his eyes.

The hasty first report that a student had been found in Chidley Hall on North Carolina Central University's campus; identical with the overdose deaths of five other men proved discomfiting but true. Meanwhile, matching the death with the others --- a subject of a seven-month old probe was added to the list.

The now-burgeoning investigation centered around the University's men's dormitory --- enclosed and security protected --- located on the corner of Alston Avenue and Lawson Street.

It was there that Ron Humphrey's dead stiffened body had been found. Humphrey was a native of New York, scholarship basketball player and campus drug dealer. When Homicide Detective Jake Morris arrived, uniform policemen were stationed outside the dormitory entrance, and inside paramedics from the Fire Rescue were treating Essie Bagley for shock.

Detective Linda Graves and Solomon had preceded him. The media, alerted by an exchange of urgent calls on police radios were assembled in force outside in the parking lot facing the dormitory, where they were being restricted from entering by uniform police, acting on behalf of Solomon's orders. Reporters were already debating how the student had died.

Solomon on arriving had already been stopped briefly by reporters from WTVD, and WRAL T.V., holding microphones to the open window of his car while cameras shot close-ups. Their shouted questions overlapped.

"Detective do you know what killed the young man?" "Is his death due to a drug overdose, and if so, is it related to the other unsolved overdose deaths under investigation?"

"Is someone really distributing killer dope in our City?" But, Solomon had shaken his head and continued driving, stopping his Impala in a far corner of the parking lot facing Alston Avenue instructing a uniform officer, "Call Headquarters and tell them we need someone here to deal with the press."

Chief of Police John fletcher arrived shortly in an official car, driven by Sergeant Seagroves. The Chief was in uniform, his stars of rank displayed. Solomon nudged Detective Graves asking, "How many times this year have the Chief showed up at a homicide scene?" I'm sure the call concerning the media made him grab his coat and get down here."

Detective Jon Parker, the Chief's sidekick who arrived a few minutes earlier met the Chief as soon as he stepped foot on the ground.

The Chief ordered in a low voice, "Show me the scene and direct any media my way."

"Yes sir, this way."

Some thirty minutes later the entire second flood of Chidley Hall had been condoned off by official yellow tape ---- POLICE LINE DO NOT CROSS." Chief Fletcher approached Solomon who had made his way to the second-floor bathroom.

"Detective King what do we have?"

"Looks like more of the same." Solomon reported. "We haven't touched a thing." He motioned for Essie Bagley who was standing off to the side. "This is Mrs. Bagley. She is the custodian who found the kid."

Essie visibly upset joined them. She told the Chief "When I found him, I lost controlled. I didn't know what to do. One of the men from facilities called security."

"Did you see anyone else around the bathroom at the time you found the kid?" Fletcher asked.

"No, not a soul." She said

"Did you touch anything in the stall where the young man was found?

Everyone is a crime expert, especially when the media is close by, Solomon thought.

"We'd appreciate you letting us take your prints so we can separate them from any others." Fletcher said.

Solomon walked over to the forensics expert; he knew it was another of the serial overdose cases. He pushed the boys in white to gather every scrap of evidence as fast as they could, examine and assess it and get back with him without delay. He then relit his cigar and made his way through the crowd toward the Impala.

As Solomon stood in a daze under a glaring light outside the morgue at Durham County General Hospital's night entrance, he looked toward the sky --- the meteorologist had called for snow. He turned the collar of his London Fog up to shield himself from the December chilled air. He was aware of the night's gloom and that James Alford --- the Professor had struck again and was loose on the streets.

Thomas Stroud's voice came on the intercom, the door hummed and Solomon walked down the bright colored hallway toward the autopsy room.

Stroud was in full green scrubs from head to toe --- white sanitary cap and shoes. The front of his outfit was colored by blood. The body on the table had been sliced into a human filet.

Solomon bit down on his cigar --- asking, "What we got?"

Thomas Stroud stood dressed in green scrubs, a black rubber apron, and white hair net on his head and matching covers for his shoes. "Same damn thing, another heroin overdose. What's it been now, five in the last six months?" he asked. "No six" Solomon replied.

Solomon scanned Stroud up and down as he clamped down on his cigar with his teeth. He walked over to the stainless table where the corpse looked like a human filet. He turned and blew a circle of smoke above his head.

"I'm no detective but this and the other deaths are no coincidence.

Five people in the last six months all overdosing on junk strong enough to kill a horse. Nobody --- puts dope on the street like this. All those deaths have been HOT SHOTS. The mobs don't even have dope that potent." Stroud preached.

"You singing to the chore. I know this thing is deliberate. But all I have is circumstantial evidence and what's in my gut on this thing." Solomon mumbled.

"I put the autopsy ahead of some of the others because I knew you were chasing a ghost with this. The science don't lie, it's the same type high quality heroin that killed this kid. He was dead before he finished running it in his arm. Sorry, but there's no physical evidence that leads to anyone."

"Somebody sent their child off to school in an effort to better his life, and now this. He was probably a nice kid --- who messed around with a little dope here and there, like a lot of college kids." Stroud said with dampened eyes.

"We'll he's a dead kid. Just a pawn in the game of a sick man. What's troubling me right now is that the guy responsible for this has gone all the way out of control --- over the edge. I don't know exactly why he started but it's turned into a murderous game. It's like he's challenging the police to try and catch him."

Solomon held his cigar between his fat fingers, slowly walked over and thumped ashes in the trash can in the corner of the room. "This guy would kill me if he could get to me and anyone else, he thinks have figured this thing out."

"I know you got your eye on who's doing this. The pattern you figured out probably make sense. I know you gonna walk this guy down. I can't wait to see who's responsible for this type of thing."

"Yeah, right now he's stalking around trying to get next to his next victim --- like a wolf in the night.

Clara Banks wore a white terry rob that was loosely tied at the waist, exposing her firm breast and smooth chocolate thighs. She sipped green tea from a mug and leaned into the dim light over the bathroom sink using alcohol pads to clean the make-up off her face. Then she leaned closer into the mirror to examine her face.

The figure of a man peeping in her window, through the dark fell back into the shadows as she turned.

She carried a turkey sandwich and potato chips on a plate as she switched on the lights in the den and hit the answering machine to play back her messages. She listened as she nibbled on her sandwich. There were two calls from Dwayne Newkirk, the church choir director remaining her of the special call rehearsal, a call from Bertha Beasley who worked with her at the hospital asking for a ride to work and one from Detective Solomon King --- asking her to call him as soon as possible. She flipped the machine off and thought for a moment, disregarding both the choir director and Bertha's call. Her mind was fixed on Detective King and the urgency in his voice. She ate chips from her plate as she made her way to the chair beside the stand that held the phone. She dialed Solomon's office and got his answering machine, "You've reached the Office of Detective Solomon King, Durham Police Department. I'm not able to speak with you right now, please leave your name at the beep and I'll get back with you." She thought for another moment --- went and got up her purse and found Solomon's business card with his home number. She dialed the phone again. After three rings a voice echoed in her ear. "Sorry, I'm not able to answer you call right now. At the tone leave your name and number -- I will get back with you." She slowly placed the phone on the set and seated herself in the recliner in front of the T.V. Solomon's urgent voice resonated in the back of her mind as she perched in front of the T.V. aimlessly finishing her sandwich and chips. The call had robbed the taste of the sandwich. She didn't know what to do so she flipped the T.V. from channel to channel, surfing. Finally, she decided on BET'S SISTER'S. Her instincts told her that Solomon would call her back, if it was important.

At 9:45 Clara turned off the den light and headed for the shower. The secret figure crouched, watching as she undressed. She got into the shower and turned on the water as hot as she could stand it. The man in the shadows seized the moment, moving to the back of the house to pop the backdoor lock. He had to get in the house before she finished her shower ...in time to turn on every gas outlet and the water heater, the eyes on top of the stove and the oven. Then he'd waited for her to finish showering while the natural gas fumes silently filled the house. With the gas fumes sipping, he shook his head in the dark and waited behind the door. Cars hissed down the street. Five minutes, eight minutes. The intensity growing, his blood pulsating, the pressure rising. How long was she going to stay in the shower? He needed to get out.

He heard the shower stop. Then the phone rang as Clara toweled herself. She rushed to answer the phone, not seeing the figure in the dark. Detective King's baritone voice broke the silence. "Ms. Banks, this is Solomon King. I want you to listen to me carefully and do as I say. Lock all your doors and windows. I'm across the street in view of your house, along with two other officers. James Alford has been spotted in the area around you house. He went around the house toward the back and we've temporary lost sight of him. I don't know what he's up to for sure but we're not taking any chances. Don't panic, do as I say. We got him surrounded. He's not going to get away --- without explaining why he's stalking in the dark around your house."

She didn't question Detective King. For some reason she trusted him and his advice. She listened with total concentration. Then she placed the telephone back in the set. At first, she didn't hear anyone or any strange sounds inside her house. But could smell her owe fear. Then she heard the floor crack or thought she did. Her pulse raced and heart felt like it was in her throat. She stayed still for a nervous second and headed to the front door to check the lock.

For the first time since Ronnie's death she realized how vulnerable she'd made herself, living alone. She slipped to the back of the house toward the back door to check the lock. She felt the coldness of the tile under her stocking feet.

Bam! A glove hand came down over her mouth and nose from nowhere. She felt the strength in the arms that wrapped around her. It had to be a man. Her mind raced. She knew it was Alford. She was right all along --- he had something to do with Ronnie's death. But, why come after me? She thought.

He was cutting off her air supply. He knew what he was doing. She could see flashes of a white cloth as it covered her nose and mouth. It was toxic, suffocating, and odorless.

She struggled and twisted her body but there was no use. Suddenly the room started to spin. She tried to break his grasp. Her heart was beating so fast she thought she was having a heart attack.

"Help me! Somebody please help me!" As she let out a muffled sound through the damp cloth. She could feel herself losing consciousness. In a daze, she thought of Ronnie and how he was alive one day and dead the next. She kicked her legs one last time and passed out.

James Alford "the Professor" dressed in black running outfit, black skull cap on his head and running shoes. He'd plastered a two-inch black beard onto his face. As he walked through the house, he stuffed the Halothane soaked cloth into the waist band against his holstered sixteen shot 9mm Glock handgun. He knew the drug would put her out long enough for the gas fumes to take over and steal her life. He crept through the house toward the back door, took one look and disappeared into the night.

He was playing the ultimate game. No, the academic game of chess; playing a game of life and death. Choosing who would live or die. The joy and excitement caused a rush ---and addictive euphoric charge as he made his way toward his old rust color Honda.

CHAPTER 50

THE NIGHT WAS MOIST AND quiet. The fog rising from the low ground had the image of campfire smoke.

The Professor had taken the bait. He hadn't spotted the surveillance. Solomon stood in the dark at the edge of the trees. He whispered into his radio. "This is King, get ready to dance guys?"

"What we got?" a voice shot back.

"Our pert dressed in black is heading my way, coming right down the street from the back of the house — right side." Solomon's voice cracked with an edge of excitement and intensity.

"He'll be in sight, under the streetlight in one minute. He's walking like he's on a nightly stroll."

Solomon thought of all the lives that had been lost. The dreams crushed — Ronnie Banks, Trevor Hall and Ron Humphrey, all college kids killed in total disregard of their value to their families. Leroy Watson found dead on Green Street — what had he done to anyone but himself? Ray Kelly peddled poison for sure, but it wasn't Alford's call to play judge and jury. James Alford a man with no concern for human conditions, driven by a selfish motive. As he waited, vengeance tugged at his heart.

"Where is Graves?" He asked.

"She's on foot, behind him, staying out of sight. I'm staying where I am; he has to pass where I'm positioned. Harris said, "He's probably trying to make it to whatever car his driving."

"The only car I see is an old rust color Honda down the street, about a half a block between your position and where I am. I'm gonna stop him before he gets into the car. You guys get ready, start moving in from your positions." Solomon whispered.

The Professor looked around --- he heard footsteps behind him as he grabbed for the door handle of the Honda. He turned --- Solomon was standing behind him in a beige London Fog trench coat, his hands deep in his pockets with a cigar stuff in the corner of his mouth.

The Professor's eyes danced in his head as he froze in place. He knew he had been suckered.

"Step away from the car. Keep your hands where I can see them." Solomon ordered in a slow even tone. "Now back away from the car." Solomon trusted his pistol at the Professor's upper body. The Professor stepped back slowly and turned toward Solomon. "Now don't move," Solomon said as he reached for his radio.

The gun appeared out of nowhere. Alford come up with his Glock 9mm like a trained gunman. He'd switched his passive approach to murder to that of a gun slinger. He fired three shots at Solomon in quick succinct rhythm --- bang --- bang ----bang.

Solomon hit the ground — diving behind the back of the Honda. He held his Smith & Wesson .38 with both hands as he lay on the ground, waiting for Alford to show his face. He'd been hit in the thigh. His body was shaking but he was able to pull himself up and lean on the side of the car.

Detective Graves and Officer Mark Harris raced toward the gun fight — running low with their guns drawn.

The Professor eased toward the back of the car, holding his 9mm with both hands, easing, inch by inch ---- he knew he'd hit Solomon.

Solomon kept still — lying in wait. He knew Alford wasn't finished. In a flash Alford made his move. Solomon looked up and there he was.

Alford pulled the trigger — the automatic jammed. He blinked his eyes, confused.

Solomon impulsively got off three rounds into Alford's chest. He flew back around the corner of the Honda. He let out a growl like a wounded animal. Numbness was spreading through his body. Blood cover his chest and sipped from his mouth. He realized the game was over.

Detective Graves and Officer Harris made it in time to kick the gun away from Alford's reach. Graves ran over and squatted beside Solomon. "Don't move Solomon, you been hit. Don't move" She shouted into her radio, "Officer down --- need assistance. Send EMT, now."

Solomon looked up at Graves, "Give me a hand, this damn ground is cold on my backside. Help me up."

She placed her arm under Solomon's shoulder, helping him to his feet. He leaned against the Honda and reached inside his jacket and found what was left of a cigar. He fished for a book on matches and lit his stogie.

Officer Harris stood over Alford. He watched as Alford's eyes turned upward and disappeared into the back of his head. The whites of his eyes were the only thing that showed. His arms jerked three or four times, and then stopped. James Alford died in the middle of the street --- never having answered anyone's questions.

Solomon sent Officer Harris to check on Clara Banks. He pounced on the front door, bam, bam, bam. There was no answer. With one hard kick the door flew open. Harris scooted in with his weapon drown. He moved from room to room.

Clara was unconscious, sprawled on the floor. Harris put his gun away. "Officer needs assistance," was heard over the radio. The gas sipping from the stove almost took his breath away. He made his way to the kitchen and found the source. He went through the house opening the doors and windows. He didn't take any chances --- he raced back to the hallway, placed his arm under Clara and carried her out the house.

CHAPTER 51

POLICE LINE DO NOT CROSS. Yellow display tape had half the block by the rust colored Honda cordoned off.

Some thirty minutes later Dearborn Drive was overrun with police cars, officers, orange and white EMT wagons, and crime scene technicians mingling, stepping over each other while people stood in their yards whispering --- trying to piece together what the hell had happened.

In the parking lot outside the Green Candle take-out dinner on Fayetteville Street, two days later a gusty December wind blew drifts of paper wrappers, styroform cups and leftover debris across the pavement. Solomon sat in his old Impala with an unlit cigar in the corner of his mouth reading the article about the death of James Alford standing at the hands of the Durham Police. A photograph of Alford standing at a podium speaking at a recent science seminar and a page worth of prose were spread over the front page of the Durham Herald Sun — matching the non-stop television coverage of the days before. For the ten minutes it took him to read the piece, he knew had no solid proof that James Alford was the one responsible for the drug overdose deaths. All he had was circumstantial evidence, his gut feelings concerning Alford's involvement --- and questions of why Alford had attempted to murder Clara Banks and why he'd chosen a shoot-out over being arrested.

The black headlines made him flinch even though he'd expected some cynicism. **LOCAL UNIVERSITY PROFESSOR KILLED BY POLICE** --- but he was further incensed by the subheading written in smaller letters. **Community cries foul! City manager asking for a full report.**

He knew sooner or later every detail of the investigation and the night in question would be raked across the coals --- analyzed, processed and viewed from every possible angle.

He felt a little dumped on by the article's implication of some type of police misconduct in the shooting.

He examined the photographs after reading the article. The reporter had used pictures presenting Alford as the dignitary he was known to be. There wasn't one shot of Alford, the man in the all black outfit he'd worn the night of the shoot - out.

The second picture was one of Alford standing in front of his classes at North Carolina Central University. He was recognizably in a zone, lecturing as his students appeared to be mesmerized.

Solomon was convinced of the power of the media and how it could spin a story in either direction — swaying opinions; simplifying facts to the point of fiction; confusing the public; all for the sensationalism over substance for the sake of ratings and sells.

He read the article for the second time, slowing himself with gasp and grunts. Typical of newspapers, it contained errors, but the text was mostly true. The subtle spin is what was irritating, news reporters typically seeing a bad cop in every case.

Folding the newspaper, he whispered, "Thank God we didn't let him get away and Clara Banks didn't die. At least we were able to save her."

Again, he told himself no matter how the newspapers slanted the story --- the night in question was by the book. No matter how he processed it in his head, he still felt dumped on, and his mood didn't change. Talking to himself about it didn't help.

He turned the key and started up the old Impala. As he drove out of the parking lot, he was still troubled that the case with Alford hadn't ended the way he'd like for it to.

A gust of wind caused a whistling sound through the crack of the window. He pulled on his cigar and made a left turn onto Fayetteville Street --- with no destination in mind.

CHAPTER 52

HE DIDN'T GO HOME. HE went to visit Clara Banks at Durham Regional Hospital. He took slow measured steps, using a metal cane. A total of thirty minutes passed before he made it to her room. She looked haggard; she was ashen; her hair frizzled and looked like she hadn't eaten in weeks. Her voice sounded weak and tired.

"Surprise, you got a visitor." He said as he walked through the door into the pastel green room.

"I heard you got shot." She whispered with a dull smile. It was the same withdrawn Clara he'd met months ago.

"Yeah, I caught a bullet in the thigh. It's not as bad as it looks. I'll be back to normal in a month or so."

"If you say so," she mailed a honeyed smiled --- talking slow and deliberate.

"Do you think it will all end." She asked

"I don't really know we'll have to hope and pray. I do know he was more than just a Professor. He had his hands in this thing more than we know. If no more addicts come up dead, then maybe he was our guy."

Solomon pulled a card out of his coat pocket and handed it to her. She took the card and flashed a wide smile. Solomon could feel energy between them — a rhythm not felt before.

Three days later Clara was back at home unsure whether she could live alone again. She stirred around cleaning, putting things in order, trying to move on with her life. Although the Professor was dead --- his voice and presence resonated in her mind.

At home, Solomon wiped the sweat from his forehead as he struggled to push the peddles on the stationary bike. It had been two weeks since the shoot-out.

It was the first of January, the air was crisp, outside the cold weather had a sting to it. He'd taken two weeks off so he could stay off his leg. That's what he'd said anyway.

He had ten more minutes of peddling. Junior and Sarah Anne had both come home for a couple of days --- to watch over him.

Although he didn't solve the overdose case outright, the bad guy might have been Alford, or he might be still out there lying low. In all, Durham's got a pretty good Police Department. Crime in the Bull City ---- like most places is on the rise and the Police are trying to keep up with it. Other than the crime which is mid-range these days, Durham is a great place to live.

Solomon headed for the outside porch after finishing dinner with Sarah Anne and Junior. As he pulled on his cigar, for some reason he felt like someone was spying on him --- watching in the dark. He put his cigar out and walked back inside.

EPILOGUE

The afternoon was overcast; the sky appeared hazed with smoke. Solomon drove from Roxboro Road in route to the Macaroni Grill on Chapel Hill Boulevard to have lunch with Clara Banks. He arrived and parked his old Chevy Impala near a big black 500 Mercedes. He opened the door and swung his legs out the car --- he could barely feel any stiffness in his hip where he'd been shot a month earlier. He made his way through the congested parking lot to the front door of the restaurant.

As he entered the door, he could see Clara setting in the far corner dressed in a dark blue business-like suit, cream blouse with a ruby studded pin on her lapel. Her hair was pulled back in a French Roll and her face was perfectly outlined with make-up. It was the first time he'd ever seen her properly dressed. She looked like an entirely different from than haggard woman who had shown up at the police station months before shyly offering information concerning her brother's death. She now had a different glow and confidence about herself.

"Hello Detective King, I didn't think you were going to make it. I was beginning to think I would have to eat alone." She said.

Solomon pulled off his gloves and laid his beige overcoat over the spare chair as he sat at the small table across from Clara. As they settled in the quiet atmosphere of the restaurant, Clara felt a touch of nervousness in her stomach.

"Yes, I will have the filet of chicken salad, and ice-tea." Clara told the waitress when she came to take the orders.

Solomon looked at the menu for a moment before closing it. "I'll have the salmon cake with a tossed salad and ice-tea as well."

"Your lunch will be ready in about ten minutes." The waitress said as she hurried away.

"You're moving around like you were never injured. I'm happy you're doing so well." Clara said as she looked at Solomon.

"I'm doing okay. Not quite a hundred percent yet, but I'm getting there. I've been back on the treadmill for a week --- I think I'll be fully recovered in a month or so. Enough time about me." He said. "Will you do something for me? If you will ---?" he asked. Clara nodded her head in agreement. "For the time we're having lunch, please call me Solomon. The Detective King thing seems so official and formal. How do you feel about that?" Clara offered a slight smile, saying "Solomon it is, then. I like the way it sounds."

Solomon twisted his cigar out in the ashtray as the food arrived. "How have you been since leaving the hospital and getting back to work?" He asked.

Clara shrugged "All my co-workers have kinda been over-reacting --- tip toeing around on egg shells, making sure they don't mention Ronnie or anything about the case. I appreciate them for caring for me, but I wish they would just relax. I'm probably in better shape than I've been in a long time. I now have closure. So, to answer your question, I'm feeling fine and doing well."

Solomon looked around at the lunch crowd, who were stealing quiet time in different corner booths, whispering and nodding as they sipped coffee and periodically noticing their watches --- tracking time.

Solomon spoke, "one or two reporters are still calling, or should I say hounding and begging me to give them an exclusive inside scoop -- on how we connected Alford to the case early on. They just don't give up."

‘If you don’t think you should talk to the Press --- then stick to your guns.” Clara said.

“The media have gone from crying foul play to job well done, since more of the evidence has come out. Alford’s hideaway --- the safe house apartment did the trick. When we found that — it sealed all doubt of whether he was our guy or not.” He said.

“I’m glad you asked me to meet you for lunch. It’s been a long time since I’ve met anyone for lunch or had lunch with anyone outside by Duke Hospital co-workers. I think I need to do more of this kinda thing. It feels good to relax and chat like this.”

Solomon grinned. Well it’s good for me too. My daughter has been getting at me about my social life --- says I have a one-track life which includes nothing but work. I’m trying to lighten up and take her advice slowly. And to be honest, I’m enjoying myself setting here eating with you and going over things. Maybe we can do this again soon.” Before she could respond he throws up his hands saying, “Now! I don’t want to impose myself on you. But if you can manage it --- I think I’d like the company.”

“Sounds like something I’d like to do.” Clara said.

Solomon looked at his watch as they finished the last of their food. He thought to himself that Clara was still not the most talkative woman he’d known, but he could see a different side of her beaming through.

He looked into Clara’s eyes, “I’ve enjoyed our lunch and if it’s okay --- I’ll give you a call soon so we can get together --- maybe for dinner.”

“Just give me a call. I’m usually home after work on most days.” She said.

He glanced at the clock on the wall. “It’s about time for me to be heading for the station.” He said.

Clara reached for her coat and handbag, stood up and waited for Solomon, he left a tip with the check on the table and they headed for the door.

Solomon walked to his old Chevy Impala, waved by to Clara as she pulled out of the parking lot and slowly moved toward Chapel Hill Road — merging into the flow of traffic. By the time he'd traveled far enough to make it downtown his radio sounded — "gun shots reported at 1709 Kent Street." Hmmm, let me drive by Kent Street --- I'm headed in that direction anyway. He thought.

He was still thinking of Clara fifty minutes later when he had his knee on the small of Tommy Lee Hayes' back, pressing his face in the dirt, charging him for shooting into an occupied dwelling as he informed him of his Miranda rights.

He heard the sound of sirens loudly into the haze smoked sky as they approached the scene. It was a perfect day in the life of a cop in Durham the "Bull City."

As soon as Solomon was half-settled in his office, he was summons to Captain Fletcher's Office. Fletcher greeted him with kin words, asking for an update of his injury and overall health. Solomon thought to himself "what is this son of a hound dog up too," Right at that time, Fletcher informed Solomon saying " we have concern related to several homeless veterans who have been found murdered in the last two weeks or so in abandoned houses, park cars and in the woods over our fair city. I'd like you to take a look at the cases and get back with me. Solomon bit down on his cigar without a comment and excused himself from Fletcher's office.